Gillian White is a journalist and lives in Devon. She has four children.

Critical acclaim for Gillian White

'A novelist of the highest quality . . . an intense and vividly-written novel which takes you by the throat and won't let go' *Sunday Independent*

'Bitingly brilliant . . . complex, witty and sinister' *Daily Mirror*

'A wonderful mix of storytelling and hilarious entertainment' *Annabel*

'A gripping read' *Today*

'A rich and wonderful tale of conspiracy and domestic infamy' *Fay Weldon*

'Creepy and insightful' *Ms London*

'This is clever, clever writing, to mix tragedy and comedy and present it as easy reading . . . it is a Martin Amis with heart' *Glasgow Herald*

Dogboy

GILLIAN WHITE

PHŒNIX

A PHOENIX PAPERBACK

First published in Great Britain
by Orion in 1995
This paperback edition published in 1996
by Phoenix, a division of Orion Books Ltd,
Orion House, 5 Upper St Martin's Lane,
London WC2H 9EA

A CIP catalogue record for this book
is available from the British Library.

ISBN: 1 85799 436 1

Typeset at The Spartan Press Ltd,
Lymington, Hants

Printed and bound in Great Britain by
The Guernsey Press Co Ltd,
Guernsey, C.I.

To David Gribble
With lots of love
'I know, let's pretend . . .'

The Ban dog, Cerberus, from hell he bare away –

I

All the little brown birds of England chirp and flit from tree to tree; the sky is a blue marquee pegged out between the hills. All is warm and well with the world, so we know that as sure as eggs are eggs, something dastardly is about to happen.

So summer is the time and Fingles Ponds is the place. Now let us draw nearer in order to observe this intriguing setting bang in the heart of the countryside.

At its conception Fingles Ponds broke the hearts of the county planners, although, by day the one at Melrose is just as Kirsty Maggs sees it, 'A really lovely day out, everything laid out so nice and convenient and so much to do for the kiddies, you don't even have to pay to get in.'
By night, of course, it is quite different.

Is there one in your area?
There are four Fingles Ponds complexes dotted around the west country, a mutant's response to the dreams of children with its very own turrets and towers astring with fairy lights. What would you call it – well, it is a hotchpotch of zoo, fairground, park and shops from cash and carry to petrol station and a garden centre that sells wood chippings that smell of Austrian mountains. Motorways snake like rivers alongside, and the buildings themselves rise, pantomime

castles clamouring for attention from a contemptuous back-cloth of sky.

Clever work with plaster and beams creates a Ruritanian kingdom on a disused airfield.

You have to ignore the chain-linked fences, or just imagine they are there for protection against the hordes without. Summer is the time and Fingles Ponds is the place and Hump Bass works here. At dawn this morning, just before Hump Bass set off on the last of his rounds, the dew made sparklers of the spiders' webs that draped the wire, but Hump is not the sort of man to notice artistic little touches like that. He is bleak and military, soulless as the place itself, the kind of man who might play the part of janitor in a horror motel. The occasional scream of a peacock. And gaunt stands of fir trees serve to break the monotony of wire, just as conifers act as sentinels in all the world's most Godforsaken places where men and women are kept in, or out. So why does the death tree grow so abundantly here? For this is a shoppers' paradise, surely? A shrine to seconds and bargains where you can get the cheapest thrill in the country, bungee jumping from a rusty crane.

Nearly noon and here comes the aforementioned Kirsty, she and her sister lumpy in leggings; along the spiralling pathway they come, between the ponds spotted by mangy wild fowl, under the willows, Kirsty and Sheralee Maggs droop fatly over their pushchairs with their overfed children leaping along behind them, threatening the geese. All the flowerbeds are red, white and blue interspersed with empty styrofoam cups. Heathers, and other such stringy rock plants, have been gouged out by the roving geese. Kirsty throws a fag packet down, somebody else can clear up the mess. Monkeys' piss from that row of cages mingles with the smell of chip fat and vinegar. Ugh.

In the past there have been numerous complaints about the treatment of the animals here; the llama, the donkeys, the angora goats on display, but bureaucracy's wheels never creak too fiercely against the buffers of Fingles Ponds and the tyrant behind the fantasy. I mean, if the planning departments are powerless against Zak C. Oliphant, what hope for anyone else?

Last year, egged on by a squeamish public, the RSPCA timidly suggested that a trained person should be employed to deal with the livestock on all four sites. But no, that would prove far too expensive and anyway, old Hump Bass once had his own greyhounds, didn't he, he knows enough about animals to keep them alive.

Something dastardly.

Consider the plight of Old Mother Hubbard.

Unknowingly, Kirsty and Sher and their children are now passing Hump's private domain. Hump, a bleached and knobbled dog-bone of a man and buried away in the daytime, has his own territory cordoned off by a square of corrugated iron fencing. PRIVATE! KEEP OUT! The words dangle in angry drips of black gloss paint. In here are the kennels that house the guard dogs that come out with him at night. In his shed within the fence Hump keeps his condensed milk and all the supplies that he needs to care for his little menagerie . . . bedding, disinfectant, sacks of animal feed, ropes and chains, hard leather gloves and all manner of broken junk that one day might come in handy.

He keeps something else in here too.

Something that nobody knows about, but which satisfies an inexpressible need within him.

Hump's shed smells of turpentine and sawdust and dog.

On they go amongst the crowds.

'Dirty buggers, chimps,' says Kirsty sourly as all the machinery of her face struggles with the fatness there to sniff. She raises a pencilled eyebrow which covers the shavings of darker hair. 'Always fiddling about with their bums.'

'They can't help that,' says her sister idly, hardly concentrating but pulling a child away from one of the gingerbread-house-shaped shops, one of the many small businesses that rent space off the management and sell a selection of tat: tasteless telephones, pizzas and jokes like wrinkled plastic sick. 'You'd piss yourself locked up in there all day with nothing but a tyre to amuse you. You'd probably start fiddling with your arse as well.'

'Well I manage not to piss myself at home, and what's the difference, Sheralee? When all's said and done, what's the difference? Four bare walls. I hardly ever get out anyway.'

Sheralee shakes her head and tuts. 'You're out now, aren't you? Grief, stop your moaning. Jesus – see that bloody peacock after Jason? It's vicious, look. It's caught up with the little bleeder. It's going to kill him before it's finished. Get off you bugger, sod off!' And Sher sets off to protect her yelling four-year-old son. After the rescue she shakes him and smacks the bottom of his baggy jeans. 'What did you do to it? What did you do? That bird wouldn't have come after you for nothing, I know.' And then, flustered by the exertion – the tops of her burnt arms are an angry red that matches her cleavage, because Sher does not tan well – she turns to Kirsty and says, 'If they're going to have animals running free they should bloody well make sure they're tame. Look at the eyes of that bird. Look at its livid little eyes. I'd swear it was still watching Jason.'

Maybe Sher should get a doctor to have a look at those spreading freckles. With her pale colouring, Sheralee Maggs should probably use a total sunblock.

'Serve him right probably,' says Kirsty, safe to criticise her sister's child.

The four complexes of Fingles Ponds are popular places. There are more cars parked in the carparks than there are in the nearby towns. All the little pathways are packed with people, and there are queues for the children's rides, the hot dogs and the ice creams. On a Sunday it takes half an hour to get in, the traffic is nose to tail for at least half a mile, almost back to the motorway.

But this is a midsummer Tuesday morning, and the only chance Sher has to borrow her neighbour's car, a red Capri and hardly large enough for pushchairs, two large adults and five children. After a journey like that no wonder the children are scratchy and keen to be free. Kirsty and Sher ignore the threatening notices as they near the entrance to the main building. Exclamation marks stand like one-finger gestures all over the place. THIEVES WILL BE PROSECUTED! KEEP YOUR CHILDREN UNDER CONTROL! NO SMOKING, NO DOGS, NO PUSHCHAIRS! THERE ARE HIDDEN CAMERAS IN THIS STORE! But Kirsty and Sheralee stop and stare as a uniformed town crier goes past, ringing a bell and covered in sandwich boards which list the names of members of the public who were caught shoplifting last week.

Customers leaving the main store wear dated stamps on the back of their hands so they cannot sneak back in again to nick something after they have been cleared.

Neither Kirsty nor Sher appear to see this treatment as offensive. They do not seem to find it degrading. Perhaps they believe that the store is doing them a favour by letting them in.

'I don't blame them one bit,' mutters Kirsty, struggling to release the child in the pram, puffing at the wad of hair that falls forward over her face. Same hair as her sister's, and brittle, the colour and texture of last year's hay. She sides with the establishment who will stamp the back of her freckled hand when she's done her shopping. She will offer it to them gladly, so much safer to side with the strong. 'I mean, they have to do something. Stores like this lose millions of pounds every year, and it's you and me has to pay for it in the end with higher prices. Good luck to them I say, if this idea puts people off.'

'Later,' hisses Sher, for the umpteenth time. She drags at the reticent limb of a child as she enters into the mêlée of people. Around the door it is like a stampede and inside the store there's a crush of bodies under a sweet musky smell. 'If you lot behave yourself in here we'll go on the rides later. If you don't, well, it's up to you. Aunty Kirsty wants to choose some wallpaper for Sandra's bedroom. And it's up to you lot how long we take to get finished.'

Something dastardly.
Wait for it . . .
In sorrow thou shalt bring forth children.

Two single mothers, Kirsty and Sher – horror, the scourge of the economy, and can't you tell? Their appearances tell against them, their button blue eyes surrounded by purple, eyes that already acknowledge defeat. Look at their cardboardy shoes, the wrinkled heels that make raw red skin. Look at all that pink polyester – thrust together by fate into neighbouring flats in Montpellier Court.

It's a jolly good thing they get on so well together.
Living so closely as they do, even their periods have come into line.
They breed together. They bleed together.
Single mothers, a breed despised by Godfrey Halkin, their Member of Parliament, who can cope with life and therefore detests those who cannot. They both voted for him because of his smile and his dark striped suits. Nudge nudge, wink wink. 'Bit of a sexy sod.' It is far too late for Sher to declare that she'll never do that again, that she won't vote for anyone next time because they are all exactly the same. Single mothers, and yet this state was inflicted upon them, not chosen.

Ah yes. Both these young women have been betrayed.
By whom? By the men they chose to father their children? Or

6

by their own low self-esteem – and where do people get that from?

Heaven only knows, perhaps they were just born damned.

But when Sher's man abandoned her for a woman with larger breasts, at least he left her something more than sad black eyes, bills and the kids. He taught her to drive, didn't he, and for that she is mightily grateful.

Oh what a struggle it all is.

Kirsty and Sher Maggs verge on the obese and yet they carry no weight. They have no clout. They can shout as loudly as they like but they will never be heard – not even by their own children.

Even the threat 'Just wait till your father gets home' is denied to Kirsty and Sher, and most of the other women who live in Montpellier Court.

Billy and Sandra are impressed by the date stamps on their tiny hands.

Smack goes Kirsty as she struggles out of the store carrying her share of the wallpaper of a *My Little Pony* design requested by bored little Sandra. The wallpaper is awkward as Christmas wrapping and topheavy in the carrier bag. She slaps at her children as nonchalantly as a Memsahib might swat flies. 'I've just about had enough of you lot and I warned you . . . I warned you . . . what did I say before we went in? *What did I bloody tell you?*' And her voice is toneless and deadly.

'The rides!' they shout with one jarring voice. 'You said we could go on the rides.'

'IF, I said, if, IF you bloody behaved!' The sweat itches, same as their screams, as it trickles down her sides, between her breasts, down the crease of her back. There are unpleasant stains on the zig-zag material underneath her arms. 'Christ I could do with a fag.' She forces the hot chubby legs of her child through the wellworn webbing of the pushchair.

7

'That's not fair!' The whining pierces Kirsty's head and she shouts:

'Life's not pissing well fair.'

'Jason's gone already.'

Kirsty is instantly frightened. 'Jason's gone where?'

'He said he'd gone to look at the peacock.'

'The fucking peacock nearly killed him. What the hell's the matter with that kid?'

'I'll kill him, so help me,' murmurs Sheralee, her boiling face contorted with hatred. 'So help me, if that damn bird doesn't get him I will!'

Two safely in pushchairs and two being dragged by the arms, the depleted procession of Maggses makes its hasty way back up the hill, the way they came, in search of the missing son. 'Jason?' yells Sher every now and again, and her fag moves with the coldness of her voice.

Where is that peacock what pecked me?

His leather belt is slung low round his babyish hips.

When he was breast feeding, Jason Maggs used to stare at his mother with his iron-hard eyes and chew on her nipples till they bled.

Now Jason is a stocky child who wears a permanent scowl. Accident-prone, hyperactive, there will always be solid little bodies like Jason to haunt the dreams of primary school teachers, little girls and timid boys.

'Jason did it, Miss.' 'Jason took it.' 'It were that Jason.'

Can such an infant be motivated by malice? No, the thought is quite incredible.

A four-year-old gust of turbulence, and already his language is rich with obscenities and his knees are scabbed and full of grit.

'I'll get 'im I will, if'n it's the last thing I do.'

Jason arrives at the place where he remembers being chased by the peacock. He did not understand the fear he felt in his chest – a novel experience, it made him breathless, it was exciting – but he liked it and wants to feel it again. There is no sign of the creature with the hooked beak and the piercing black eyes, dragging its tail along in the dust. Jason wouldn't half feel wicked if he could get himself a tail like that. All he has got to do is find the thing and pull it off and say that he found it on the grass.

There is no sign of the bird, but here is a likely hole and is that a feather . . . only a little hole, mind . . . leading under this high fence as if a rabbit might have burrowed under. Fresh earth. As if there's been some kind of scraping. Maybe even a giant rat . . .

Lying flat on the sun-burnt grass, Jason thrusts his grubby little hand through the gap and pushes, and clenches, and scowls, and grits his sharp baby teeth.

Nothing. No good. With one open eye he watches a wasp drowning in the bottom of a lager can, he thinks he can hear the roar of its wings and its heartbeat. A hunter now and at one with the earth Jason concentrates harder, never a man to give up that easily.

'I can, I can, if'n I can just . . . ' In his excitement he dribbles. If he angles himself even lower, and shoves right up to the fence with his shoulder, he can gain another six inches. There's something there, he can hear it, he can hear the earth tremble close to his ear and there is the sound of something heavy listening.

On the end of his arm his little fist flexes. Grabbing to see what he can get and pull back through the hole.

'Jason, you little bugger, where the sodding hell are you?'

Severe shock numbs the pain.

It is the grip of a red hot vice on the end of a vicious, slathering breath.

Jason hears his skin ripping open.

9

He hears the gnawing on bones that crack.

He hears the tearing of tender flesh and the spurting of blood from the severed vein.

And then all he hears is his own voice screaming as he tries to retrieve his missing hand.

It is a long time since Jason Maggs has cried such babyish tears.

2

Just down the road the ramshackle convoy approaches the Melrose site of Fingles Ponds. Belligerently. Defiantly down the A38, heading for the vast expanses of Bodmin Moor where the locals wait with furious pitchforks and tractors parked in strategic places. Never again, they say to each other, fired by a wartime fervour; after last year, no, over my dead body, never again. Flanked by police, the convoy travels with a three-mile queue of demented drivers, roofs glittering in the sun behind it.

Only a couple of miles away now, they might even hear the shrieking ambulance as it rushes the hapless, handless, Jason Maggs to hospital. Poor little Jason, however despicable he may be, nobody wants a child of such tender years to suffer such a traumatic ordeal . . . as Sheralee says to the ambulance driver, and rightly, 'It's a right fucking scandal.'

Behind the iron the ban-dog sleeps, with Hump snoring drunkenly on the rag-strewn bench above him. But not for long. Hearing of the accident and sweating about the repercussions, already Zak C. Oliphant has his fat, businessman's finger on his buzzer.

'Get your arse up here. What the hell's going on?' he orders his terrified manager, a hen-pecked man called Cavendish.

They picked up Fergus Johnson as the convoy stopped for repairs on the A303 somewhere around Salisbury. He was hitching at the time, a teenage lad with patched jeans, an earring through his right nostril and wearing smart new Reeboks.

He carries a pork pie in his pocket and revenge in his heart. And why is this creature of the city travelling westwards so far away from his own patch?

We would do well to ask.

His label was bestowed upon him by a bored court reporter who made a bomb by selling the story to the nationals, and since that day 'Dogboy' has stuck like a lump of mud.

'Give us a ride, then, mate.' A product of Lambeth with time spent in Durham, his accent is tricky to place. Nothing to set him apart from the crowd, nothing smart about him apart from the Reeboks, and now he sits, staring forward, squeezed on the tatty, sun-blazed seat beside Dianne and Ramon Sinsemilla, shoved up beside their foul-smelling mongrel dog.

'Why not come with us all the way? asks the gentle Dianne, swinging her home-made papier mâché earrings. A beautiful girl, Fergus wonders what she is doing wasting her time with a pale apology for a poof like Ramon.

'Ner,' he mumbles, 'not my style.' He takes the wrapped pork pie from his pocket and begins to peel it as if it's a grape.

Dianne smiles earnestly, her pale skin wrinkling like the cellophane. She smells of earth and roots and foreign grass. Her silver hair flows and covers the side of her face as she turns towards him. A vegan – to her an egg is anathema – the smell and sight of the pork upsets her. 'What is your style, then, Fergus?'

Fergus, who inspired the bored reporter because of his unsavoury habit of leaving his mark in the houses he burgled, forces his eyes from her breasts; the top halves bulge fruitily from the top of the folded curtain secured so tenuously under her arm. What the hell's the matter with the bitch? None of the women he's ever had would be seen dead wearing an old curtain, but he wouldn't mind grabbing a handful of that. He wouldn't turn down a suck at those tits. 'I don't mix,' he grunts. Fergus licks his lips free of pastry as a wolf cleans its teeth after a meal. 'I'd rather travel alone.'

Ramon is silent in the driving seat, fighting a steering wheel which is so loose that even the joy-riding Fergus is relieved to be travelling at under thirty miles an hour.

Jesus, and not even pulled over by the pigs. Funny how these bastards manage to get away with it. While he's with them, Fergus considers, stroking the Swiss army knife in his pocket, while he's travelling in a van with a rose painted on the side, he is relatively safe.

'My child, my child!' cries Sheralee Maggs, isolated in a plastic chair at the hospital casualty department.

'Cool it,' comforts Kirsty. 'They'll come back in a minute.'

'But I want to know . . . ' wails Sheralee with understandable drama. 'I am his mother, after all.'

'Please Mrs Maggs, do have some consideration, for the sake of the other patients,' snaps one of those passing angels, a nurse, with a hard-faced frown.

'Put your shoes on Sher, come outside for a sec and have a fag,' orders Kirsty.

Ah, but Fergus Johnson is wrong, he is not safe at all. The convoy is nearing the end of its journey, about to arrive at the point of no return. This is the point where tolerance runs out. Society has reached the end of its tether. A trap lies in store. When they reach the next junction – these New Age travellers with their ragamuffin kids and their dogs and their giros and their anti-social behaviour – the Devon Constabulary have been instructed to peel the vehicles off, one from another, this one to Melrose, this one to Hartwell, and the third string will be directed to the next roundabout where they will have no option but to return the same way they came.

'Jesus, there's not even a radio in this goddamn wreck.'

Half a mile along the road there are barriers up and an army of police, restricting traffic to one lane only. Any travellers opposing the plan will be held on the hard shoulder to be dealt with later. It is a good thing the ambulance bearing Jason Maggs left half an hour earlier. If the vehicle had been delayed by the tailback, who knows what might have happened to the wretched child.

There is something wrong with Fergus Johnson, something dull and brutal, some uneasy thing you can sense but cannot see. Whatever our ideas about decency, most British mothers, knowing nothing about his history but going by instinct alone, would rather their problem children turned into hippies like Dianne and Ramon than someone like Fergus Johnson.

'What the fuck's going on?'

Fergus Johnson's slitted eyes stare through the fly-spattered windscreen. Tense and alert at once, he points out, 'Everyone's slowing down. Look, they're stopping.'

But Dianne and Ramon, this placid couple, do not appear to be phased at all. With long dirty fingers Ramon slides through the gears and the vehicle groans with relief. They might have all the time in the sodding world, but Fergus Johnson has not. Already he can see the sun glinting on uniform buttons. He can smell a gathering of rozzers a mile off, more acrid than sunburnt tar. Only the dog beside him looks worried; thirsty for water its tongue lolls out wet and slick as a slice of liver.

'It's a road block,' says Dianne. And whispers maliciously, 'The bastards.'

Fergus turns, amazed. 'You sound as if you expected it?'

'It's happening more and more these days. You just get used to it in the end.'

'So why don't you do something about it? Why do you let them do it to you? Why do you travel together and fall straight into their traps?'

'Some of us'll make it in the end.'

'Not far you won't,' says Fergus contemptuously. 'That's crap. Not through this sodding lot.'

The van pulls to a throaty halt. 'Shit, I don't need this. I'm off.' He pushes the cowering dog to one side and lets himself slide down till his feet, in his brand new Reeboks, touch the dusty road. Half a pork pie is crammed in his mouth. 'See you. Thanks for the ride . . .'

'Turds,' he mutters flakily to himself, and he slides out of sight down beside the concrete struts of the viaduct.

At the makeshift door to Hump's cage, Peter Cavendish rattles the chain of the padlock.

Silly in his office suit among the dresses, plimsolls and shorts, he shouts, 'Mr Bass? Could you spare me a moment, if you please?'

Silence.

Members of the public passing by start staring as Peter calls again. 'Mr Bass? Mr Bass?' He would much rather not be the one to have to confront the security man.

'Is that where it happened?' some morbid yob yells at him. 'Is this the place where that young kid lost his hand?'

'That is a matter for an enquiry, and I cannot comment,' says Peter stiffly, rapping once more upon the iron.

When Peter learned ballet, back in the kindergarten days, he remembered having to knock on a door and then, in silence, all the little girls and boys had to flit, like fairies, away.

Because of the sleeping guard dogs nobody is keen to set a foot inside Hump's special enclosure, least of all Peter, not a dog lover, but a man trained for softly carpeted offices, and accounts tapped out on computer. His dream was never to end up working for a spiv at a place like Fingles Ponds, but it is a step up the ladder, and there is no doubt that the 28-year-old Peter has much to learn about life.

As he is discovering more, to his dismay, day by day. But Peter Cavendish is not the only employee of Fingles Ponds to loathe his boss and the high-handed way his businesses are run. Extraordinarily, in spite of the methods used by Zak C. Oliphant, contravening most of the country's employment laws, let alone those of common humanity, no-one is man enough to best him.

Zak C. Oliphant is a thug, and ruthless to anyone who threatens his powers, yeah, even to the lowest, most common handyman or humble tiller of the soil.

Peter's recent meeting with his boss was not a pleasant experience. 'Sort it out, Cavendish, with no fuss, no publicity, no loss of face and no compensation! That's what you're paid for and that's what you'll bloody well do.'

'But Mr Oliphant,' Peter spluttered, appalled, 'the child has lost his hand. One of the dogs must have . . .'

'Sod the fucker's hand. No doubt he stuck it where he shouldn't have stuck it. If his sodding parents are too damn stupid to be able to read warning signs, then what am I supposed to do about it? Bleed? Not bloody likely. Go and have a word with that piss artist, Hump. Tell him to come up here if necessary. Directly.'

So, 'Mr Bass! Mr Bass! Are you in there?' calls Peter again, wiping anxious wet hands on his jacket. He has already attracted an interested crowd, who should be over at the bungee jumping.

Throaty growls.

The four alsatians are already on their feet, nosing along to the end of their chains. Rattling as they go.

The ban-dog twitches its smooth black ears and lays them back against its head.

Inside his hut Hump twitches, coughs and spits onto the earth-packed ground. 'What the hell . . . ?'

'Mr Bass? It's Mr Cavendish here . . .'

'Hang on. Hang on.' Who the hell is goddamn Cavendish? The padlock keys dangle from his pocket as he hitches himself

16

off the bench, shakes his ill-fitting trousers around so his cock settles comfortably, and pads towards the gate.

He opens it a fraction and squints through.

It is a grunt. 'Yeh?'

Peter Cavendish edges in, though not too far. His eyes are on the alsatians already, checking to see that they are chained before he dares to move his face into a conciliatory smile. The ban-dog he does not see. Hump may look stupid, but Hump knows that dogs such as that one are strictly taboo in this country. That's why the brute cost what he did. No, the ban-dog is chained inside the hut and Hump has pulled the door to.

'There has been an accident, Mr Bass.'

Hump gobs, and glares at Peter with rheumy eyes, so bloodshot they set Peter's off, he feels his own eyes starting to run. Is it that, or the fumes of whisky?

'Don't know anything about that,' grunts Hump, scratching his dirty head, thinly streaked with strands of grey, and greasy to a crispness. 'Been asleep. Not on duty till eight, boss.' Through the water, Hump's eyes still manage to look accusing.

'This is an emergency, Mr Bass. Earlier this afternoon a young boy . . .'

'No young boy bin in 'ere.'

'No, but the police think he might have stuck his arm through a hole.'

'The law? They bin 'ere, 'av they?'

The dogs' eyes never leave Peter Cavendish, who shivers, he cannot help it. Hell, that boy's hand was severed in seconds. 'Yes, they have, and they are still in the offices now. The awful thing is, Mr Bass, that this young boy had his arm savaged and that resulted in the loss of his hand. Now do you see how important this is?'

'But nowt to do with me, Boss.'

One of the grey alsatians is baring its teeth. Razor sharp, they shine yellowly in the sun. Hump ignores the brute. Peter is

17

forced to carry on regardless although those restraining chains seem thin, from here.

'Mr Bass, I am sorry to say that it is. It is to do with you, unfortunately. This accident, this terrible accident, is bound to bring unfortunate repercussions, and it is important that we, the management of Fingles Ponds, are aware of the events which took place here this afternoon so that we are in a better position to defend ourselves. Now, Mr Bass, could we look round the outer perimeter of your fence, so that we can see if what the young boy's mother is alleging could possibly be true?'

Hump shakes his head and spits again. Peter's novel suggestion takes some understanding. Nobody ever comes in here. 'Go round 'ere you mean?'

'Yes, Mr Bass, if you don't mind. It's either myself or the police. Just to check, you understand.'

'For 'oles, or for 'ands? My dogs 'ave been chained up all afternoon. You can see that much with your own eyes ... none of them could reach the fence ... unless they broke their chains and was cunning enough to put them together again after.' And to Peter Cavendish's disgust, Hump gives a phlegmy chuckle, stretching his lizard-scale neck to the skies and revealing the filthy line of his collar.

'You better come in then so's I can close the gate behind you. We don't want any more of these so-called accidents, do we?'

'No we do not, Mr Bass.' And Peter watches in trepidation as his way out is bolted securely behind him.

Peter Cavendish's boss has ways and means of dealing with his friends the police.

'So why don't you leave it to us, Derek? Young Cavendish is sorting it out now. So far he has reported finding neither hand nor hole.'

Zak Oliphant slaps his old golfing partner on the back as he goes on, 'If we can't prevent children burrowing under walls, in spite of strict warning notices, then where do we go from here?'

The Inspector, on his way out, nods in agreement. He slides his hat round in his hands as easily as his conscience.

Zak opens his office door and bows sycophantically to his friend. 'We have to keep tight security here, as you know, and our dogs are chained up until we have closed for the night and checked that no member of the public has inadvertently been left behind. No-one is more sorry than I . . . '

'I know, Zak. I know. The lad was probably thieving anyway.'

'At four?' Zak feigns disbelief.

'Oh yes, certainly at four. And if you'd just met the mother as I . . . '

Zak Oliphant laughs easily. 'I know, Derek. I know the type. And the trouble is, these ill-disciplined little buggers are beginning to outnumber the rest. Part of an underclass of uncontrollable children. Sadly, no matter how much money you spend you can't protect yourself against all contingencies, Derek, as you and I well know.'

'Exactly. And let's just be grateful it's only a hand, and nothing worse. Will you be popping down to the clubhouse for a jar this evening?'

'With a bit of luck, on the way home . . . '

Bloody kids.

The hospital lights go on as dusk begins to fall, a late summer dusk, filled with the smell of cut grass, and mosquitoes bunch round the light like flowers opening and closing.

'Jason is out of danger now, Mrs Maggs. If you like you can pop in and see him, but only for ten minutes. He is still under heavy sedation. Shock, you see, can cause worse damage than the injury itself if care is not taken . . . '

'Go on Sher,' whispers a bleary-eyed Kirsty. 'It's okay. I'll wait for you here. Mum'll be fine with the kids, and Cheryl says it's okay to keep the car. I've just managed to get hold of her at work . . . '

'I better take the tissues with me,' sniffs Sheralee, her cardigan clutched anxiously round her, shuffling across the linoleum in her broken-backed shoes.

While deep in the grass beside the motorway, unseen save by late-browsing rabbits, Fergus Johnson, otherwise known as Dogboy, slithers towards the slip road and the bright arc lights of Fingles Ponds. He licks the blade of his army knife in the way he was taught at Durham, revenge slides pleasingly over his tongue. Durham – they called him disturbed, my arse, and no wonder after what that bitch did to him, after everything she promised, *everything she led him to believe*. He had learned quite a lot of other, interesting stuff at Durham, too. His thieving habit, his craving for excitement, makes him wonder if there's anything worth having behind this wire, if he can cut a way through . . .

Probably not.

It's like a fucking concentration camp, although they probably don't take security all that seriously, not in this horse's arsehole of a place, talk about the back end of nowhere.

He won't press on till the morning. Best wait . . . not get mixed up with the dregs of the convoy. Plenty of time to find the cunt. He has waited for so many years already, sod it, another twenty-four hours won't hurt.

3

Nothing but a bundle of nerves since she gave up her Ativan, Mrs Maggs senior comes screeching from the flat when she sees her daughters passing the window.

'Oh my sweet Jesus. Holy Mary Mother of God and it's gone midnight. How is the poor little soul, I cannot believe this, Sheralee, come in the door, come in, you look dead beat, I just cannot believe it.'

We have to bear with the Maggs family no matter how irritable they make us feel. We have to bear with them because they play an important role in the downfall of Zak C. Oliphant.

'Thanks, Mum.' The flat sounds ominously quiet. 'Are they asleep?'

'Only just. I've been on the go since the cops rang my doorbell and brought me over and blow me not five minutes later the kiddies arrived in a police car, all bawling their eyes out and ever since then I've been backwards and forwards like a blue-arsed fly . . .'

'You ought to have put them all to bed in Kirsty's . . .'

'How could I? I needed the second cot for Billy. Oh Lord the shock of it all, Sher, the shock, I just don't know how I managed to cope . . .'

Kirsty kicks off her shoes and slumps on a sofa of bobbly Dralon donated by the community chest. Absolutely exhausted.

Kirsty and Sheralee Maggs are lucky, their flats are on the second balcony of Montpellier Court. One with a cheery lemon door, one with a red one. Okay they get the kiddies playing on the landing, knocking their balls around every hour of the day, but the yobs mostly go up to the eighth – almost abandoned now, and the windows are only burnt-out eyes – and it's on the stairways that the dealers hang out so they don't have to push past them every day like poor Laura on the sixth does, with three kiddies and a pushchair.

'He's gonna be okay, the little bleeder. Jesus, Mum, I never knew I had such pain in me . . . ' And, for the first time since the incident Sheralee Maggs stops swearing and bursts into predictable tears.

'But his hand, sweetheart . . . ' Dulcie Maggs, the only married woman among them and that was for just three weeks in the fifties, says, 'The cops said Jason had lost . . . ' The tea tray rattles as, with difficulty, she lowers it to the glass coffee table. Her two daughters stare as she fights with the words in her mouth, slipping her plate in position to get the awful concept round all its slippery pinkness, 'they said his hand was bitten right off.' And then she adds in a quaking voice, 'at the wrist, if you please!'

'But he's going to live, Mum. At first they thought . . . ' It is too harrowing to go on. They said that Jason lost so much blood.

'But Sheralee – *what about his hand?*'

'You wonder what sort of dog, don't you?' And Kirsty takes over from her mother, pouring the heavy brown tea into fluted cups without saucers. 'What sort of dog could do that?' The kids have broken most of the saucers, using them to mix up paints.

'Never mind what sort of dog, Kirsty. You wonder what sort of people they are to make it possible for little kiddies Jason's age to get in that position in the first place. I mean, where do they keep these monsters?'

22

Kirsty heaps sugar into Sheralee's tea – sugar, for shock. 'It's a kind of store. For the animals. Feed and that. It's a fenced-off place in the middle. No-one but that little sod Jason would have dreamed of sticking their hand inside . . . under the fence, for God's sake. He stuck it right through the fence, Mum.'

'Hang on, Kirsty, what was a hole doing under that fence in the first place?'

'I suppose they can't keep their eyes on everything. Jason might have dug it himself. Knowing the little swine, I wouldn't put it past him.'

'Rubbish. It's their responsibility. Jason could never have dug a hole like that – a hole large enough for him to get his arm in. No, it's their responsibility and it's them who will have to cough up!' Dulcie Maggs rolls baggy blue eyes. Her lips smack tightly together with righteous conviction. Her head is covered with tight white curls, the fashion of coach-party women. Over her dress she wears a button-through overall and, having lately found out about pop socks, her legs bulge veinily at the knee where the grip of the dark nylon stops. Perhaps Dulcie Maggs, smoking as heavily as she does, should think a little harder about the possibility of thrombosis.

As Zak C. Oliphant's Jaguar approaches the driveway to his house his progress is floodlit by a system of hidden sensors.

The chippings on his drive glint like diamonds embedded in snow.

Zak lives in a house of chimes. There is a wind chime under the porch, and the doorbell itself plays 'Alas, my Love! ye do me wrong to cast me off discourteously' – the first few bars of *Greensleeves*.

But Zacharias Cornelius Oliphant has his own key, which opens the back door leading from the garage; he enters his house through a kitchen of English Rose and is hit by the feral smell of geraniums. And a fine kitchen it is, too, nothing cheap and shabby about the Oliphant kitchen, nothing you might find in tawdry places such as Fingles Ponds. A breadboard from there will warp after a couple of months of wear.

Oh dear, being poor costs money – what with repairs for worn out cars, jumble sale clothing, badly wearing clothes and bedding, let alone warped breadboards.

But Zak and Kimberley Oliphant know nothing of this because they have never been poor. But they have an inbuilt terror of it, all the same.

'It's me, darling. I'm afraid I'm later than I promised.'

Kimberley Oliphant, annoyed but pretending not to be, switches off *Coronation Street* and moves to meet her husband in the kitchen. She turns on the microwave and goes to the built-in bar to pour her husband a welcome brandy.

'How was your day?'

'How was yours?'

Neither of them answers immediately, but they mime the procedure of pecks on cheeks.

'I went to the golf club to buy Derek Hooper a drink. Spot of bother this afternoon . . . ' Zak sips his brandy with relish and flings off his heavy dark jacket.

'I heard. It was on the news. A little boy lost his arm . . . '

'A hand, Kimberley, a hand! There's no need to exaggerate. A little boy fooling about where he had no business to be fooling.'

Kimberley is silent as she sips her gin, coming to sit down beside him. Heftily built, ageless and painted, she looks like a tango contestant out of *Come Dancing*. Eventually she asks, 'Did they find the hand?'

'No, the blessed dog must have eaten it up.'

'Are you expecting trouble?'

His answer is irritated. 'Why would there be trouble?'

Kimberley shakes her hard groomed head. 'No reason. I just thought. I mean, if you went to have a drink with Derek . . . '

'I often stop by to have a drink with Derek.'

'I know dear, I know.'

24

Kimberley was sickened by the news item. But then, Kimberley is sickened by so much that she sees and hears that she has her own form of defence. She was already on her third gin when she heard it, and went, at once, to pour herself another.

Zak is not only a tyrant at work, but here in his neat and cared-for home, without any need for physical violence, he terrorises the lounge, the conservatory, the dining room, the kitchen, the study, the bathrooms and the bedroom.

Even his smell is a terrifying mixture of cigar tobacco and plaque mouthwash.

But Kimberley chose a dominant man, so why should she complain? She prefers dominant men. With a dominant man she can remain passive, and sweet and pretty; even at forty-nine she has the knack of curling up like a kitten without looking ridiculous.

Once she was a model and posed like that on a calendar. Before she married Zak she ran her own mobile hairdressing business, supported by her father.

Kimberley Oliphant is dependent on Zak for everything she is and everything she does. And she enjoys a life of exotic holidays and shopping sprees – not much culture, granted, and she might feel uneasy with his taste in furnishings . . . the coffee table with the Prince of Wales feathers carved in the oak, for example. Or the ornamental telephone in the shape of a grand piano.

But some things you just have to put up with . . . don't you? He is hardly home, anyway. Zak is a man's man and a good ol' boy with the fellas. A workaholic, successful Freemason, chairman of the local Rotary, this year's captain of the golf club.

And what is Kimberley?

Sometimes she sees herself through the bottom of a beautifully cut glass, darkly, and then she closes her long-lashed eyes and smiles, ruefully.

25

Zak undoes his waistcoat buttons, prepared to enjoy his meal to the full. 'Anyway,' he says, expanding, 'they're not the sort of people to know how to make a fuss.'

'Oh?'

'A couple of tarts, apparently, not two halfpennies to rub together.'

'Well that's a relief then, isn't it dear,' says Kimberley.

At eight o'clock on the dot, just as Zak is starting his sprouts, Hump Bass oils his runaround truck, loads it with bedding and straw, throws on the shovel, and sets off in electrical silence to tackle his first job of the evening, cleaning the animals out.

Mr Oliphant prefers this to be done at night because the public don't like it. There is another reason, also, and Hump sympathises with his boss's point of view. He doesn't want his security man lounging around all night doing fuck all and if the animals find it most natural to sleep at night, as humans do, and would rather not be disturbed, then bad bloody luck to them.

'They're here for our convenience, not theirs,' as Mr Oliphant is wont to point out.

And Hump, who admires Mr Oliphant, agrees with him absolutely.

It is not until an hour later, when he has checked that all is secure, that he will let the guard dogs out. No names. No need for names, after all, what sort of a handle is Hump for God's sake? No, there's One, Two, Three, Four, all the alsatians respond to the calls, and what is the matter with Dog for the big one . . . that's what he is, isn't he?

Dog is an honest name and a good enough description of the creature acquired by Hump last year from the salesman from Cresswells, the animal feed people.

'Straight from the US of A. No kidding,' said Alan McCabe, his eyes shining. 'Jesus, you should see the bastard. Like nothing on earth, I can tell you.' A tall man, he bent only slightly to indicate the ban-dog's extreme size with an excited open hand.

Hump's sharp nose grew sharper. 'Who's got 'im then, Alan?'

'Client of mine, farms out in the sticks near Launceston. He's got some good dogs already, pit bulls, crosses, terriers and the like, and he paid a fortune for this one thinking he could start to cross-breed in this country, make himself a fortune. Bit on the dodgy side, but worth a try. Talk about sod's law. One week later the government, which'd been fairly lax until then, panicked, clamped down on dangerous dogs. Christ, Hump, I dunno what he thinks he's going to do with this baby now. Trained and all. Covered in bloody great scars. There's no other breed can touch it. 'Course, prestige is what it's all about, has to be that when you think about it, but if the law gets wind of this little darling . . . '

Hump understands about prestige; it is something he has always wanted but never come anywhere near attaining. He would pay anything, do anything to get his hands on just a smattering of this sort of power. His mouth fell open with awe. Two blackened incisors hung from his jaw like a couple of fangs. 'How'd your friend get him into the country?'

'Ah, well, that's another story. The poor brute was anaesthetised for twenty-four hours and nailed up in a crate under a pile of fucking computer software. Hell of a risk, of course. Not just a fucking fine . . . a hefty stretch if you're caught with something like that in your back yard, and the bugger might have died on him.'

'Yep, could have.'

'He comes from a line of fine fighting dogs, well known in America. Crossed with ruddy great mastiffs, see. 'Course round about here, folks think different . . . Them Yanks is more easy going than us.'

'If he were so good, why did the Yank want rid of 'im?' asked Hump shrewdly, closing one wily eye.

'Ten a penny out there, mate. No rarity value, see. No, only joking, more likely this black bugger was more than even he could handle.'

Hump nodded and scratched his head, stared at the contents of his nails and admitted, 'Proper job.' And then, almost begging, 'Jeez, Alan, I'd badly love to see 'im.'

'Well, maybe I can arrange that. My client is an agreeable sort of bloke. No doubt he'd welcome the chance to show the bugger off. What else can he do with it? He can't breed from it. He can't fight it. Waste of money when you think about it. But don't go spreading the dirt, Hump. Keep this strictly to yourself . . . it's a big one.'

'Who the bloody hell do I see? Am I likely to spread the gossip around with my social life as it is, damn it?' Hump spat on the ground with disgust while Alan was forced to step back to protect his suede Hushpuppies.

That is how it started and that is how Hump Bass acquired the Dog, the love of his life, for five thousand smackers, everything he'd managed to put by during his fifty-two years of working life, from a boy of twelve picking up coal, which is when he was given his name, to security man at Fingles Ponds. A life he was used to by then, a life spent in darkness with only occasional glimpses of the sun to warm his withering, sodden soul.

Someone else's soul is withering on the vine not very far from here, someone who is creeping along in the darkness, someone whose soul started to decay the day his mother died, when they lived up in Bolton and Fergus was eight years old.

That's when he first met *HER*. She was young, then, very young, and keen, eager to do well when she came round with that stern older woman, 'to learn the trade' as she jovially put it.

She can't have been more than twenty-one. Just out from some snooty university or other and she smelled of the countryside, and those straggly wild roses that grow around ruins, the way that they give out their scents in the dusk.

Can you fall in love when you're eight years old, and can it last? Can it be something you can never shake out of your head, something you are forced to endure even when you can feel it driving you bloody well crazy?

Anyway, Mum had married four years previous to that and she and Fergus moved from the room and into Roland's house – Roland, the wanker. The prat. Randy, rabid, rancid Roland.

A shitty little house that frowned at Fergus under all that brown paint, a huddled house full of lino, in a narrow street where Fergus spent most of the time outside, sitting on the step, or running errands, while Mum screwed with Roland upstairs.

Funny really, Mum must have been dying already. They said it had been growing inside her for years. Of the womb, it was. Cancer of the womb. Having a child had possibly triggered it, that's what they told Roland.

Cancer is just like love. It grips you without your permission. It grows bigger and bigger and eats you up until it takes you over completely, sobbing with pain, and then, if it's kind, it kills you.

Fergus had never known about his dad. Till he was eight he had not considered it strange that he didn't have one. He hadn't realised, had not understood that his dad could be a real live person made of flesh and blood who might have taken him in. Not until it was too bloody late and there was no-one to tell him.

Fergus and Roland never got on, so no wonder he wanted to get shot of Fergus after his Mum died of the cancer. He wouldn't even nurse her himself at the end. Said that he couldn't do that and keep working as well; someone had to bring home the bacon, said Roland. He never even gave Fergus a chance to stay home from school and do it. Roland packed her off to a hospital and she hated that. She'd told Fergus how she hated that but Fergus was helpless, what could he do?

'You've got me, now, Fergus, and I'm not going to die. Between us, you and I, we are going to work together to find you a home where you are going to be very happy. And we'll stick at it till we do. I'm not giving up on you, Fergus. Now, come on, cheer up and give me one of those gorgeous smiles.'

Snotty great kid that he was, eight years old but still, she had let him sit on her knee and burrow into her hard little bosoms.

'What shall I call you?' asked little Fergus, clinging to anything that was solid, lost and angry in the chaos of childhood loss.

'Call me what my best friends call me. Call me Jem,' she said. 'My name is Jemima but nobody wants to bother with that. What a mouthful. What do you think my mum and dad were thinking about when they gave me a name like that?'

When she smiled her lips made a nice, unsticking sound.

'Well I like it,' said the fawning Fergus, beginning to wonder if the best thing possible hadn't happened to him after all. He'd been lonely for a long time, since they'd moved in with Roland. He had lost that early closeness he'd shared with his mum. He couldn't feel sad for her yet, not then, that came later as a kind of emptiness, a dull thudding when his heart beat faster at night and he couldn't breathe when he realised how small he was, in a world without family, friends or relations.

The long and the short of it was – he never brought that certain smile to anyone's face any more.

'I care,' Jemima had told him, seriously. 'I care now, and nothing that happens in the future will make me stop caring about you, Fergus.'

Jemima was new to the job, so surely Miss Bird, in her supervisory capacity, should have warned her new social worker about the importance of impartiality.

*

You can only cut so many Js into the skin of your arm. The more deeply you cut the more you divert the anguish of obsession.

She lives down here somewhere, in a village just outside Melrose. It had not been difficult to find her new address, he had just stalked into the office, like he always had, and demanded it. They were wary of Fergus at the office – tossers – Dogboy and his unpredictable behaviour. Jemima Hardy-Brown, the receptionist told him with a sugary smile – not working any more but the mother of her own two lovely children since she married three years ago while Fergus was locked up in Durham.

'But I'm sure she'd love to hear from you, Fergus, if you'd care to write. I know she was always very fond . . . '

But Fergus was gone, leaving the door swinging behind him, snuffing out the stench of charitable cardboard boxes and jumble sale socks.

Yes, fond enough to betray him. How many times had she done it before, and now this!

Write, my arse.

Fergus Johnson leans his back against the fence, plugs in his Walkman, and glares accusingly at the moon as he listens to the reggae plea:

> Doan worry.
> Be happy.

4

One a.m. and the moon has gone in, all the available space has been taken up by the pushy stars.

The dog's approach is a stealthy one in spite of its giant size. The pads on its feet are large and soft, efficiently splayed to carry the muscle, bone and sinew required of them, all that strained tension which is now poised and crouched silently above them. Red eyes stare from the slits in the mastiff's bullet head. Two hundred pounds of fighting power housed in a package of hard black silken dog-skin.

Fascinated by the unfamiliar smell of cannabis and LSD, the creature is drawn towards the fence, not soft here, like the place where it fed yesterday. Where it ripped, tore and swallowed and filled a small hole in its belly.

Hang on. Let's be reasonable. Before we depersonalise this animal any further, we have to stop and talk about the bandog's antecedents, and now is as good a time as any, before we become too involved.

But don't worry – this is not the real life story of Old Shep, nor is it a caricature of the Waltons who lived in a shack on the Blue Ridge Mountains during the years of the thirties depression, although it has to be said that Ethan Adams was as near to a present day Huckleberry Finn as you are ever likely to get.

Dang me, look at the lad, an all-American boy in his L.L.Bean tartan shirt, his rugged blue jeans and his sneakers. He even carries a battered straw hat, nagged into taking it with him by his ma. If only he would suck on a straw, and give us the total effect.

Satan had been blessed with his name for only twenty-eight days when he was unceremoniously hurled from the back of a Ford pick-up truck somewhere in the wilds of West Virginia. See how the dry, dry farmland spreads out as far as the eye can see till it wrinkles against the mountains, and yellow buses like browsing wasps call for the children each morning to take them to school, buzzing along over dusty tracks.

Rather puts Fingles Ponds to shame, with their assortment of bruised little acres.

Where West Virginia borders Kentucky, far from the steel mills of Pittsburgh and the factories of Detroit, there is a mining valley which huddles between the foothills, a valley in the wilderness. And it was in this valley, in the early morning light, just as the sun started to filter through the trees, that Ethan Adams, aged twelve and a strange sort of kid, found Satan, not fifty yards from the highway.

Darn it. He'd never seen anything bigger than a coon hound before. And sheeit, this was a puppy, hardly weaned.

In under five minutes Satan's name was changed to Scooby-Doo and he found himself lugged towards the nearest cover available, a clump of prickly brush down by the river.

The dog snarled sweetly.

The reason for the ditching of Satan was simple. The look-out car in front of the pick-up carried a CB mast, a silver wand which waved like an ant's antennae over its hot, bulging forehead. It radioed back to the pick-up, 'Holy shit. Say Cy, ditch them pups, there's a goddamned police checkpoint ahead . . . ' There'd been too many warnings already; the next time, the law insisted, the breeder would be prosecuted. The rest of the message was blotted out as the pick-up roared to a halt, the back was lowered, and the box of puppies tipped upon the road.

On went the pick-up. The bitch with the dumb but worldly eyes lay mystified in the back as she was carried on her wobbly way, through a sea of thick dust, till the box faded from sight and even when she stood up she could not make it out from the boulders.

The box emptied overnight and the puppies staggered off squeaking, each going its own way.

Satan stuck to the road, where the going was easier and less prickly.

Scooby-Doo was moved several times after that, finally taking up residence in a cave on the ridge which became the den of the gang led by Ethan Adams.

Brave lads who leaped on and off the trains as they steamrolled through town coughing cinders.

'What kind of dog is this sonofabitch?'

'He's wild, that's what he is. Could be a wolf. Yep. Darned right he could be. Hundred percent.' And Ethan drank from a carton of soda pop.

'Naw,' protested Leroy, the cocky one with the longest dick and the furthest pissing power. 'Wolves ain't that colour. Wolves ain't jet black like this feller. And wolves have sharp muzzles, his is all flabby and soft, all this hangin' skin round his face.'

Every day the ban-dog grew and every day they would set off, Scooby-Doo and the gang, doing nothing much but exploring and climbing the ridges, swimming in the rivers – they would throw sticks in the swiftest currents for Scooby-Doo to retrieve, laying bets on whether he could or not, playfully tossing walnuts at him. They hunted rabbits and coons. They camped out overnight as the long summer holidays stretched endlessly on.

As he grew older, and only by a matter of weeks, Scooby-Doo became a problem. When he had food, which they took it in turns to scrounge for him – mostly hog bones with rank

34

chunks still attached – from the bin behind the stores, he would coil himself up, snarling, while he worried and tore at the meat, his eyes fixed angrily on them. 'Must've bin starved or fed on nothin'.' They grabbed for the meat in fun, daring each other to get closer. They watched him warily, never quite certain when they were safe to approach. It seemed to be something to do with his nature. And then one day, for no apparent reason, he went for Ott Hammer's balls.

'Call him off, oh Christ get him off me,' the boy was shrieking, pounding the dog's head with his fists, and although the animal shifted his hold it took two of them all their strength to move him.

There were deep teeth marks in the soft place at the top of Ott Hammer's thighs.

'Shit, and he's one mean sonofabitch, no kiddin'. What if he's got friggin' rabies?'

To check on the state of his fear of water, one week later they threw Ott into the river.

'Nope,' they sighed with relief, watching him swim calmly to shore. 'Nope, he ain't got rabies.'

Summer, fall, and a lonely winter of dripping icicles holed up in a hunter's cabin, fed when the gang remembered. And when summer came around Scooby-Doo, a hard and muscled twelve months old, had lost all of his sweetness and his novelty value was falling fast.

But one day they cleared a space in a cornfield ten rows in, a natural theatre hidden from view, and they fetched the meanest mongrel from town, a grey, lanky thing with a tail like a rat's, which belonged to Horse Parsons, a crusty old man who worked on the railroad downriver.

None of the other town dogs would go near it, cringing on their bellies in the dust when they saw the mongrel approach.

Ethan's gang lured the sly-eyed creature to the cornfields by dragging a piece of meat along before it, on a rope. Its tongue

35

rolled out like a party blower. Whenever the animal grabbed the meat they let it stop and take a bite before chasing off down the track with another piece of dubious bait tied to the end. In this jerky fashion they led it through the path in the cornfield, careful to pull the cornstalks closed behind them.

'Atta boy, Scoob.'

Boy Hennessey snickered.

At the sight of his wiry opponent – the first dog he had ever seen other than his brothers and sisters – Scooby froze for a second or two before he went foaming mad, an awesome sight to behold. Ethan Adams clamped his hand over his mouth, realising murder was about to be done but it was too late to stop it. Half the size of the mongrel, yet Scooby was twice as heavy. None of the kids gathered round felt like laughing any longer.

The smell of fear hung in the air like the red hot sun on the browning corn.

'Shit, reckon we've gotta find a bucket of water.'

'Goddamn fool, where are we goin' to find a bucket of water out here?'

With a slathering snarl the ban-dog threw itself onto the bitch and embedded his teeth in its neck. Having first unbalanced the mongrel – who let out a steady high-pitched scream that set the hairs on your head on end – the jet black dog shook it just as if it was made of straw with no weight at all. Quick as sprung steel he let go of his howling prey only to take a firmer hold, clamping both jaws tight for the kill.

This was no fight, therefore this was no fun.

The boys had expected to see the old mongrel punished, taught a lesson for its mean and wicked ways. Ott Hammer, remembering the nights he spent spreading antiseptic on his bite marks, was the only one who had secretly hoped the mongrel, with its greater experience, might win. But now even Ott was worried. The railroad man, Horse Parsons, had one helluva temper and if he discovered his bitch had been deliberately led into a fight where she'd end up worse off than merely bloodied, the game would definitely be up. Better to see the mongrel killed, so they could take it away and bury it, rather than see it crawling, wounded, dragging its bloody, mangled tail back into town.

But the devil dog was not just out for the kill, he was tearing and maiming instead, wreaking an unholy carnage. The victim's two front legs dangled in the dust, both broken. A crunching sound then, as the mighty teeth began cracking open the skull. Ethan picked up a hoe and beat it down on the black dog's head, but it made no impression at all. Finally, saying nothing, but grimacing and picking up his gun, the youngest among them, Boy Hennessey, sprayed pellets into the black dog's side.

Afterwards the young boy's face was tight and white – he'd only shot at squirrels before.

The bang made the cornstalks rattle.

The dog yelped, leapt in the air and rolled over, while the loser, in mortal agony, cringed and began to pee. Jesus effing Christ, the stink, the pungent liquid flowing into the dust and clinging to it in crimson puddles along with half its innards, foam, scum and gristly bits. And its eyes begged for pity.

Except for the pellets the ban-dog wasn't wounded. Not a scrape was on him. Nor a cut. They warded off the ban-dog using the hoe as a pole until they could reach him and tie him again.

Boy Hennessey re-loaded his shotgun to put a quick end to the loser's anguish. They buried the mongrel right there in the cornfield, and avoided Horse Parsons like the plague for several months after that.

As the hardwoods broke into the brilliant colours of autumn, the clouds began to clamp their wintery lids onto the mountain tops. Ethan's gang were forced to abandon the tough restraining ropes which the dog chewed through with worrying ease, and use a chain instead. The hunter's cabin could not be made sufficiently secure. They hammered the link into the rock at the back of the cave when they left Scooby for the night. They made a new rule; no-one must approach Scooby-Doo without someone else being around.

School was open again and Scooby-Doo spent most of his time alone, dry and protected from the wet and the blow under his ridge. The boys, now one year older, had better things to do than wrap themselves up in their winter gear and venture out into the swiftly falling darkness. There was football again. And they'd rather hang around Ruby's Diner with its steamy windows, smoking and listening to the juke box. Rumour had it that Ruby would show you her cunt for twenty dollars, but nobody raised enough money to prove it.

Finally, after three days had gone by and no-one had visited Scooby-Doo, the water in his bucket was all iced over and Leroy told Ethan, 'Tain't no use, Ethan, you can't keep him out there in the freezin' cold. Reckon you'll have to hide him some place else, maybe somewhere nearer to home or he'll be wild directly.' There was no fun in keeping a dog you didn't dare go near and the trouble with him was, you couldn't see his mood in his face. If Scooby-Doo was going to turn, he'd turn on you without changing expression.

'That fucking killer is wild already. And he's costin' me plenty more than I reckoned he would.'

The next time Ethan and Leroy went up to the ridge they made the final decision together. They shared the nerve-racking chore of leading the ban-dog to the outhouse next to Ethan's house. Pa kept an old anvil which even the ban-dog would be pushed to shift. They could anchor the bugger to that. It was funny, you seemed to be able to follow his smell right up and into the cave. Wolf. Wet fur and evil energy. It was extraordinary that no hunter had accidentally stumbled upon him. Their bodies tense, their eyes watchful, Leroy carried his gun and Ethan kept a rock in his pocket in case the bastard turned ugly when they led him down the dirt road into town under cover of darkness.

'The trouble is, you never trained him right,' said Leroy.

'Jesus, whenever I tried the sonofabitch eyed me up wicked and took a lunge at me . . . '

'Too soft. Pa says these fightin' dogs is evil, and has to be ruled with a rod of iron.'

'Yeah – but goddamnit, when I first had him I didn't know he was a fightin' dog, did I, Leroy?'

It wasn't too long before the outhouse was shit high and stinking worse than the pig-man's dung heap. Ethan couldn't find enough time to get in there with his shit bag and shovel what with everyone prowling around. The rest of the gang had lost all interest. It seemed that he was stuck with his dog.

So he wasn't sorry when he was in there one day, shovelling shit with one hand and holding his nose with the other, and trying to watch Scooby all at the same time while the dog rattled his chains to get loose as usual, when the low voice came from behind him, 'What you got in there, boy?'

He had grown more nervous of Scooby than he was of his pa. The most he could get was a whipping, and he could cope with that.

'He was nothin' but a pup when I found him a year ago, Pa. I didn't know what I was doin'.'

Ethan's pa stayed at the door, his eyes fixed on the growling ban-dog. He spoke without hesitation. There was none of the expected anger in his voice. 'Good God Almighty. I've only once in my life seen a critter like this before.' He swallowed nervously, took a step back, and in a very calm voice he said, 'Back out of there, Ethan, don't make any sudden moves but back out and close the outhouse door.'

Ethan turned, surprised, to look at his father.

'Do it, son, and do it NOW. That bastard'll rip your arm

from your body as easy as takin' candy from a baby. That sonofabitch is straight from hell.'

'I know a man,' said Ethan's father, and before the evening was up, before the mountains and ridges and pine trees gave up their shapes to the darkness, the ban-dog was on his way once again, penned up in a sheep truck, just eighteen months older than when he was ditched on this same highroad by Cy Fitzgerald.

'You done real well, boy,' said Pa, with a wink, giving Ethan a straight twenty dollars . . .

Back to Fingles Ponds again, and in silence the creature watches the boy as he nods his head in time to the music. Steady with anger, the ban-dog edges closer to the fence, hackles raised in the back of his neck. He knows that the fence divides them, he has explored every inch of his compound a thousand times over and has no particular wish to escape. By night he is free to roam at will, called in by Hump for raw meat at seven in the morning, sleeping and resting in Hump's hut during the day and never a hand or a stick raised against him.

It is a good life for this killing machine, no longer the potent mixture of pleasure and pain that it used to be. He should be feeling something by now, but the nothingness inside him will not dislodge itself.

As if it has been beaten there, or poured into his damaged brain like lumpen, molten metal.

5

It's going to be another hot one.

You might not have noticed, and it is understandable if you have not, but Fergus Johnson made a special effort before he set forth on his journey yesterday. The way he looks matters to him for two important reasons – 1, in spite of his fury he wants Jemima Hardy-Brown to like him, and 2, if all else fails he will look sharp in front of the TV cameras. Sharp = threatening and unfriendly.

No blanket-over-the-head job for Dogboy.

No huddling on the back seat of a pig car.

On his white T-shirt is printed the web of a spider.

His nose ring sparkles.

His Reeboks cost him nothing.

Nor did his genuine baseball cap which is worn back to front, (although this is a mistake because it drags his hair back and makes his greasy brow seem more bulbous than ever). And his leather jacket is slung over one tattooed shoulder.

Quite comfortable in the spot he chose for the night, it is a good spot, with some good cover, nevertheless he is forced to move on before the traffic gets heavy in case the pigs come by and stop him to ask where he is going.

> Mrs G. Hardy-Brown.
> The Old Schoolhouse.
> Middlehempston.
> Near Melrose.
> Devon.

Posh eh?

Who the fuck does the bitch think she is and what sort of arsehole has she married?

He has got that address scrawled on the back of his hand, where it has been since he was naively given it by the receptionist at the social services.

No fear of it getting washed off except by a torrential downpour of rain.

He overcame his natural inclination to break into Fingles Ponds in the night. No point in attracting needless attention when he has more important business to attend to. Anyway, he has got all the dosh he needs for the few days of his visit.

He pats his pocket, reassured by the feel of the army knife, and sets off down the Melrose road wondering what the shit has happened to all the buses.

The next movement of any importance comes from within the Fingles Ponds enclosure itself. Propping open the door of the stores, Hump calls his dogs home with a high-pitched whistle. Free to roam the twenty-acre site all night where they forage for skinny rabbits and rodents, yet they need no encouragement.

With his bare hands he slops the bloody melts from the galvanised bucket into their individual bowls, sprinkles the mess with dry biscuit and makes sure to put the black dog's bowl down first.

'Get on, yer varmint.'

Once the ban-dog is totally engrossed, tucking into his meal of the day, then, and only then, is Hump safe to serve the others.

When he is done Hump wipes the slick off his hands onto the back of his trousers. He clicks the chains to the alsatians' studded collars while they are otherwise occupied. He waits until the ban-dog has finished before he approaches that one, and for this job he dons a pair of thick leather gloves.

Yesterday, fool that he was, he'd made the fatal mistake of trusting the bugger. After his return to the compound, after checking that it was safely padlocked, he took a snap and foolish decision to avoid the risky procedure of securing the blasted ban-dog. After all, the corrugated fence was twelve feet high, the brute was hardly likely to find his way out.

How was he to figure that some goddamn kid would come shoving his hand under the fence? He must have slept deep, he hadn't heard the screaming. Hump does his job, doesn't he? And he does it well. Can't be expected to start sussing out all the faults in the sodding system. Never was much good at brain work, leaves that to the bosses which is what they are frigging well paid for.

Tossers, the lot of 'em.

However, this morning he takes the risk, and clips the ban-dog to his chain the moment he has finished eating.

'But are you sure you'll be able to keep this bugger well out of the way and give him the exercise he needs at the same time?' asked Alan McCabe's client, after Hump had made his offer. 'Take a bit of feeding, too, these types. Not like your daily tin of Chappie.'

Hump gobbed and the burly farmer recoiled. 'What d'you take me for? It's a dog, isn't it? And I know dogs.'

The farmer winked slyly at McCabe, who had promised to find him a sucker in return for a handling fee. They would have accepted a quarter of Hump's ridiculous price. The Launceston farmer had confided, 'I'd never have touched a devil like this if I'd known what I know now, fortune or no fortune. Yep, I reckon for the first time ever the law has done me a favour. You'll never tame a beast like this, not in a thousand years you won't.'

'But Hump Bass doesn't know that, does he?'

'Hump Bass knows fuck all. He's missing up here, isn't he? Tells everyone it's the result of a cave-in!'

'Cave-in my arse. Cave-in of the brain, most likely.'

'Lucky for us, in the circumstances.' And the two men chuckled together as Hump drove away in his sagging van.

But not for one minute does Hump regret his decision. Really, his set-up is ideal. He is left entirely to his own devices, and nobody comes near Fingles Ponds after eight o'clock at night without pressing the alarm buzzer on the gates first. This gives Hump the necessary time to call in the dogs.

And no bugger in their right mind would go nosing round the perimeter fence at night. Hardly a pleasant place for a stroll, right beside the motorway with its fumes, junctions and bridges. No bus stop for miles, and a hard shoulder bristling with briars and nettles.

Nope. Hump runs his seeping eye over the glowering ban-dog.

Power.

Prestige.

Nobody knows of the ban-dog's existence but him, the farmer, and McCabe. But nobody needs to know. Hump knows.

Good morning!

Rise and shine!

The Maggs family are awoken, as usual, by children's cries.

This morning it is Scott and Sandra, Kirsty's kids. At least Kirsty, with her two fatherless brats, has more restraint than her sister, the tramp.

Next door Billy and Kelly are woken by the racket coming through the paper-thin wall. This is unusual. Normally they would have woken at dawn, battered awake by Jason.

With old make-up soaking into the night-creases in her face, Sheralee rises to face the day, dozy with those extra few hours of sleep. Her nightdress used to be rose; now it is dead petal grey, and quite a sophisticated colour if she had bought it like

44

that. But Sheralee is a poor sort of person and not sophisticated at all. There is old boiled egg down her front from yesterday's breakfast, and little holes burnt into the nylon where hot ashes have fallen from her rollies.

Sheralee has never been a pretty sight first thing in the morning. It takes her an hour to wake up. Maybe this is why her man left her. 'Unwholesome,' he called her, before he disappeared out the door.

She did not grieve.

After he left her for the bigger-breasted woman Sheralee unwittingly entered the contest. Not bothering to wear a bra any more – for what was the point? – this liberation caused her breasts to gain both weight and vigour. It is a secret she keeps to herself, and enjoys.

'Come on, come on, let's get you lot dressed, we've got to get to the hospital . . . '

'Want to stay here with Nana . . . '

'Nana can't stay here with you. Nana's got to get back to her house to look after her pussies.'

'Want to go with Nana . . . '

'Nana doesn't want you with her. She had you all day yesterday. Nana's nerves are in shreds, you know that, I'm always telling you that. That's why you have to behave . . . '

'Where are Nana's nerves? I've seen them. In her hair.'

'Oh shit, in her arse, probably. Now get out of that bed, Kelly, and let me change this frigging sheet.'

Sheralee is going to have to lug them with her to the hospital on the bus and put up with the sharp jibes of authority all day long unless Kirsty can be persuaded . . . just this once . . .

It is an unwritten rule that neither sister will fob the other one off with her kids unless it's a real emergency, and, living on each other's doorsteps it is a rule that really ought to be kept, for sanity's sake.

However, if this is not an emergency, what the fuck is, and so, in towelling gown and slippers, crumpled fag hanging from

45

the smudged corner of her mouth, Sheralee Maggs shuffles needily along the landing to say good morning to her mother, Dulcie, who has spent the night on the sofa, and to her sister, Kirsty.

'Oh, I thought we would all go together,' says Kirsty brightly, kettle on already.

Is this a cunning entreaty? Is Kirsty so nervous of being left alone all day with little Billy and Kelly?

'After all, Sheralee, you're going to need support, aren't you?'

Shit it, thinks Sheralee, but she wishes she could have a few more mornings like this, with Jason safely out of the way, with Jason in some other bedroom under some other roof.

And then, when she thinks of the poor little mite and his poor little hand, the guilt makes her hate herself so much she nearly retches on her acid build-up of wickedness.

Good morning!

Rise and shine!

Zak's dressing gown is the russets and browns of a man's Easter egg packaging.

'These things escalate, that's the trouble, and that's why it's important to slam the lid down before they're allowed to get out of hand.'

Down in the kitchen, down from his early morning shower with his energetic energy deadening all it lights upon – wet towels, bath mat, weary slippers and toast – Zak Oliphant picks up the morning paper and growls at his wife.

'Look at this!' He shakes the limpid organ at her. 'Look at this crap!'

Kimberley sags as usual while she tries to rinse the smell from the dishcloth. There is old milk in it, and she really ought to throw it away but she sees it as a challenge.

'As soon as I get to the office I'm going to ring Cyril.'

Cyril is Zak's solicitor.

'Take legal action you mean?'

'Take out an injunction to stop these goons blackening my character and threatening my living!'

'I don't see . . .'

Zak pours sauce on his eggs and booms, 'Parasites!'

He can be so vindictive, once he gets a bee in his bonnet. 'It looks like a fairly straightforward report to me, dear. The journalist probably picked it up from the police during a routine visit. I would have thought it might be better to let sleeping dogs lie.'

'Under the circumstances I consider that a particularly thoughtless remark, Kimberley, and since when have you been privy to the habits of the local press?'

'I'm not privy to anything . . .'

'Damnit, I'm trying to read!'

Silence, as Zak's angry presence seems to deaden even the cat who slinks from the room, ghostlike, and the radio crackles with static.

Kimberley wants to argue, but her mouth will not say the words and her heart is not in it. She has bigger things on her mind today. She is off to the hospital this morning having found a lump the size of a pea underneath her right armpit. Not a pimple or a blackhead but a lump! *A flaw in the marble!* The flaw she has always known she had, buried somewhere inside her, like a worm, the flaw that will be held up for all to see and examined under a microscope.

She will end up bald and breastless.

At first of course she couldn't believe it – you read about women . . . And when she realised, when it dawned upon her that she had no-one to phone, no friends with whom she could discuss this most frightening, this most personal thing, the biggest disaster of her life, she sat on her garden sunbed and wept among the butterflies.

The GP said she must not worry, most lumps like that are

benign, but dear God . . . She decided to go national health, not private, because she has a horror of Zak finding out.

If she had had children and breastfed them she would not have a lump, and whose fault is that?

Nuns gets lumps. Nuns and spinsters. Barren women.

Ah, but her fear makes her irrational. After all, it was Kimberley who chose to remain the doll, Zak's little lambkin, indulged with designer teddy bears and Victorian dolls' house furniture. She decided against children and Zak, not particularly bothered, merely agreed with her.

No, she is wrong to blame the man she still calls 'Daddy', but the thought of a day in the general hospital! Many times she has almost rung to cancel the appointment.

Oh my God.

Good morning!

Rise and shine!

And here we are in the charming old village of Middlehempston, and as daylight settles and yesterday's parched air puffs across the main street, a pair of pretty gingham curtains is drawn back across The Old Schoolhouse windows. Whitewashed walls. Thatched roof. Porch with clinging clematis. Stream running through the garden filling the natural ponds.

Oh, wouldn't Sheralee give her right arm for this?

And from this gem of a home – similar to bingo prizes handed out by the *Daily Mail* – Jemima Hardy-Brown, the victim-to-be, waves happily at the milkman before she turns back to finish squeezing the orange juice.

'Breakfast in the garden today I think, Hannah. Come on, bluebird, let's go and get the table ready under the chestnut tree.'

Hey ho and out through the stable door they go into the cottage garden. Fresh from last night's illegal watering, hollyhocks, snapdragons, pansies, poppies and rampant bushes of lavender wave at them on a fragrant breeze because

48

Jemima and Gerry both prefer things natural and wild. On the way out they pass the crisp white awning which provides the shade for the infant, Felix, asleep in the pram.

'Have I,' Jemima asks herself, as she gazes up through the green branches, 'have I any right to be so happy when there's so much sadness in the world?'

The light is so brilliant that sometimes Jemima thinks she will have to start guarding her soul, in case it thinks she is dying and has already found Paradise.

6

Who the hell would choose to live here?

Fergus, passing through the sleepy market town of Melrose, quite understands why the police were directing the hippies through here yesterday afternoon. Anyone in their right mind, passing through Melrose, would only be concerned with reaching the other side and putting as much space between themselves and this godawful town as possible.

Hell, *what do people do with themselves round here?*

The high street, and presumably there is no other, is a combination of shoe shops, antique shops and building societies, mostly closed until ten o'clock. Jeez. He passes through with the flickering eyes of a natural born hunter. It wouldn't take much to lever your way into most of those windows, or ramraid the electricity showroom. Shit. But there's nothing round here worth nicking.

The only pub he passes looks like an old coaching inn with a cobbled track running through the middle to the carpark, all beams and timbers, overhanging the street with its dimpled glass windows. The smell of bacon and fresh coffee makes his stomach rumble. They probably sell real ale at the bar, and those disgusting Tortilla chips – fucking posers.

There is a bus stop, but it's not worth it now. Middlehempston is signed two miles, and Fergus can just about cope with that.

He has stayed somewhere like this before with the Burchalls, on holiday. He remembers, they bought him a pair of fucking Ladybird pyjamas. 'You can't sleep in the altogether, Fergie,' said Mary Burchall, laughing at him. 'What will the chamber-maid think when she comes to tidy your room?'

That was the first holiday Fergus had ever had, and it was shit. He had hated being away from Jemima, for a start, 'But it's only a fortnight,' she told him, 'hardly a wrench, and I'll write if you like, and you can send me a card. Two cards then,' she saw his miserable face, 'or three if you want to!'

He had clung to her then, just as he had clung when she took him, in her little red Mini, to meet the Burchalls for the first time.

'But I want to stay with you!'

She smiled down at him, earrings jangling. 'Oh Fergus. I can't have you, even if I wanted to . . . '

'Do you want to?'

Jemima, who could turn sharp and cruel when she liked, said: 'Hey, I'm certainly not going to be coerced into playing these little games of yours. Now listen to me, Mary and Patrick Burchall have two older boys of their own, they are experien-ced foster parents who have taken care of several of our children . . . '

'How long have I got to stay there?'

'Oh Fergus, this is your home, now. Please try to keep an open mind and give these good people a chance.'

He felt like an invisible guest passing through that front door with the horses riding through wavering glass.

The house stank of pine disinfectant.

There were dolls with skirts covering the bog paper.

He had looked round at the neat little garden, as square and tidy as the house itself with names on all the doors . . . even the bog had 'Toilet' written on the door, softened by rabbits and forget-me-nots.

Shit. On his bed was a trucker-style bedspread, with CB jargon scrawled all over it and pictures of all kinds of lorries.

His hands, at night, looked very small and still when they rested upon it.

False, false, false. Because it wasn't his bed and it wasn't his bedspread and if this wasn't a cover for the truth what was, like the doll in the bog, like the flowers in the fireplace, like the plastic sheet on his mattress. This was the kind of bed and bedspread decent little boys ought to like – or probably a hand-me-down from one of their own children.

He was taken out and forced to pick blackberries in order to make jam. Yuk.

And Fergus knew, deep down, that although she praised the place up to the skies, Jemima, disdainful and beautiful, would not want to live here herself.

All new. No atmosphere. Jemima would laugh and call it suburban. And it lacked class.

Was this, then, all she thought of him? Did she consider that this place was good enough to be the centre of his universe?

Did she think he would settle here without any fuss so she could take herself and her briefcase out of his life forever?

His humiliation was total.

He used to light a candle at night and see how long he could hold his finger over the flame. Trying to burn out the great, passionate wanting inside him.

'But he is perfectly all right between your visits,' Mary Burchall confided to Jemima as, with smouldering eyes, Fergus listened from the top of the stairs. A confidential chat, hah, you could hear anything in this house, even Mary and Patrick screwing together and people wiping their bums in the toilet. 'He only behaves so sulkily, becomes so disruptive, when he knows you are due. I don't know what to suggest . . .'

'He is bound to find it difficult at first. Fergus, as you know, has already led a fairly traumatic existence, losing his mother so young, enduring, for years, the open dislike of his step-father. He has identified with me, and that's not unusual. That is something that is going to take time to work itself out.'

'I just wonder,' said the devious, sweet-faced Mary Burchall, 'if it might not be wiser for Fergus to be transferred to another social worker, a man, perhaps, someone to whom he could relate with a little less emotional involvement.'

Fergus almost screamed out loud.

'I understand what you are saying, but I do think we ought to give this some time to work itself out, as I said before. A move like that, so soon after gaining his confidence, would be bound to cause Fergus some resentment and he would see it, quite naturally, as a betrayal of our mutual trust.'

'But we are seeing an almost complete character change. Both Patrick and I find it quite hard to deal with. He is so quiet and compliant, reasonable, gets on well with the boys, eats well, when we're on our own, it's just before you arrive he becomes quite badly disturbed, and afterwards . . . well . . . ' And Mary Burchall leaned back against her floral patterned sofa and nearly disappeared, because her summer dress almost matched it.

Bitch bitch bitch.

Fergus shrank back against the pale pink wall. Something had to be done, and quick.

Fergus Johnson found the avocado bog brush in the upstairs bathroom and started taking it into his bedroom with him at night. Eight years old but wise enough to know about sexual abuse, things like this happened all the time.

The sun beats down on his head as he goes.

Every so often some sticky grass, or a bramble, tangles itself round his ankle, like arms pulling him back from his fate.

He had toyed with the idea of taking a car . . . the journey would have been quicker but there were obvious risks attached to that, and anyway, he quite enjoys the time he has to savour the reason for his mission.

Fergus cannot recall feeling such blazing emotion before.

Revenge. Natural justice, and the exultation, the glory of righteous battle.

So acute it is almost spiritual.

It is a nightmare.

But we have to go with them.

By the time they manage to take their seats on the bus, Sheralee and Kirsty Maggs are at the end of their tethers and already loathed by the other passengers staring darkly from their seats. Billy's face is a sea of snot, and what rests warmly and stickily in his nappy is obvious to all within twenty yards of the whingeing lad.

Kelly insists on standing up on the seat, wetting her finger and drawing squeaky pictures on the windows, and one grumpy old man leans forward from the seat behind her and says strictly, 'You should learn to do as your mother tells you.'

Naturally Kelly licks her finger and stretches towards his shiny bald head, making it imperative to stop her.

So that deals with Sheralee's kids. Thank God Jason's not with them this morning.

Sandra and Scott, Kirsty's two, have spilt a trail of popcorn from the back of the bus right through to the front, and old ladies exclaim and point every time there's a movement.

'Mind that mess, dear.'

'Dangerous, someone could slip on that . . .'

'What sort of mother . . .'

'Fancy allowing children of that age . . .'

'Hasn't she heard of children choking?'

What do they care, thinks Kirsty, these old biddies who had the war to save them, safe with corner shops and coupons, safe with their bakelite radios, their coal fires in the evenings and an easy hatred everyone could share. The world must have been different then, else how could people have survived, sheltering communally with their kids and facing this sort of nightly distaste?

It is no better at the hospital. Wouldn't you think that with so many patients being children, a few more activities other than Lego tables and dog-eared books could be provided?

But we all know that a good mother like Jemima Hardy-Brown would have arrived prepared, with a bagful of favourite toys and a pocketful of sensible rewards in exchange for good behaviour. She would have been surprised if she had needed to use them because, of course, good behaviour is naturally expected from three-year-old Hannah.

So here we are in the waiting room of the children's ward, waiting for visitors to be admitted, waiting until after the morning treatments have been dealt with. Sheralee could have stayed the night in one of those little rooms allocated for mothers with special concerns, but Jason was hardly conscious and would not have known the difference. Anyway, Kirsty has enough on her hands without lumbering her with Scott and Kelly. And Mum, struggling to come off her Ativan, has a fit if she's asked actually to stay *overnight* with the kids.

So Sheralee's hands are tied.

'Ah, Mrs Maggs. A word?'

Sheralee looks sorrowfully over her shoulder at Kirsty as, like a naughty schoolgirl, she follows the crackling sister into her office of glass.

'Now, let me see, Jason!'

Sheralee perches on the edge of the chair, rests her plastic bag on the desk and wonders if she should . . . is it sterile?

'He had a good night,' says Sister brightly. 'And he is wide awake this morning. He even managed to toy with a little breakfast.'

Sheralee caves in with relief.

'He has a wonderful spirit, hasn't he? And that's what we like to see. A determination to overcome the odds, and that, more than anything else, is what we are going to require now, from Jason.'

'But his hand?' ventures Sheralee timidly.

'Now, now, Mrs Maggs, by the time we have finished with Jason no-one will know that he has no hand.'

'What do you mean?'

'Well, it might have been better if we had been able to retrieve the natural appendage, but then again, in Jason's case, the bones in the wrist and the lower arm have sustained such severe damage that it is unlikely they could have been effectively reconnected. But that is not a problem. These days the prostheses we use, and the after-care Jason will receive, will ensure that he can do everything he managed to do with his left hand, anyway.'

'You mean, he won't be handicapped?'

Sister smiles, briskly patronising. 'No, assuredly he will not be.'

'And how long will all this take?'

'You will be surprised, Mrs Maggs, to see how quickly children heal, and adjust. Jason will be home in the blink of an eye, and then there will just be weekly visits to the physio-therapy department . . . '

Jason? Home? With a bandaged arm? Frustrated and angry, needing special care? A future of traipsing across the city to the hospital, waiting indefinitely for Jason's treatment? 'It's not Mrs, actually.'

'Pardon?'

'I'm not married. It's Miss Maggs, actually.'

'Makes no difference to me, dear. No difference at all. We see all sorts here.'

And Sheralee wishes she had not bothered to say it.

'Can I see him?'

'Certainly you may.'

'And his brother and sister?'

'It will do him good to see them, but please make sure that Jason does not become over-excited. And it goes without saying that the children should not disturb the drip in his arm, and, of course, he has a catheter attached at the moment. I should see him alone, first, Mrs Maggs, if I were you. Some mothers can find the sight of their child distressing the morning after prolonged surgery.'

And so it is with some trepidation that Sheralee follows Sister along the cheerfully decorated corridor, averting her eyes from the little tragedies she passes, the crutches and the miniature wheelchairs spinning along beside her.

Sister says, 'Hello again, Jason, let's have you sitting up a little bit straighter, here's Mum to see you.'

Jason scowls, his little red face peers from his pillow out of bruised, pained eyes.

'Oh Jason, Jason!' cries Sheralee, breaking down. 'Oh Jason.'

'Please, Mrs Maggs,' whispers Sister, a hard hand on Sheralee's arm. 'Remember, the child is looking for reassurance, not pity. You'll frighten him if you go on like that. I know it is difficult, but please try and pull yourself together.'

Sheralee edges up closer to Jason's bed, and lays a nervous hand on his forehead. It feels so hot. She turns anxious eyes towards Sister but the woman is busily reading her notes. 'We're all here. Kelly and Scott, Billy and Sandra and Aunty Kirsty. Nana stayed round at Kirsty's last night.'

Jason pouts, his right arm looks very bare and small with that rubber tube running into it, and there is blood round his nostril where the tube disappears up his nose. His stump, because that's what it is, a stump, is fatly bandaged and lying across his chest.

'Does it hurt very much?'

Jason shakes his head. Oh why doesn't he say something? Sister, standing there listening, will be convinced by now that Sheralee is a bad mother, unable to handle her son's injury, *unable to communicate with her own little boy*.

'Is there anything that you need?' What a ridiculous question. The child can hardly move. Lying here like this, what the hell would he need? 'Is there anything I can bring you?'

'Cars.'

'What's that?'

Jason clears his throat. 'Box of cars.'

'What box of cars?'

'Like what Pete's got.'

Sheralee is perplexed. 'Who's Pete?'

Sister interrupts helpfully. 'Oh, Pete is the boy in the next room. He visited Jason this morning, and probably showed him his car collection . . . '

Sheralee jumps at the opportunity. 'Is that what you want, love? A box of new cars? I'll go and have a look at Pete's in a minute and see if I can't find something like that to bring you tomorrow.'

There is a look of something resembling triumph on Jason's ruddy face.

'But Jason,' Sheralee speaks without thinking. 'What good are cars to you at the moment? You can't even . . . '

A sharp cough from Sister prevents her from taking her thoughts any further. 'Oh yes, of course, you can look at them, anyway, can't you . . . '

'Did you say that Jason's brother and sister were waiting outside, Mrs Maggs?'

Sheralee nods hopelessly.

'Well then, now might be a good time to bring them in, break the ice so to speak.'

'Oh yes, yes of course. I won't be long. I won't be a moment, Jason.'

'Don't care if you are,' says her eldest son.

The whole morning has been so ghastly that when lunch time comes, and they have a break, Sheralee collapses completely.

They are sitting in the hospital grounds eating expensive sandwiches. The canteen was too clean, too organised a place for the Maggses to eat there comfortably. And smoking is not allowed anywhere in the hospital which declares itself in moral signs to be a 'Clean Air Zone'. If Sheralee or Kirsty needed an expensive heart operation there is a good chance they would be refused by the sinless, Godlike specialists working for the national health. And monetarily speaking, who could blame them?

'Kirsty, I just want to be by myself for a sec, take a walk round the grounds, perhaps, get my head together.'

'Well of course you do.' Jason has been a deliberate pain in the arse all morning, making the most of his situation, milking it for all it is worth. Kirsty knows that. So does Sheralee. Although it seems too cynical, too insensitive to remark upon it. After all, the poor little chap, just think what he's been through . . .

'You go, Sher. I'll be perfectly okay.'

'If you're sure?'

'I'm sure. I'll take the kids over to the swings for half an hour.'

Sheralee lets her shoulders sag. The tension in them feels like steel bars knitting a jersey in the back of her neck.

She is relieved, of course she is relieved, to discover that Jason will be all right, but what about her? She couldn't even keep her eye on him long enough to prevent him falling into danger. She couldn't even be a good enough mother to prevent her child from being savaged.

And how is she going to afford a box of cars like Pete's? Having promised Jason she went next door to look. The little boy had burns all over his legs and yet he smiled and chatted to her pleasantly. No self-pity. No nasty manipulation, using his situation, as Jason does, but a nice, cheeky-faced, happy child . . .

How is she going to cope with Jason?

Mum won't help. Mum's in no state to help. She can't.

And Kirsty is wrapped up with her own problems.

At the edge of the carpark Sheralee decides to cross the road and call at the newsagent she spies a few yards further along. She is out of tobacco, and she is sure Kirsty could do with a packet. She might even find some suitable sweets for Jason, glucose perhaps, with energy in them. Cheaper than in the hospital shop. Shit. That would impress that capable Sister. And a poster, maybe, for him to look at.

Her thoughts elsewhere, Sheralee steps out, grubbing about in the bottom of her bag to check how much money she has brought with her. Inadequate as ever, she ought to have cashed her giro before they set off this morning. But spare change often falls to the bottom or gets trapped in the torn lining.

She does not see the car, or hear it.

She is on the bonnet in milli-seconds.

She is over the roof and up in the air in less time than that.

She is back on the road, slapped on the road, banged on the road, slumped on the road.

All she can see is red-hot tar and all she can hear is violent roaring.

White-faced and distraught at the windscreen, all paint and hair with a vacant, *Come Dancing* smile on her face, Kimberley Oliphant checks that the road is empty before she drives speedily away.

7

Well. What a toing and froing there is.

Gorge rises in Zak Oliphant's throat as, rehearsing his approaching conversation, he passes the hospital where porters are hurrying Sheralee Maggs to casualty on a stretcher.

His wife's car is long gone, on its terrified way back to the garage by now.

After breakfast Cyril warned, 'Play it cool, Zak. I've already given you my professional opinion, and that is – leave matters well alone. It was a standard report on an accident. You don't think the general public would put up with being deprived of a grisly story like that! You'll see, nothing else will appear precisely because there is nothing else to report.'

'What if that bloody rag gets stuck in to dig the dirt on me, Cyril? They've done it before over wages, and layabouts we've given the boot, and all that equal employment crap.' And Zak flicks his thick, grey ash into his onyx ashtray with angry urgency.

'Okay, the *Western Express* doesn't particularly like you or your style and they've criticised you quite reasonably in the past, but there's no need to take this personally and go off at the deep end.'

'Well, I've already arranged to have lunch with their goofy editor.' Zak had not been able to wait for Cyril's advice. Bloody solicitor, not arriving at his office till gone ten and extortionate with his monstrous charges. In his angry impatience, Zak could

61

not sit there twiddling his tingling thumbs any longer, he had dialled the offices of the *Western Express* and, typically, the wanker refused to discuss the matter over the phone. In the end it was Zak who suggested lunch with the editor, and was taken aback when the bugger accepted.

'Well Zak,' said Cyril calmly, and Zak could imagine him reading his mail while he gave his half-hearted attention to the call. Perhaps even writing while he spoke, Zak has been in the office and seen him do that before now, damn the man. 'Just remember my advice, Zak. Handle with care. You don't want to get these chaps' backs up deliberately.'

'For Christ's sake, Cyril, give me the credit for some nous. I didn't get where I am today by going around with my eyes closed.'

And Cyril, stirring his coffee, thought to himself, 'No, you did not. You got where you are today because your father was a mean, cut-throat little spiv who diddled everyone in the retail trade, drove a few more to bankruptcy, and left you enough dosh to cover every crass, insensitive blunder and then some.'

But Zak is not worried. He has met Gerry Hardy-Brown many times, at public functions, at Rotary meetings, and knows he can eat that sort of bearded wonder for breakfast.

The *Western Express* will learn not to tangle with HIM again.

Let's sidetrack while Zak drives on to his meeting and take another look at the victim.

She eats meat, but mainly chicken.

She mixes her own breakfast muesli.

She prefers brown rice and makes her own wholemeal bread.

She does not buy birthday cakes from Marks and Spencer.

Jemima Hardy-Brown is off out to lunch with a friend. She

has packed a large bag full of swimmers, baby feed, towels, nappies, and everything else to ensure that she can spend a peaceful afternoon with Jacqueline, relaxing beside her kidney-shaped swimming pool.

She need not head home till around four o'clock which is when little Felix begins to get scratchy, and Hannah, too, is easier to deal with at home at the end of a long, hot day.

To see her walk along the village street would gladden the heart of the most pessimistic. Surely all the old values worth preserving are alive and well here in Middlehempston. To see her is to see hope for the future in the shape of a beautiful young woman, in her early thirties and in her prime, wearing a dress of sky blue liberally speckled with daisies. Her hair hangs loose and free to her shoulders, a chestnut brown with golden highlights, and her skin is a healthy light tan.

Somehow she is timeless.

Goodness oozes out of her, and that's nice. It makes a change. She could be carrying a basket of eggs on her arm in the manner of Little Grey Rabbit. She could be going about good works, taking soup to the poor, off to comfort the dying, in the manner of Marmee from *Little Women*.

But no, she happens to be going swimming.

The baby is propped up on pillows in his pram, top of the range, and her little girl travels happily strapped safely into the pram seat.

They sing to each other and giggle together as they go along . . . *'There was a Princess long ago, long ago, long ago . . . '*

'There was a Princess long ago, long, long ago.'

No, her children are no weight to her, her children are planned and longed for, the apples of her eye.

Surely this young woman who trips along the road so happily knows nothing of the dark secrets of the underworld, the despair of the cities so sunk into sadness and sin, knives and needles and 'niggers', the predatory streets and estates of destruction where fear and the smoke from burning tyres fug the air and blot out the light.

Oh but you're wrong, she does know.

She probably knows more than most, and perhaps you can detect the knowledge glinting there in the vulnerability behind her questioning eyes.

And she carries the burden of knowledge with her in the form of fear for the fate of her children. A terror that, one day, they might fall so low. A terror that has already influenced her to put their names down at the best public schools in the country.

You could say that Jemima has done well to overcome her knowledge and stay the sweet-natured, kindly-thinking woman that she is. Others might have become embittered by ten years' experience in the social services, first in Bolton, and later for Wandsworth council.

Does she remember Fergus Johnson, who is watching her, even now, from the red phone box with the hanging basket above the door?

Yes, of course she does.

How could anyone forget Fergus Johnson? The child who, in her eagerness, in her naivety, she had placed with a family of abusers, proved beyond doubt to her mind anyway by the medical check and report from the doctor that his anus was sore and distended and that there was no question that the child had been interfered with.

And she believed it, *then*.

She was firmly on the child's side.

Quite gratified by his transparent worship . . . and so unsure of herself.

How easy it was for her, though not so easy for Mary Burchall who could not understand why this sweet, fresh-faced young social worker removed little Fergie with no satisfactory explanation just when he was beginning to settle down.

'You can't win them all,' said her husband, annoyingly. Patrick Burchall, who would no more dream of interfering with a child than would the Archbishop of Canterbury or the Duke of Edinburgh.

Jemima's supervisor, a wise and worldly spinster from the ranks of the old Children's Department, suggested, in spite of Jemima's outrage, that they should take no further action.

'Although it is your case, Jemima, and if you feel this family are unsuitable foster parents for Fergus it is quite within your rights to remove him.'

She was incensed by this flaccid reaction and appalled that the police should agree. The doctor explained how most people, not wanting to believe it, preferred to do nothing rather than face unpalatable facts.

(This was long before the Cleveland scandals hit the headlines.)

So remove young Fergus she certainly did, and was all the more determined to do better for the lad next time.

Sometimes Jemima Hardy-Brown still dreams about Fergus Johnson.

Fergus had gone to town with that avocado bog brush.

And it worked. Jeez, it is so simple to convince right-minded people. The only ones you cannot convince are the sharp ones, like yourself.

There she goes.

To see her again after three years gives him one helluva shock.

If only he could be free.

Exactly the same. She has not changed her hairstyle, or the kind of clothes she wears. She always stood out in the town, she always looked as if she ought to be living in a cottage in the country. He often laughed with her about that and she made the excuse:

'That is because I come from the country, Fergus. And yes, I do miss it.'

65

'Mummy and Daddy have a nice "hice" down there, I suppose,' jeered Fergus jealously.

'Well actually, yes they do.' She was careful not to add that Daddy was sheriff of the county.

'And you're doing this job to find out how the other half lives?'

You could see he had unnerved her. He had probably hit the nail on the head. Guilt, see. These do-gooders, these community workers and churchgoers, prison visitors and the posh bastards who stand up for the workers, why do they do it? Well, thinks Fergus, it's partly guilt, because they're the haves. And it's partly *because they want to see*! It's like gawping at an accident, and you can feel more safe and secure in your own car when you see somebody crushed to death in theirs. They have failed. You have succeeded. More by luck than judgement, and yet you are still alive. Like seeing one of those poor sods with a bottle of meths, sleeping under a cardboard box. These do-gooders can go home to their warm fires and their families and feel even better than before because it's not them. They're not the poor bastard that's fucked up his life. They might have made their mistakes, but shit, they've managed to get away with theirs. He eyes Jemima menacingly as she disappears off round the corner while his anger burns and his obsession festers.

So this is where she lives.

How bloody typical.

The village is dead; all he can hear is the wretched crow of a distant cockerel.

He crosses the road and wanders round to the back of the house, through the little gate and along a footpath bordered with roses. Jeez, there's a bloody Morgan in the garage.

Into the back garden he goes, dazzled by the scents and the rainbow colours there.

Christ, the bitch has even left her door open.

Real life is taking its time wending its way towards Middlehempston.

Kitchen. Pine. Aga. Dresser with matching mugs on hooks. Blue and white striped china. Colourful Habitat druggets contrast with all the straw-coloured coir – leading through to the massive playroom which used to be the main schoolroom before this was converted into a house. Rocking horse, dolls' pram, dolls' house from Galts . . . all that predictable wooden crap.

Sitting room overwhelmed with plants. Beamed fireplace with ancient bread oven and cushioned seats. Bookshelves stacked and battered and worn. Sofa in cottage garden print with lots of scatter cushions. Straw matting on the floor and expensive CD equipment stacked in the recesses. Bowls of freshly gathered sweet peas softly scent the room.

With his army knife open in his hand, Fergus climbs the twisted stair.

Whoops, wrong room. Airing cupboard, nothing of interest in here, but he notices the clothes, sheets and towels are incredibly colourful and neatly stacked.

Bedrooms two and three, all cribs and frilly bedspreads. Windows open. Curtains fluttering. And smelling of Johnson's babies.

Bedroom one. Framed pictures of Mummy and Daddy on the side. Canopied pine bed. Patchwork quilt. Window winks out from the roof with window seat beneath. Her side – Penelope Lively. His side – Martin Amis.

Fergus opens the built-in cupboard and sniffs at her clothes.

And weeps for something he's always known he could never reach.

Zak has arrived at his lunchtime venue.

It is dark in here, a tobacco brown, after the bright light of day.

'Jolly good old man.'

But Gerry Hardy-Brown eyes Zak Oliphant warily, noticing the bracelet the man wears round his wrist.

'They do a good steak here,' Zak is encouraging, but Gerry dislikes steak, he dislikes chips, and you have to say if you want alternative vegetables here.

It is a pub Gerry would never have chosen. And anyway, he would rather not drink at lunchtime.

'Good of you to agree to meet me,' says Zak, leading the way from bar to dining room, carrying his whisky and Gerry's alcohol-free lager. The prat. He sits down heavily at the table and deliberately lights an offensive cigar.

The menu is stickily wrapped in a cover of red plastic with the name of the establishment – The King William – embossed in bold type.

'Now I personally don't believe in beating about the bush,' says Zak, puffing smoke from behind his menu. 'I'd rather clear the air and come out with it, man to man.'

'Oh?' Gerry frowns, wondering what the hell he can choose without making himself feel sick for the rest of the afternoon. Prawn cocktail . . . that old saviour, or perhaps the melon, to start with. It is bound to come bubbling with sugar, with cherries on cocktail sticks.

'Sometimes I get the feeling, and tell me if I'm wrong, but sometimes I get the feeling that your esteemed organ has got it in for me.'

'I am sorry to hear that, Mr Oliphant.'

Pompous arsehole. 'Oh, none of that bullshit, please, call me Zak. No, we don't see eye to eye on very many important issues,' Zak continues truculently. 'And I therefore decided it might be useful for you and me to meet.' He puts down his menu and beams across the table unpleasantly. 'Right?'

'I assume you are talking about yesterday's article on security.'

'Yes, I am.'

'You objected to the slant?'

'Not so much of a slant, more like a sheer drop from where I'm standing.'

'But, Zak, most of what we said is fairly well accepted opinion.'

'You implied that I had no right to secure my own damn property.'

Gerry Hardy-Brown laughs lightly. 'We implied no such thing. We merely reported the unfortunate accident that took place on your premises, and listed a number of similar occurrences which have happened locally within the last few months.'

'And what made you think you had the moral right to print such a list?'

'Sorry?'

'The moral right! The goddamn moral right! Is it my fault that thugs have been hurt climbing over dangerous railings? Is it my fault that thieves were injured while tampering with what you called a particularly vicious electronic security system? Is it my fault that some bastard broke his leg after getting it trapped in a mechanical door? Is it? Is it? Are any of those things my fault?'

'No, no they are not,' says Gerry flatly.

'Well then, why did you fucking well list them right underneath my picture? And what about all the rest of the crap? That chappy I sacked a couple of months back. That private memo I sent round about working overtime. That stipulation that all my workers should turn self-employed and provide their own . . . '

'Mr Oliphant, it is the proper duty of a local morning newspaper to take up issues . . . '

'You pompous, self-righteous bastard . . . '

And they haven't got round to ordering yet! His solicitor's sensible warnings are the last thing on Zak's mind.

'I am sorry, Mr Oliphant, but . . . '

Zak, puce-faced, half rises in his chair. Most of his weight rests on his knuckles, red and pudgy on the table like trotters. 'And I have heard that you intend to interview the Maggs sisters with a view to taking this matter further . . . '

'I must say I don't know where you . . . '

'No, I'm sure you bloody well don't.' Zak stabs at the air with his cigar. His raging pupils glitter. 'You interfering bugger. But I have friends in useful places, and I can tell you . . . '

'I am sorry, Mr Oliphant, but I just don't believe this conversation is serving any useful purpose . . . '

'That's it! That's it, you spineless cretin! Back away as soon as the going gets hot. Typical of your type – silver spoon, private schools, so-called pissing intellectual . . . '

Aha. So that's it. Gerry Hardy-Brown gets up quickly and replaces his chair. This incident is becoming far too unpleasant, and the other diners are being disturbed by the commotion.

'Let me give you this little bit of advice, my friend.' Zak is nowhere near finished. The veins are standing like worms on his forehead and his blood pressure is well up. He just cannot stand bearded men who wear sandals to work. And as for those wire-rimmed spectacles . . . pretending to be national health but costing an arm and a leg. Designer spectacles, dear God in Heaven. 'If those little whores so much as speak one word of slander to you I'll take them to the cleaners, so help me . . . You tell them from me to watch themselves. And if your pathetic rag dares to print any more damning suggestions about me or my businesses, I'll . . . '

Gerry interrupts the spluttering with a calm, 'You'll what, Mr Oliphant?'

'You'll see, Mr Hardy-Brown. Damn liberal leftie. Let's just leave it at that. I bloody well warn you. *You'll see!*'

Oh dear.

Just one hour later Fergus Johnson lets himself out of the editor's house, replacing the silver blade of his knife.

8

'Can I be of help?'

Help? What sort of help? Her sister is probably dying somewhere.

Kirsty's ears are banging. Her face is blank with desolation as she half hears the question put to her by a crisp, no-nonsense person who looks and sounds like Edwina Currie.

The hospital social worker explains. 'I was told by the casualty sister that you have a problem.'

Well, and can't she see the fucking problem? Already a doughty middle-aged woman in a bright pink shell-suit has whispered loudly to her friend, 'No control, some of these people. Breed like rabbits.'

They think all four children are hers.

Kirsty, vaguely watching as Sandra and Kelly construct a ship out of canvas chairs, is too exhausted to respond, too shocked even to bother with a two-finger reply.

'Is there anyone I can contact?'

Kirsty continues to rock the two pushchairs backwards and forwards, backwards and forwards one in each hand, in a hopeless effort to comfort the screaming toddlers trapped within. 'There's my mother,' she says bleakly, nibbling a frayed lower lip, 'but she's not on the phone.'

'Has she a neighbour . . . ?'

Mum's neighbour gets furious when anyone uses her phone for messages. She used to be okay when she first got it, it was a novelty then, but her attitude has steadily changed: now it's,

'Who did you say you wanted? Mrs Maggs? There's no Mrs Maggs here.'

'This is her daughter, Mrs Crosby . . . ' As you well know, you cow.

'And you expect me to go out of my house, across the landing in the freezing cold, and stand there waiting till your mother takes it into her head to open her fucking door?'

'I know, I'm sorry.'

The doctor is pleased with Dulcie Maggs. He says she is coping well considering how long she has been hooked on her Ativan, but part of her current problem is that she won't go out, and is afraid of people. There is only a fifty-fifty chance that she will respond to the bell. 'It's mostly kids, anyway.' She uses the kids as a thin excuse to stay in hiding.

But maybe that old crab Crosby will respond less chillingly to a social worker. The strident tones of authority might do the trick.

'I can give you a neighbour's number, but she might not be too happy . . . '

'Good Heavens, this is an emergency, Mrs Maggs.' The social worker has to shout to triumph over the kiddies' cries.

As Kirsty searches through the meaningless bits and pieces in her bag her hand trembles and her eyes blur with tears. 'If you could try and break it to her gently. My mother's not very well, you see, and the shock . . . ' She imagines her mother's hysterical face. But Kirsty has no safety net, no ring of neighbours and friends and uncles and aunts and well-wishers who might come to her aid, no support system. So inadequate are they that she and Sheralee have failed to construct even this. She misses them now. There is only Mum. Suddenly her life seems shattered and empty.

Her MP, Godfrey Halkin, for whom she voted and who has three cars, one for himself, one for his wife, and a jeep for when they go to their house in the country, would say she should have thought about this before she opened her legs to all

72

comers. After all, and it's true, why should society pick up the pieces?

'Leave it to me, my dear, you certainly need somebody with you to help get all these children home.'

'Oh, I thought I might get a lift . . . '

'A lift? This is a trust hospital now, Mrs Maggs, there aren't the spare people around any more to cope with situations like this. No, the most we could do would be to help you out with a taxi, refunded by you in due course, naturally.'

They say they don't know about Sheralee yet. Dear God, they say that she has gone into coma. And Kirsty Maggs cannot help her next wicked thought – she envies her sister her freedom.

'And don't you miss working?

Jemima Hardy-Brown stands like a nymph in the sparkling water of Jacqueline's kidney-shaped pool. No chlorine in this pool; it is environmentally friendly, with salt. She raises Felix high in her arms until he kicks and laughs, and then she lowers him into the water, gripping him terribly firmly. How people can allow their new-born babies to swim, how they can let them go, to sink and gasp and cough and kick, lowering them to their spluttering fate, is beyond her.

In the shallow end little Hannah and Jacqueline's daughter, Emily, splash happily in their arm bands and the water spangles like diamonds in the sunlight.

'No,' answers Jemima in her soft pretty voice. 'I don't miss it at all.'

'Won't you go back when the children go to school?'

'No.'

Hannah and Felix, like Emily, are going to the village school – a school with an excellent record, where all the children wear blazers and no wonder, when you consider the socio-economic status of most of the residents of Middlehempston – until they are eleven. They will be home at three-thirty for the next nine years, giving Jemima a reason for a daily walk to the school gate, with a retriever on a lead, perhaps, in all weathers. Even when they go away Jemima expects to have them home most weekends, and then there are always the long holidays.

'You don't sound as if you liked it much.' Jacqueline is pregnant. Her stomach bulges wetly and shinily under her emerald costume. She is creepily fertile like a frond. After all, Emily is three now and it is the ideal time for another. One of each, like Jemima's, would be nice.

'I did to begin with,' Jemima laughs uneasily. 'I thought I could change the world. Didn't we all? But it's awful, the older I get the more my views are changing. I sound more and more like my mother.'

'I know. I know. Isn't it ghastly? So do I.'

'Tight and narrow and angry. Bring back hanging and flogging!'

'Manners and attitudes. They're catching. Lock 'em all up and throw away the key!'

'Castrate them! Mutilate them. But seriously, Jacky, I think we were wrong. I think we went too far and now we're seeing the repercussions.'

'You're so old-fashioned, Jem. Such a contented little home bird. Perhaps you think that going back to work would be bad for the children. You're young, beautiful and talented. If you don't go back to work, where are you going to put all your pent-up passion?'

'I do not feign orgasm yet,' says Jemima, feeling that she is being attacked as a chill of water runs down her spine.

'Give it another couple of years,' says her good friend Jacqueline.

Oh God oh God oh God help me.

And if there is a God He is probably chuckling to himself in all the great safety of his Heaven, because Kimberley Oliphant has not been near a church since she married, a good twenty years ago.

'It's no good calling on me now,' God says self-righteously.

The ice in her glass trembles and clinks like her wrists against her bracelets as she paces her luxurious drawing room. Lady Macbeth with blood on her hands. I am now a hit-and-run driver. Probably a candidate for Holloway Prison. She turns up the local news on the telly at two o'clock . . . nothing; at three o'clock . . . nothing; but at four she stares at the set in horror.

She keeps going over the events of this morning, over and over and over in flashes of bright red nightmare as the woman steps out into the road and her terrible zig-zag top passes crazily over the windscreen, the lumpy bang as her body thumps over the roof of the car.

And then the terror.

Kimberley had been drinking.

Well, only three or four, but she had to find the courage from somewhere to keep the hospital appointment and the consequences of what she has done are more than she can stand.

Her mind was not on her driving. So relieved, so totally happy to be told by the specialist that the lump was a boil that needed lancing, she hadn't even felt like a fool.

She allowed him to examine her breasts – 'Might as well while you're here,' he said. And he showed her the correct way to do it in future. She found it rather soothing. Hell, if she handled them like that and Zak was about, it would set him off in no time. He liked to see her touching herself with her own cool finger. It drove him wild when she dangled her legs apart wearing black stockings and suspenders, and he lay at the bottom of the bed, drooling and watching.

So demeaning and undignified, like the thought of eggs in your body and milk in your breasts. Zak enjoys it, but Kimberley thinks it rather ugly, tasteless, you know, like his love of Black Forest gâteau and his gold *Reader's Digest* cutlery. Private parts. Ugh. She never likes it when he makes her look at his revolting magazine pictures. They give her the creeps and she was always against satellite TV.

Kimberley jumps when, on the four o'clock news, they give the first report on the accident. A 23-year-old mother of three is unconscious in hospital after being involved with a car, the driver has not yet come forward. Extraordinarily, the as-yet-unnamed casualty was visiting her son at the time, the very child who had his hand chewed off by a dog at Fingles Ponds in Melrose yesterday.

How tragic!

Talk about sod's law.

If accidents come in threes – my God, the mind boggles.

They will catch her. They always do catch middle-class lawbreakers, mostly drivers. They are easier to deal with than the menace of persistent offenders; old lags, joyriders, thugs and thieves. Less paperwork and a little respect while they're at it, which helps. Middle-class criminals wait for the law, they respect the law and are therefore caught by the law, as they skulk, tearing their nails and their lips behind their lined and pleated curtains.

Kimberley has searched the car and the only give-away sign is a deep dent on the roof. Nobody sees the roof, save lorry drivers and people in buses.

Oh God help me. Should she tell Zak? What would Zak's response be? Would he tell her off, a naughty little girl driving badly again, his attitude when she has over-spent and she pouts at him sweetly and confesses. He certainly would not worry about damage to the car. He certainly wouldn't shop her; no, even if the woman should die Zak would stand paternally beside her.

Loud and strong in her defence.

But what about the fact that the woman is involved with the accident at Melrose yesterday? How will that affect the situation? It wouldn't look too good, would it? She imagines the *Sun*'s headline, *Isn't a child's hand enough for this family? They took his Mum's life as well.*

Oh God oh God oh God help me.

And poor Kimberley Oliphant collapses on her white leather Chesterfield, slobbering there in a drunken stupor.

When she wakes up the studs will have left dents on her pretty pink cheeks.

'Gerry, it's me!'

'Jem?'

'Come home,' she sobs. 'It's awful . . . '

'The children?' His voice is desperate.

'No, no, nobody's hurt. They're both here with me now. At home. Gerry, someone's been in the house while I was out . . . '

'Jem, calm down, I can hardly understand what you're saying. Have you phoned the police?'

'Yes, I dialled nine nine nine as soon as I saw it. They say they'll come immediately. But I want you home, Gerry – now!'

'Of course. I'm on my way. Have they taken much?'

Jemima is struggling to control her voice. 'No, I don't think so. No, I don't know. Gerry, I just don't know.' And then an aside, 'It's all right, darling. Daddy's coming home. No, Mummy's not crying. Not really. Gerry, I can't describe it. It looks as if a madman's been in here and . . . '

'Jem, listen to me. I'm going to call Clara next door to come and stay with you until I arrive. Now go into the kitchen, shut the door on the mess, pour yourself a brandy and wait there for me. Will you do that?'

'Yes.'

'I'm leaving the office right now.'

'Okay.'

'I'll be as fast as I can.'

'Oh Gerry.' Jemima sniffs.

'Hang on. Just hang on till I get there.'

It is so quiet when the phone goes dead and she is alone with the dialling tone. Weakly, she hangs it back on the wall and does exactly what Gerry says: she closes the living room door behind her.

At least the kitchen is recognisable.

'But who's been in here, Mummy?' asks the white-faced Hannah. 'Have they been upstairs? Have they hurt Rosebuddy?'

Jemima kneels on the kitchen rug. It is a hot, sultry afternoon and yet she needs the warmth of her Aga. She hangs on to her pretty child. Felix is still parked in the pram outside the stable door. He will be wanting his four-o'clock feed in a minute. 'I shouldn't think so, Hannah. Rosebuddy is tucked up in your bed, isn't she?'

Jemima has not been upstairs. She couldn't cope with that. The chaos in the living room was bad enough, and she only caught sight of the playroom.

Who would do this? She knows very well who would do this.

But Jemima forces her mind to a blank.

'What's that awful smell, Mummy?'

How can she tell her child it is shit? How can she tell her innocent daughter that someone has come into their house, pulled down his trousers and crapped on the living room rug before smearing it . . . ?

A stranger?

Hardly a stranger.

She accidentally looked in the mirror, only to see the reflection of her own shattered face, in broken slivers. Her eyes were black holes and only her hair was still beautiful.

And the curtains have been ripped off their rings. The sofa cushions have been slashed into shreds, feathers and horsehair all over the place giving her home, her safest place, the look and the stench of a slaughterhouse.

Dear God, *what if she hadn't been out when he came?* What if she'd been indoors, upstairs, resting perhaps, with the children?

What if he comes back? Or is hiding, upstairs?

She feels dizzy. Confused and dizzy. Trying to hold herself together Jemima gets up, takes the grizzling Hannah in her arms and shuffles out into the green enclosure of the garden. She shrinks from the house itself, she feels shy with it, and disgusted, as if it is an encroaching stranger muttering obscenities into her ear. She steps back and looks up at the bedroom windows but can see nothing there, no movement. No movement at all. The curtains are no longer at the windows and there are smears of lipstick on the glass. Something written? She cannot see properly from here.

Jemima groans. Whoever was here was savage as a wolf, mindless as an ape. A madman. A killer. She imagines him moving quietly as he went about his total destruction, breathing out fumes of black malevolence.

Oh Gerry, where are you?

And two minutes, a life-time later, when Clara Cotty, her kindly neighbour, arrives, she finds Jemima Hardy-Brown huddled on the grass feeding her baby, with her other arm clutched round her eldest child. Panting with fear, she is shivering and sobbing, sharing her darkest secrets with the hollyhocks.

9

Even Fergus is horrified by the extent of his regression. Frustrated and humiliated, as he stumbles along the disused railway track that runs somewhere behind the market town of Melrose and away . . . as far away from that house as he can get.

Fergus moans.

As if he has been tortured, maimed or burned. He curses wildly to himself as he half walks, half trots, out of breath – Scout's pace, but he would not know about that – and his mind thuds as he staggers along between the deeply scratching, raw-edged undergrowth that rises steeply either side of the track.

There is nobody in sight. But if there was they would have been shocked to see Fergus like this, a nineteen-year-old yob with a face so oddly childish and unformed, blood pouring down his arm and dripping onto the brambly ground.

It was not meant to be like this.

Fergus is ashamed of his own pathetic performance. Dogboy. Drifter. Mugger. Joyrider. Burglar. Vandal, addict, obsessive and would-be killer.

Product of the system.

This young man should have been locked up and the key thrown away years ago, for his own good and everyone else's.

Fergus had planned to wait for her, there in her crappy house, to mooch round until she and her two brats came home and then to surprise her. He wouldn't be violent – oh no, not at first. He would be cool, controlled, polite while he let her get over the shock. He would accept a cup of coffee . . . she always used to laugh at his request for four sugars . . . he would sit quietly menacing, cleaning out his nails, maybe, with his legs crossed on the table, and listen to her as she talked. As she desperately made her excuses for her monstrous betrayal, couched in her easy middle-class accent.

When Jemima Hardy-Brown lies, it does not sound as if she is lying. But if you know her, like Fergus does, you can tell what she's up to because her cheeks flush slightly, prettily.

It was being in her wardrobe that did it. He should never have taken her dress off its hanger and gone to lie on her side of the bed, he should not have picked up that photograph of the two of them smiling so lovingly together.

What a fucking freak HE looked.

Why had she chosen a git like that? Shit, he looked like a mad professor, fucking four-eyes peering gormlessly through those spindly spectacles.

He shattered the shroud of glass with one easy bang on the pine of the four-poster bed. He picked up his knife and prepared to thrust it deep into her heart and score across that face of kindliness, self-righteousness and patience. Christ, it was hot in there. Fergus sweated. He gritted his teeth and blinked to clear his filling eyes.

Putting an end to his dream.

Putting to death.

'Trust me, Fergus.'

'Of course somebody cares. Don't be so silly. I care.'

His brain could not control his hand. As if in spasm, it took the glittering edge of the knife back to his own forearm where it cut a deep slit in the skin till the two halves of flesh peeled apart and blood welled from the gape in the middle like a Christmas decoration.

The pain brought beads of sweat to his forehead.

Nevertheless he enlarged the cut until it formed a J, super-imposed on the old, aching scars of all the others.

He stood alone in his own world where no-one had ever entered, or seen. He bled, and then, making deep, guttural sobs, he wanked himself off over her patchwork quilt.

A product of the system?

After four failed attempts at placing Fergus in foster homes, each one proving more disastrous than the last as he either ran away and was brought back by the irritated police, bullied the couple's natural children, refused to attend school or just failed to eat, Jemima finally decided that he might find it less emotionally demanding to spend some time in a children's home.

She took him to St Thomas's, stopping on the way to buy him a cream tea and the pair of new baseball boots which he craved.

'Don't you want to know a little bit more about St Thomas's?' she asked him.

He sulked, 'It's no big deal.'

She said, 'Oh Fergus, I wish you could be happy.'

Oh yeah, I bet. She was always bent on stripping away his veneer. And that's why you're bringing me here then, is it?

Jemima knew the supervisor there, a young man obsessed with sport and dedicated to giving his charges everything they naturally lacked. A quaker. When they arrived they sat in the cosy office together beside a roaring fire in chintzy, homely, comfortable chairs, dunking ginger biscuits.

By now Fergus was ten.

And wiser.

And could see by the way Crispin Oliver looked at Jemima that he fucking well fancied her. She was wearing a ribbed grey polo neck that accentuated the shape of her breasts and made them look like hanging pears, and her knees were crossed so you could see halfway up her thighs. Fergus felt nothing but anger. Couldn't she see that the guy was fake, from his sloppy, homeknit Fair Isle to his faded blue jeans and leather boots?

He was saying, 'We haven't got many rules but those we do have . . . '

Fergus switched off in contempt. He didn't bother to listen. He didn't plan on being there long enough to break their sodding rules.

'Give us a fag,' he said to Crispin Oliver who smiled, pretended not to look shocked, pretended to take the question quite seriously.

'We don't allow smoking, but not because we do not approve of the habit. We don't allow it because . . . '

Bullshit. Fergus studied his nails but the blood was banging inside his head in time to his own heartbeat.

She was telling Crispin Oliver all about him. Making him sound like a right git. Making it sound as if nothing which had happened was his fault, as if life was against him and everyone else ganged up against him. Is this what she thought Fergus felt? Some fucking schizo with no brain at all? A candidate for a lobotomy?

She'd be dropping him off at the funny farm next.

Couldn't she see why he was doing all this? Was she totally unaware of the confused gift that Fergus was so intent on giving her? So hungry for her love that he lived in a state of perpetual agony. He had worked so hard to grab her attention, but every time she took his side and tried to understand him.

He had messed his whole fucking life up on *her* account.

Why didn't she swear at him, shout at him, bash him? Show him she fucking well cared enough, as if he was one of her own?

He was nothing but one more sodding client. Another file in the cabinet. Another note in her diary. And every time she talked to him she probably discussed him afterwards . . . or wrote about him in her clever, green handwriting.

Well, Fergus thought to himself after she'd kissed him lightly and driven away, while he was being shown his room by a well-meaning lad called Dirk, well, this time I'll make myself so bloody interesting that you can't just turn round and walk away.

This time I'll do something that pissing well matters.

His hunger burned.

In despair he gave his baseball boots to Dirk the trusty.

Fuck you and see if I care.

Gerry Hardy-Brown, an intelligent man, and not one to flip easily, does not trust the direction in which his angry thoughts are taking him.

He had been disturbed enough when he'd heard that the Maggs girl was in hospital, unconscious, after an incident involving a hit-and-run driver.

Zak Oliphant was quite correct when he accused Gerry of planning to meet her. Heaven knows where the man got that information from, but then again, it had been no secret. He considered the savaging of a child required a good deal more attention than it was getting – from the police in particular.

But surely Zak Oliphant is no more than a bully and a seedy business operator, greedy for money and power, little else.

A small fish. Anyone more ambitious and capable, the upwardly mobile criminal, would be living and working in London. Gerry is aware that he himself could have 'done better' as his headmaster would have put it. But he has never been an ambitious man, neither is he short of money. A peaceful soul and a lover of the countryside, his chosen lifestyle suits him completely. There is no mafia-style organisation in this insignificant part of the woods. There is nothing to be plundered down here, save a smattering of cannabis every now and again as little boats pull onto the beaches. But nothing bigger than that. Nothing that would merit . . .

And he even smiled at his own paranoia.

But that was an hour ago, before he entered his house and saw it.

Good God.

Jemima and the children are next door with Clara. The police have been and gone leaving little hope in their wake, and Gerry is attempting to clear up the mess with the help of Mrs Haddock and Hilary Randall.

Zak Oliphant would never arrange anything like this.

Just to warn the editor off future editorials?

We are talking about the *Western Express*, for Christsake.

Funny, though. A strange coincidence. And one which he pointed out to the police.

They had not taken it seriously, and quite right. Probably.

'I've never seen anything like this in my life,' says Mrs Haddock, Jemima's regular cleaner and an old friend of the family. 'It's that little kiddy I feel sorry for. If Hannah had walked in and seen the state of her room the poor little mite would never have got over it, I know.'

'What scares me silly more than anything is the fact that someone who is capable of carrying out this sort of frenzied attack is out there somewhere, walking around, quite free to enter somebody else's house and do it again. I do wish it was you who came home and found all this, Mr Hardy-Brown. These things can affect women badly,' says Hilary Randall, who helps at the pub. 'And they won't find him. Well, they just don't bother these days, do they? I mean, there's so much of it going on.'

'But not in Middlehempston, that is, up until now,' points out Mrs Haddock, almost crossing herself with her brush. 'I never lock my door myself. Never have and don't intend to start.'

'Well that's going to pose a bit of a problem,' says Gerry, down on his knees brushing feathers from the herringbone coir matting. 'You see, the insurance won't cough up once they know the door was unlocked. They will call Jemima's behaviour irresponsible . . .'

'What nonsense. Any excuse not to pay out. Sometimes I wonder why I bother to keep mine up at all.' Mrs Haddock does not keep her contents insurance up and has not done so in years. She considers that in her small cottage there is nothing worth insuring.

'What I find so odd,' says Hilary, puffing, plastering on the sweet-smelling polish, 'is that nobody saw anyone strange lurking round the village. I mean, with this being a Neighbourhood Watch area, and he must have looked pretty odd. You're not telling me that anyone with the sort of mentality to carry out these disgusting acts would look normal. Or ordinary. I've put all these cushion-covers into black bags, so Mrs Hardy-Brown can take them to be re-done at Storeys in town when she's feeling better.'

'She'll probably want new ones,' says Mrs Haddock, raising a sage eyebrow. 'I know I would if I could afford it. Well, no matter how clean they come up you know what's been on them, don't you? I admire you, Mr Hardy-Brown, I really do. I couldn't have dealt with it, even wearing thick rubber Marigolds. I couldn't have faced it dressed in a wet suit and a snorkel. Ugh. The thought. These people should be hanged drawn and quartered.'

'At least the smell seems to have disappeared,' says Gerry, breathing in the dusk through the wide open windows.

'Or have we just got used to it?' asks Mrs Haddock worriedly. And then, 'Why do you think whoever did this picked on The Old Schoolhouse? Was it because there was nobody home, and he knew it, or was there a deeper reason?'

'Who knows. I don't expect we will ever know,' says Gerry, worried sick, thinking about his wife next door and wondering

86

if he should leave her there for the night, with the children. Felix could sleep in his pram in Clara's hall. It might be too early to expect Jemima to return after the terrible shock she has suffered, but he does not want to let it build up in her mind until her return becomes an ordeal in itself. And although the house is clean now, after three solid hours of sorting and scrubbing, there are signs of damage everywhere. To put it right is going to cost thousands and then there's the papers, photographs and books which are irreplaceable . . .

Apart from the whole ghastly experience there are little pointers about the attack which unsettle him. *Bitch! Bitch! Bitch!* was scrawled across the upstairs windows with bright orange lipstick. The word 'cunt' was scratched out on the living room wall. It almost seems as if the lunatic who wreaked this havoc was directing his vengeance towards Jemima . . . But then again, there aren't many male words that would make such an impact, apart from 'balls' and 'prick', and neither of those are half as aggressive, much more childish.

'Perhaps you should get a dog,' Hilary suggests.

'One of those rottweiler types,' agrees Mrs Haddock.

'I think not, not with the children the ages they are,' says Gerry sensibly.

'Or a gun,' pursues Mrs Haddock.

'I've got a shotgun, it's chained up upstairs,' Gerry muses, half to himself. 'But what's the use of a gun? Anyway, you wouldn't be allowed to use it.'

'Huh,' says Hilary Randall sharply, 'I know what I'd do if I heard some bastard – excuse me Mr Hardy-Brown but I do feel strongly about all this – if I heard him coming up my stairs I'd blast his bloody head off, no messing.'

'Oh Gerry, what are we going to do?' cries Jemima, that night, wrapped in his arms in Clara's spare room, cool in sheets of Egyptian cotton.

She looks as if she has been ill.

And no wonder.

The past has a habit of catching up, but this is Jemima's first experience of it.

'We are going to try and carry on as normal. We are going to try our hardest to put this behind us. You are going to go round that house tomorrow with a pencil and paper and the Laura Ashley catalogue and work out exactly what you want. Then we are going on holiday, we are going to get as far away from all this as we possibly can, and while we are gone Mr Harding and his men will come in and decorate.'

'I loved that house,' sobs Jemima. 'I loved it. I felt totally safe inside it . . . '

'And you will again, Jem. Now dry your eyes and look at me. We are bigger than all this . . . we have to be. Think about our little family and the love that we share, and then consider the poor soul who was driven to do this awful thing today. Think of the sort of despair . . . '

Gerry is a *Guardian* reader.

If only he knew. If only she could confide in him. 'I can't, Gerry, I have tried but I can't see it that way . . . '

'Think of the sort of mental state . . . '

'Sick, you mean, not evil?'

'Not sane, Jem, you know that.'

'But out there somewhere, Gerry, out there in the darkness, maybe still watching, maybe he hasn't finished. And Hannah? And Felix?' She must keep her secret. In order to survive she must keep her secret from him. So she asks the predictable question, 'And I keep thinking, why us? Why us? Why not somebody else's house?'

'Oh Jem, Jem, you'll feel better in the morning. You've been to hell and back today . . . '

'No, Gerry, no, I have been to hell, but I haven't come back yet. Believe me.'

She will not come back until she has dealt with Fergus Johnson.

*

Fergus Johnson returns like a fox to his lair of last night, too agitated to sleep. Today he has failed and is sickened by his failure, but tomorrow or the next day he must do better.

Tomorrow he must build up his strength again. He must eat.

There was no pleasure in being in her house today, in seeing her happiness, only pain.

The only way to free himself is to finish the bitch, cut her and black out all memory. *Same as what happened when his mum died*.

But he hadn't even been able to damage her photograph so what chance would he stand face to face with Jemima herself, so close he could smell her hair and her soft honey breath on his face.

Like when she held him tight in her arms after he'd burned down St Thomas's, and he'd whispered so low that she could not hear him, 'Please love me.'

10

Squatters.

Horror.

'I can't take much more of this,' says Mrs Maggs despairingly.

And you really have to ask if some people chose to be victims, or are programmed that way somewhere back in childhood.

I mean, fancy leaving a flat empty in Montpellier Court.

They had decided to move all the kids out of Sheralee's and into Kirsty's flat. It was the only way, really, as Dulcie refused to sleep with Sheralee's terrible children.

This took some doing, and they weren't properly settled down until after *This is Your Life*. Some old cricketer. Not worth watching anyway.

The kids were over-excited, you would think they were off on holiday, not merely moving next door where they spend most of their time anyway. There was an infuriating discussion between Kelly and Scott about which toys they should take with them.

Both flats were tiny and the move involved re-arranging most of the rickety second-hand furniture.

'I thought there was something called the Victims' Support Scheme,' muttered Dulcie Maggs, trembling from exhaustion and shattered nerves, her distressed bones hardly able to take her into a deep enough bend to reach the cot mattress. 'Well if

Sheralee and Jason aren't victims, I'd like to know who are.'

'The trouble is nobody knows what's happening,' said Kirsty, her inconsequential ash dropping onto the rug. 'Maybe I should have rung the council, Mum, and they could have given us some help.'

'They're round quick enough poking their noses in when you don't want them, the buggers,' complained Dulcie.

See how automatically the dependent turn for help from the hand that feeds them. Big brother.

But big brother is fast asleep; he cannot afford to keep his highly paid professionals on call day and night.

Anyway, hardly an emergency situation. Two women in charge of four kids. What on earth's the matter with that?

Kirsty and Dulcie agree to share Kirsty's double bed, although Kirsty finds the thought of sharing a bed with her mother disturbing. She cannot explain the reason why. They heave one cot into the room and ram it between wardrobe and window. Now you have to climb over the bed, a lumpy sea of pink candlewick, in order to reach Kelly, Sheralee's lively fourteen-month-old baby daughter.

The second baby of the family, Billy, remains in his own room, but with him Sandra is sharing her single bed excitedly with Sheralee's Kelly.

They would have let Kelly sleep on the sofa in the lounge, but Kelly is a light sleeper – probably a symptom of life with Jason – and cannot be trusted on her own so near to the kitchen.

'Now, have you turned everything off and locked Sheralee's door?' asks Dulcie, after they have settled the kids, 'because you don't know who's skulking around these balconies at night.'

'Yeah, Mum, don't worry. Haven't we got more on our plates than that, just now?'

'I'm trying to keep some sort of control,' Dulcie answers her daughter shortly. 'And it's only by keeping busy, concentrating on the little things of life, that I bleeding well manage to stay sane. Oh God, when I think about Sheralee . . . in the dark and swathed in bandages . . . oh God . . . '

'I said I'd ring at ten to see if there's any news. But I doubt it. Not yet.'

'You're not going to leave me here on my own with . . . '

'It'll only take a second. I'll use the by-pass phone box.'

'Oh? And since when has that been working?'

'Well we can't just sit here and give up, Mum, I mean, can we? We have to go on, for Sheralee's sake, and for Jason's.'

'And how are we going to visit tomorrow, Kirsty? Have you thought about that?'

'What d'you mean, how are we going to visit?'

'How are we going to get there?' Dulcie's head falls into her veiny hands, falls into a nightmare.

'By bus, of course. Or taxi, if you've got any money. Jason needs to see the kiddies, it does him good, the sister said so, and someone is supposed to sit beside Sheralee and talk to her, in case she wakes up.'

'What more can happen to us now, Kirsty? What is there left? Here am I, a sick woman, with my grandchild chewed to bits by a dog and a daughter no more than a cabbage . . . '

'Stop it, stop it, Mum! Please don't go on like that!' Kirsty does not mean to shout at her mother like that, she knows she cannot take it. But sometimes Dulcie makes her feel so frightened, as if there is no alternative but to huddle on the floor with her eyes closed like a beaten child, screaming for help.

Sometimes she wishes her mother had stayed on the Ativan. Okay, she was a zombie and overdosed occasionally, but at least she managed to function in a bewildered sort of way. Now she is nothing but a shattered wreck.

And now in her thoughtlessness Kirsty has caused her mother to cringe in her chair, looking as if she has been battered. Perhaps she would have done better to try and cope without her, but Kirsty hasn't enough hands to deal with four little kiddies and get over to the hospital every day. It is just not physically possible. Perhaps the social services would pay for a child minder . . .

'I tell you what – I won't bother to phone tonight. Let them think what they like. If anything happens they'll send round a hospital car. Let's have a cup of tea, Mum, while everything's quiet, and then see if we can't get some sleep.'

Two hours later, and it's Dulcie Maggs who hears the banging.

'What's that?' She sits up, pink roses and gums, with her teeth in the jar beside her.

'What, Mum?'

God, look at this, now she's about to wake the baby.

'That noise! Shush and you'll hear it.'

Kirsty rolls over onto her back, opens her eyes and listens. It is many months since Kirsty Maggs shaved under her arms.

'It's not that Sandra and Kelly. I'll kill the bleeders if they're up and messing about in that kitchen.'

'No, Kirsty. It doesn't sound like kids.'

'What's the time?'

Dulcie peers at the clock. 'Gone eleven.'

'We better go and see.' But Kirsty, almost weeping, knows she cannot begin to cope with tomorrow unless she gets a decent night's sleep. Her ample chest bulges over the top of her nightie, which has no elasticity in it, and her overweight thighs are hardly covered by the shaggy hem. It said *Dolly Bird* on the label when she got it.

But wait, someone has loved Kirsty like a Dolly Bird, and fairly recently, too, by the looks of it. Someone has loved her enough to buy her enough rum 'n cokes, take her home, cover her with kisses and spread her fleshy legs apart. Someone has shot his seed up her fanny while promising her the world, else where did Billy the baby come from?

The children are sleeping. The noise comes from the balcony outside. Kirsty creeps to the tiny hallway, pulls back the net and peers out.

'It's yobs,' she turns to her mother and whispers. 'Fiddling about with Sheralee's door!'

'What do they want to do that for?' Dulcie's eyes are wide and frightened and her head begins to nod in a way Kirsty has not noticed before. Like an old woman in a home or a dachshund in the back of a car.

'Dunno. Maybe they're breaking in.'

'What for? What has Sheralee got that anyone else would want?' Dulcie's head nods worryingly on.

'Shush, Mum, don't talk too loud or they'll hear you.'

'We must get help,' says Dulcie flatly, treading the threadbare lino of the hall with blue and stringy bare feet. It is too cold to stand on for long. 'We can't just stay here and let this happen.'

Kirsty sneers, 'What help? And how are we going to get it?'

'But we . . .'

'One thing's for sure. We can't go out there. There's at least four of them. Big blokes, and you dunno what they're after . . .'

For the next two hours they sit on the sofa, tense and listening. Every now and again they hear a thump against Sheralee's wall.

'They've been in there long enough. They must've found what they're after. Why aren't they sodding well going?'

They have lit the spluttering gas fire but it gives off little heat and is nothing but a worry, because already Kirsty is being threatened with being cut off.

Kirsty shivers and pulls the spare blanket round her, Red Indian style. On her feet are last Christmas's furry blue slippers. 'Perhaps they're not going to go.'

'Kirsty, what on earth do you mean?'

'Perhaps they're homeless, and planning on staying.'

'But that flat belongs to Sheralee. There are things of hers still in it. It's Sheralee's home, and her children's home. They can't just break in and claim it!'

And how can Kirsty turn and explain to the nodding creature beside her that this is what happens round here all the time? If she was a more adequate person she would have thought about this possibility. She would never have pandered to her mother's whims; she would have forced the nervous woman to stay and sleep alone, next door.

Damn it. They could have communicated through the wall, couldn't they? They'd only have to raise their voices slightly.

The only person who sleeps soundly tonight is Zak Oliphant. Snoring like an old bull seal he grunts and farts in his sleep, fugging up the air in his whitewood, slatted, built-in bedroom far far away from the sweating, turbulent city.

For his wife, Kimberley, the long dark hours are a different matter.

How long till the wretched dawn comes?

She wanders about downstairs, pacing her mega, ranch-style home with its compulsory four-acre-field at the bottom of the garden in which she keeps three mistreated donkeys which browse amongst the furze, so you see, she cannot be totally bad. She will not mention that the donkeys are disgruntled and ungrateful creatures, refusing to come to the fence when she crosses the grass with sugar lumps to show them to her admiring callers. Old and grey, certainly, but their eyes are cunning, and then there's their upsetting private parts which slip out at the slightest opportunity.

But I mean, how can you possibly send them back?

She is not drinking any longer, but downing strong black coffee as she tries to work her difficulties out.

She was a fool to panic, earlier on. Nobody is going to find her out. If there'd been any witnesses the law would have come ringing her *Greensleeves* chimes long before now.

You are safe, Kimberley, she tells herself. Relax. Take it easy. You have got away with it – again. God must be with you.

And what of the woman, the wild-faced creature who flew through the air with her white plastic handbag, who lies in a coma slumped in the city hospital?

It was all HER fault! She stepped out without looking. Crazy. Kimberley could not help it. Anyone driving past at the time would have hit her.

Has Kimberley Oliphant no conscience at all? Is she so protected against the world by her cosy little existence?

Yes; yes she is. She prefers the world of popular romances to the real one, any day. She will whizz through four Mills and Boons in a night if she goes through a bad patch of insomnia. Or she will watch her video collection of *Roots*, five solid hours of it, so fascinated by the concept of slavery that she sometimes gets Zak to tie her up and her fantasies are all of whippings and cruel masters in knee-length boots.

Sheiks and slavemasters and helpless women in veils.

Pity it's not politically sound to write books like *Drum* any more. Kimberley still has the dog-eared paperback, and all the sequels that came after. Some of the pages are falling out, and roughened like old cardboard.

Alas, the thought of life in a cell in Holloway is not to be compared with her fantasies; no, not even remotely. Her dreams have never included beefy, warder-type women in heavy uniform skirts.

When Zak arrived home last night she waited for him to comment . . . had he heard about the accident? Was it a main topic of conversation locally? He must have listened to the news on his car radio, and, if he'd heard it he would certainly hold, and broadcast, some kind of view.

She had sobered herself up sufficiently to provide a

microwave chicken-and-vegetable dinner-for-one. There wasn't much in the two packets (who has these bird-like appetites?) so she heated up four frozen Yorkshire puddings to add a second dimension and to disguise the plastic taste.

Then she gave Zak his weekly treat – Black Forest gâteau, which she left on the wrought-iron table in the garden in order to defrost it in time.

She was determined not to mention it first. She had to wait for Zak.

'Rather unfortunate,' he said, eventually, cheered on by the sight of his favourite pudding.

'What, dear?'

'Rather unfortunate for the family.'

God, how Kimberley wished he wouldn't talk in riddles like this, expecting her to know what he was talking about.

'Oh?'

'First the kid gets himself mauled, then the bitch gets herelf mown down.'

'Who, dear?'

'You must have heard the news?'

'I think I did but there was nothing . . . '

'Name of Maggs. Mother of the boy who was attacked over at Melrose yesterday. Visiting the hospital . . . steps out into the road and gets herself knocked over.'

'Oh, Zak, how terrible.'

'Some people ask for it.'

'Oh, Zak, don't talk like that. You sound like an unfeeling monster.'

'I mean it, Kimberley. Some people are born victims and there's nothing you can do about it. Some people are just totally incompetent and unable to look after themselves. That's why folk like me have to do it . . . pay for them with our massive taxes.' He puts down his fork. There is cream caught on his stubble. 'Think about it for a moment, Kimberley. If we were a wild tribe and not so-called civilised human beings,

97

what d'you think would become of people like the Maggses?'

'I haven't the vaguest idea.'

'They'd be left behind to die, that's what. They'd be a drain on scarce resources and when times are hard no group, man nor beast, no group can afford to carry too many burdens. While we insist on carrying people like this along with us, we, as a society, cannot naturally evolve.'

'Oh stop it, Zak. You sound just like Hitler.'

'Well . . . ' Zak did not appear to take her criticism as an insult.

'I wonder if that poor young woman has any other children?'

'Probably got a whole army of the buggers. You don't know the half of it, living here, among decent people. You criticise me, but remember, Kimberley, I see families like this every day traipsing round with their litter, which reminds me. Had lunch with that fart, Gerald Hardy-Brown today. Told him quite a few home truths, I can tell you. You should have seen his face. Don't think that puny rag is going to be quite so glib with its comments in future.'

And so the conversation passed naturally on to other topics, and Kimberley, though rightly concerned by Zak's National Front approach, was nevertheless relieved to hear his point of view so firmly put.

After all, he is often right. He despised socialism for years while all the pundits and the chattering classes bowed down to it, and trade unions, and bloody immigrants. He was out of line, but he stuck staunchly to his guns and now you only have to read the papers to see how everyone's coming round to Zak's way of thinking.

No, Kimberley should go to bed and sleep soundly. There is no need for her to be pacing the floor like this at four o'clock in the morning.

She got away with killing that stray dog five years ago, didn't she? No-one found out about that, although she was hysterical for weeks and swore never to drink again. And everything points to the fact that, if she stays sensible and calm, she will get away with this one, too.

Nevertheless, try as she might to ignore it, her conscience pricks her. If only she was a Catholic so she could go and confess.

I I

No, it is not quite dawn yet; the sun is only a shoulder of fire nudging its way through the trunks of the faraway pine trees.

Is he asleep or is he in that enviable, fantasy half-state? When he was in Durham Fergus used to try to wake up before the bell went at six, just so he could dream his dreams of freedom a little bit longer. Freedom. Women. Cars. Some good hash. Booze. And over-riding all this – the *pièce de resistance*, his make-believe life with Jemima Hardy-Brown.

The law said, loosely, that Fergus should do everything his social worker told him.

Jemima told him to keep a diary in which he should write down all his thoughts, and show her it.

Taken to extremes, which is where Fergus took everything even vaguely relating to Jemima, this meant that she owned his thoughts, even before he had thought them. She had direct access to his head.

This invasive conclusion was both painful and exquisite, as the extent of her ownership of him, and therefore her control, became total.

The trouble was, if he spent too long revelling in that he was aggressive and bad-tempered all day, and likely to end up in the shit with the screws.

He was desperate to get parole.

His anguish to be near her was like an unquenchable thirst.

But no matter how hard he struggled to exclude her – even to the point of getting up and dunking his head in a bowl of water – somewhere, sometime, Jemima would monopolise his dream state. The agony and the ecstasy. In the special cells, where he found himself isolated on more than one occasion through no fault of his own, she caused him mental agony.

But now, as he nods, protected from the worst of the dew by his thick leather jacket, he senses something or someone behind him.

To begin with he does not move, does not want to react too violently in case it is some security geezer standing at the fence, sussing him out. Fergus is not keen to buck the law in this small community, not yet, not until he has achieved his mission. He must quickly invent some credible tale; he was hitching, he stopped here for the night, going on in a minute. All innocent like. Can the guy spare him a cup of coffee and a piece of bread and marmalade? 'Go on, mate, give us a break.'

So he puts a smile on his face in readiness to turn round and speak.

He turns.

He sees the ban-dog.

He raises his eyes from its massive feet, up its angular yet stocky legs, up its hefty flanks to its haunches, and then, only then does he move his startled eyes towards the face and the savage eyes that are staring straight back into his.

Fergus locks onto the face of madness, and the hunger he sees there is caused by the same starvation as his own.

On his feet in a second. Adrenalin flows, reacting to danger. Instantly assessing his level of safety, and the possibility of flight.

He will live only if the fence that stands between them is sound.

He scans his friend the fence with quick eyes, pupils fully dilated with terror. No dog could get over that, nor could any animal chew through it, even an animal with ferocious jaws like this one.

'Jesus fucking Christ.'

Protected or not, some instinct tells him not to move but to stand absolutely still.

Fuck this.

Every muscle in the ban-dog's body is taut with strain as he stands observing Fergus, well aware that he cannot get at him, aware that this is a stranger in a place where a stranger ought not to be. Although his blood lust is excited, the chain collar hangs loose round his powerful neck, swinging slightly in time with his breathing, menacingly controlled and slow.

'Shit.' No bugger would stand a chance against this murderous freak. By the force of his weight alone this bastard would have you down and torn apart in seconds.

Mustering all the control he can scratch together in his reeling brain, Fergus backs off a few inches. Slowly. Cautiously. Without allowing his eyes to move from the beast before him.

'It's okay, dog, it's okay, you fucker,' he whispers, his terror bringing a grin to his lips, already stretched to the shape of a scream. He brings up a hand in the form of a blessing and the ban-dog's eyes follow as if it's a snake.

'Steady, fella, steady. I'm going. I'm not hanging about here. Don't worry.'

Jesus, imagine walking along with this at your heels. King of the coop. No fucker would mess with anyone . . . give the pigs a fucking fright, if you went down you'd sure take one or two of the bastards with you.

Hang on. Nobody's supposed to own a dog like this. There are laws in this sodding country. Fergus knows plenty of blokes with those pissing ugly pit-bulls and there's been some new law about muzzling the bleeders. Somebody must be taking one helluva risk letting this hell-hound run loose anywhere, even surrounded by a bloody great fence.

The more secure Fergus feels himself to be the more he tries to figure out just what's going on here. What sort of place is this, Goddamnit? It's not some nuclear power station, or a secret government agency, both of which he knows the law would use anything to protect when it came down to the nitty gritty in spite of what they say. One rule for them and another for the rest of the wankers. Shipping out guns to the fucking enemy. Germ warfare and the like. For those corrupt bastards anything goes.

He has not really taken much notice of the place before now. He had just assumed it was a kind of weird warehouse, or a jerry-built prison camp left to rot since the war. From where he is standing it looks pretty much like that.

Fergus continues to back away from the ban-dog stealthily. Since their meeting the beast has not moved an inch, but stands there baring its menacing fangs and black all over, powerful as a panther, steady with anger. Strings of saliva drip from its slathering jaws and although the fence stands between it and Fergus, the last thing he wants is to enrage it further.

As soon as Fergus feels comparatively free, free from immediate danger and the kind of hypnotic effect the creature has upon him, he breaks out from the sappy undergrowth and stumbles towards the main road. He waits before crossing, waits to make sure the ban-dog knows no other secret way out, and from his new vantage point on the opposite side of the road he takes stock of Fingles Ponds.

How did he come to miss the signs when he arrived with the convoy the day before yesterday?

FINGLES PONDS – TURN RIGHT ½ MILE.
MELROSE. FINGLES PONDS. ENTRANCE.

And an arrow points the way to the slip road. It is a shabby fucking Disneyland, its turrets and towers in pink and blue pastels surrounded by concentration camp wire, as if some crazy has entered some bizarre worst-taste-in-the-world competition. Or the background for one of those fucking game shows they used to put on telly, fronted by that screaming loony, *Jeux sans Frontières* or some crap like that. So typically English, designed to make fools of all the poor sods who took part. The Royals went on it once, didn't they? Say no more.

What a mess.

But obviously popular, if you take the various pointers to carparks, filter lanes and one-way-routing.

But Fergus is fascinated by that dog. He cannot see the bottom of the fence from here, the undergrowth is in the way. He doubts that anyone can see the bottom of the fence from any easy vantage point because the whole complex is sunk in a slight dip, and you'd have to break through a wilderness of verge to get close enough to reach it.

And that is why the owner of this fucking killing machine has managed to get away with it.

No-one can possibly know of the dog's existence, or there would have been hysterical complaints.

Fergus leaves the view from the central reservation and makes for his sheltered den. The brute is still there, still slobbering, still staring, hasn't moved, not an inch by the look of it.

With the sweat soaking the spider print on the back of his T-shirt, Fergus forces himself to ignore every survival instinct in his body and approach the place where the ban-dog still stands staring.

'Hey,' he growls as he comes closer. 'Hey, what's up with you, you sick fucking mutant?'

There is no expression on the creature's face.

'Hey,' Fergus gains courage. He approaches like a child at Madame Tussaud's, ready to turn and flee at the slightest movement in the uncanny animal that stands waiting for him – the thing he dares himself to reach. As Fergus comes closer he gropes in his pocket and springs open his knife. 'Yeah, you fucker. Yeah. And it's bleeding well sharp enough to slit open your tongue for sure.

He doesn't even know if the creature can hear him, so still are its ears, so constant are its eyes, so sure is its threatening stance.

Cyrus Fitzgerald's eyes were alight, as if they were resting on buried treasure.

Cy said, 'If I believed in fairies I'd say that this varmint was one of that litter we got from that auld bitch Sara, them we let loose back along in Hudson Springs, remember, Olly? The one we named Satan.'

Olly, a rattler of a man with crafty eyes, flicked at his lips and scratched his smooth and pointed head. 'Reckon yer could be right, boss.' Olly didn't say so, but he couldn't see anything particularly special about this one. Just some young black dog, tatty looking thing, but a big bugger with a wicked temper.

The floor of the shack was covered in faeces and vomit. The stench floated up out over the top of the door, overwhelming the smell of petroleum spirit and sump oil as the two men, both garbed in tartan lumberjack jackets and peaked caps, peered inside one of the lean-tos in the yard behind the Texaca Truck Plaza.

'Well, lucky for us, some young kid's bin lookin' after it, not done too badly either by the look of 'im.'

'No kiddin'. What you plannin' to do then, Cy?' Olly knew the answer; he just wanted to hear it from Cy, his hero.

Cy, proud proprietor of the auto-truck stop, CB fanatic with his own special code and language – no 'spies in the sky' crap for him, nor the obvious 'smokies in plain wrappers knockin' on yer back door' – he was the best breeder and trainer of fighting dogs in the whole of the county, only keeping the best for himself, and his handle was Top Dog. He knew a good dog when he saw one. A compulsive liar and gambler, he enjoyed nothing better than a game of poker with his drivers, or a damned good dog fight, two ways he could raise dollars without paying out in taxes. A poor loser by nature, he went to great pains to avoid putting himself in that unhappy position. After all, as every sucker knows, it's the man who holds the best cards that wins.

He spat and rubbed his mouth with the back of a grubby hand but he could not hide the fact that he was excited. He raised himself on his toes and leaned over the top of the door, giving the dog a second poke with a long metal pole, watching the favourable reaction through speculative, half-closed eyes. 'Beautiful. Beautiful,' he murmured. 'Oh, leave 'im for a coupla days before we feed 'im. He's had it too easy, Goddamn it. Let 'im learn who's boss around here. Weaken the goddamn bastard a touch before we start lettin' 'im out, before we get into serious training, sorting out cracks and weaknesses. The beautiful, ugly sonofabitch.' Cy rubbed his money-tingling palms. He drawled on, 'After all, Olly good-buddy, we ain't in no particular hurry.'

By the cunning use of his illegal gains, Cy had torn off the label of poor white trash he'd been lumbered with when he'd started.

That night Cy Fitzgerald, who spent most of his time sitting in his office sipping cold beer and talking into his radio headset behind a wired-up plate glass window, went home to his brassy, busty wife, and told her she could now order that rock-maple and chintz covered suite for the living room she'd been hankering after for months.

Cy Fitzgerald was just about the only man who could look at the Texaca Truck Plaza and his wife and find them, not coarse and vulgar at all, but purely and pinkly beautiful.

It is all a question of patience, that, and the domination of will.

This is what Fergus decides as he stands and faces the ban-dog as the sun reaches the edge of the earth and rolls one lazy side over. He is going to wait, that is what Fergus is going to do, wait to see what happens.

Any sudden move might make the dog more dangerous.

The black dog.

The black dog of vengeance.

One of the forces of Satan himself, and his black soul shines from behind his eyes.

'I can stare you out, you bastard, if it's the last thing I do.'

Fergus's fantasies, stained by a stream of sadistic videos, are never entirely at rest in his head. Compulsive thoughts that torment him, powered by his love both horrible and glorious, until he is quite incapable of feeling properly any more. Yesterday he found himself powerless to mutilate Jemima's picture. How will he react when he has to confront her, face to face with only a knife in his hand? How incredibly right it would be if Fergus could only use this monster in his pursuit of justice; unable to strike the killing blow himself, this animal could do the job for him.

Fergus shudders in spite of himself.

And, ah! How much more satisfying a savage mutilation than the cold, precise death made by a slither of steel.

He used to dream that she would come and rescue him.

How pitiful.

So much for putting your faith in idols.

The thrill continues until Fergus is lost in a forest of wild imaginings, fevered by the visions he sees. And he might even be able to make a respectable getaway. The dog let loose afterwards, a stray, escaped from this illegal home, an unforgiveable accident on the part of its owner, whoever he may be.

The thought of a creature like this running loose is almost too terrible to consider.

There'd be slaughter on a grand scale.

Hah, they would probably hold a public enquiry.

He would bring flowers to her grave.

Since his decision to kill Jemima, Fergus has always imagined that he, buried beneath the ruins of love, would have no desire to go on living. He blots the aftermath of the murder from his mind. For surely, with her gone from the world, nothing else would matter. For in the killing of Jemima, in the murder of his misery, Fergus would certainly be putting himself to death, purification at last.

And the final denial of reality.

But there's no guarantee of this. And what if it's not like that?

What if, after she's dead, he finds himself free of his shattering obsession and at peace? Forever in the dark, this is a state of mind he cannot even remember. Unlikely, but surely possible. And a brand new concept which has never occurred to him before.

Like a wonderful vision.

He stares at the ban-dog with increasing wariness, savage, wild, with raw red rage in his eyes. How Fergus wishes that the realisation of dreams was possible.

Shit. What sort of man has the power to dominate a brute such as this? What sort of charisma would you need? Whoever he is, he must be one helluva guy. Fergus is intrigued, and quite willing to postpone his own plans in order to get to discover the truth of this simple but lethal set-up.

A high-pitched whistle from faraway.

'One! Two! Three! Four!'

Then, 'Dog!' And the banging of something hard against the sides of a metal bucket.

The black dog hesitates for only a second before giving Fergus one last evil stare, turning in magnificent tune with its whole body, and then heading off purposefully towards the source of the crude instructions.

After the dog is gone, Fergus experiences an emptiness which baffles him.

So does the thought that immediately follows.

A bucketful of meat and a sharp command?

Is that really all it takes?

I2

Morning at last. All is quiet. He must be off.

And, after paying a necessary visit to the Safeway store in the suburbs of Melrose for beer, fags and food, Fergus plans to take the railway track until it nears Middlehempston, and then follow the footpath sign round the edges of the fields. In this way he will come upon the village from the opposite direction, and avoid any prying eyes which might be watching for him, after yesterday's little fiasco.

He merely wants to watch her.

He has to be near her.

And he might find an opportunity to carry out his mission.

'Two of them are bald as coots, shaved I imagine, and the others look like those strange peace people from San Francisco, with braiding round their filthy long hair, and guitars. Foreign, I expect.'

'Oh come on, Mum,' moans Kirsty Maggs, worn out already. Dulcie has been on edge all morning, peering out of the door pretending to look for the milk while she kept an eye on the squatters. Sheralee and Kirsty no longer have milk delivered. Well they simply cannot afford it since they stopped getting their tokens. And the dry stuff is handier. She doubts if they had more than three hours' sleep last night. 'We'll sort that out later. Help me change this wet bedding, although when I'm going to have time to get down to that launderette God only knows. The whole sodding flat reeks of piss and it's already gone ten. We've missed the nine fifty-five from the station, so we'll have to walk to the corner.'

At least her mother's nodding appears to have stopped this morning.

Mrs Maggs says no more, but the thought of a day spent in public with Kirsty and Sheralee's kids makes her shrivelled-up insides quail. She's been through all that with her own kids, and she never expected to have to deal with anyone else's.

Nana or not.

And how is Sheralee this morning? Dear God, let her be better.

And what about poor little Jason with his bitten-off stump of a hand?

Is that horrible Mrs Crosby remembering to feed the cats?

It is just like living in the middle of a nightmare and she longs to wake up, or go home. If Dulcie Maggs could put her hands on a bottle full of her little green bombers she would down the lot like a shot.

Sod the bloody doctor.

Well everyone's addicted to something, aren't they, when you look at it like that? Everyone needs a prop to lean on, a God to see them through.

'Just go, Gerry, please don't fuss.'

'I would rather wait until Jacqueline arrives, or Mrs Haddock.'

Jemima smiles up at him reassuringly. 'I've got to beat this thing, as you told me last night. I can't start off by being afraid of being left in the house on my own. Jacky will be here in half an hour . . . '

'Jacky has no idea about time . . . '

'Jacky is well aware of the situation. She'll arrive on time, you'll see.'

'You should have packed a bag and spent the day at her house.'

'Gerry – look at the state of this place. Everything has to be organised, there are telephone calls to make and estimates to arrange. No, I'd far rather be here on the spot, and I think it's important for Hannah to see that we are dealing with this sensibly and not just running away.'

'Well, if you're sure.'

'I am sure. Whoever came here yesterday is hardly likely to be mad enough to come back. Now go, Gerry, just go! *And don't worry!*'

Whether Zak Oliphant's threatening behaviour has unsettled him more than he realises, or whether it was taking in the savagery of yesterday's break-in, Gerry Hardy-Brown does not know, but he is more disturbed than he cares to admit.

The police have promised, for what it is worth, to keep an eye on his house, although as Jemima says, the bastard is hardly likely to return to the scene of the crime.

But it is more than that which worries him now.

He cannot get the sight of Zak's angry face out of his head. Those mad, glaring eyes. The mentality of the man suddenly displayed like that in all the ordinariness of a pub at lunchtime, it was shocking. Acting so violently, as if he had something to hide, and then on top of all that the news of the frightful accident.

Paranoid or not, Gerry is determined to investigate further this morning. There is more to this than meets the eye, and it smacks of something very fishy. Normally such a calm and rational man, Gerry knows that his mental distress can only be relieved by following his suspicions through.

Jemima seems much better this morning, much to his relief. And Hannah, bless her heart, is dancing round with excitement, trilling to anyone who will listen that a bad and wicked man came into her house yesterday and broke her most favourite doll.

Naturally he had promised her another one exactly the same.

'No, not exactly the same, not a baby doll.' Her eyes sparkled. 'I want a Sindy.'

Gerry blanched. Oh, surely not that appalling rubbish already? Damn the TV adverts.

Children are so heartless. Such insensitive little creatures these days. Or maybe, he muses, as he drives towards the unsavoury suburbs of the city in the direction of Montpellier Court, just realists. And in Hannah's case, probably spoilt.

This morning, as Jemima is staying at home, Gerry has taken her navy-blue Morgan instead of the Volvo, with a view to taking the roof down when the day gets hotter, probably around mid-morning. Gerry glances down at his Filofax, which is on the passenger seat beside him. Kirsty Maggs, 16, Montpellier Court, Bankside. Must be down by the submarine base, somewhere off the dock road.

He needs to talk to Sheralee Maggs's sister. He needs to know everything there is to tell about that little boy's accident, and the hit-and-run yesterday. What sort of mood was Sheralee in when she went off walking by herself?

In spite of all her desperate worries over the state of her child, was she the sort of person to step out in broad daylight under the wheels of a car?

And what about the attitude of the police? Gerry wants to know a great deal more about that before he can leave the subject alone. Chief Inspector Derek Hooper has a bit of a reputation for giving a nod and a wink to his friends, members of the Rotary, the local Lodge and suchlike, and Gerry, citizen and editor of the *Western Express*, would not like to think that anything untoward was going on here.

Or that a thug like Zak Oliphant could employ men like himself to interfere with the wheels of justice.

The possibility beggars belief, but Gerry's suspicions will not go away. That monstrous man, Zak Oliphant, surely more unpleasant than sinister, issued grave threats against two people when they met at lunchtime yesterday. He threatened

Sheralee Maggs, and the editor himself.

Coincidence, more than likely. But in the space of twenty-four hours, look what has happened to both those people.

Money is a soothing balm, smoothing away all conscience.

Money is like a plaster covering a raw and open wound, keeping out infection.

Money is something Kimberley Oliphant has plenty of.

She loves it.

She removes one earring expertly before she makes the telephone call on a sudden ridiculous impulse.

Boredom probably. The whole day stretching ahead with nothing in her diary.

'Oh, good morning, I am ringing to enquire about Sheralee Maggs, who was admitted yesterday.'

'Are you a relative?' asks the preoccupied voice.

'Yes,' lies Kimberley easily, born from years of practice. 'I am her mother.'

'Hold on one moment and I'll put you through.'

A good five minutes go by, but no taped music, thank God. National Health. Probably can't afford it. Kimberley waits, tapping her shoe on the thick carpet and studying her face in the mirror. She smiles to herself; Zak would call her a fool if he knew, but she's always been a bit of a softy, she couldn't stop crying for hours after watching *Truly, Madly, Deeply*. She made herself quite ill and had to go and lie down. And then; 'Browning Ward, Sister speaking. Can I help you?'

Brrr. The phone goes dead, and Kimberley smiles at her own great cunning.

Coffee and biscuits while she gives her morning instructions to the homely char, and then she is off, completely made-up and looking as if she comes fresh from the hairdresser's, into her bright blue Astra and straight to the bank at Melrose where no-one will question a withdrawal of a fairly substantial sum of money.

Kimberley withdraws money all the time.

Flying in the face of popular opinion, she feels safer to have it on her person. In notes. Which she can feel and smell. Only victims are mugged, Zak says, so why should Kimberley worry? She's not a victim, she is one of the world's craftiest survivors.

The wife of a successful man who chose to include the word obey in her vows when she was last in church.

'Miss Sheralee Maggs. Browning Ward.' She prints it, using a black marker pen.

In the way of the criminal defying fate, she will take the stuffed jiffy bag to the hospital herself. She must do it now. She cannot wait to post it.

Yes, she thinks as she drives on. After this generous contribution, Kimberley Oliphant and her conscience are going to be able to sleep nights.

We will not go through the tiring ordeal of another journey to the hospital with Dulcie and Kirsty Maggs. By now we have a good idea of the kind of experience they have endured by the time they arrive, late as usual.

Dulcie helps Kirsty to cart the kiddies upstairs to the children's ward, says a quick good morning to Jason and then breathes a sigh of relief as she makes her way down to the intensive care unit.

Here, in a darkened room, her eldest daughter lies in a state of utter helplessness.

'I am her mother,' Dulcie whispers reverently.

'Ah!' The nurse is far too bright, shockingly bright under these terrible circumstances. Anyone would imagine that this situation – the drips, the breathing machines, the tubes and the bleeps – is normal.

'Something was delivered for your daughter this morning.' She hands Dulcie Maggs a small but solid parcel. 'It was handed in at the main reception, so I can't tell you any more about it.'

Dulcie thrusts the packet into her hold-all bag, among the packets of biscuits and the Pampers nappies.

'So many flowers!' exclaims Dulcie, standing tensely at the door to her daughter's room.

'Yes, members of the public can be very generous at times like these,' the nurse says, smiling at Dulcie's obvious gratification. 'It's a bit of a waste really, particularly with these sorts of patients, but who knows, something about the scents in the room might be the very trigger we're looking for.'

'Trigger?'

'Something to jerk your daughter out of her comatose state. The neurosurgeon has examined her carefully, and can see no reason why Miss Maggs shouldn't make a full recovery. She was very, very lucky to get away with a few broken ribs and some cuts and bruises. It is just a matter of time, and that's where you come in.'

Dulcie nods, greatly encouraged by the news. 'I have to sit and talk to her. Bring up all sorts of old memories.' Dulcie has seen enough episodes of *Casualty* in her time to know what is expected of her. She notes that her chair is already in position, close beside the bed.

She feels a fool. Playing a part. Like having to speak on an answerphone. 'Sheralee! Sheralee, it's your mother speaking.'

Silence, as she stares at her daughter's face, white as the bandages.

'Kirsty'll be down later, but they don't think it's a good idea to allow the children in here.'

Did Dulcie catch a flicker of relief . . . nothing more than a shadow really, passing across those marble features?

'Jason is doing very well. I saw him this morning. He'll soon be back to his old self again.'

Dulcie must be imagining this, for she thinks she hears her daughter's steady, remote-controlled breathing flutter. The blip on the screen confirms her suspicions, but by the time she notices it has gone.

'I spent the night round at Kirsty's. Everyone slept there together. We moved your cot across and put it in Kirsty's bedroom.'

Dulcie sits and thinks for a while. Outside there is nothing but clouds and one solitary seagull. She gets up and draws the flimsy curtains. Somewhere a woman begins to cry. And then she says, 'The kiddies all miss you.'

Actually, although Kelly asked about Sheralee once, none of the others have mentioned her absence. There has been far too much excitement going on. Dulcie must not mention the flat, or the fact that squatters have moved in. Whatever she does, however desperate she finds herself for a topic of coversation, she must not worry Sheralee at a time like this. She must find something pleasant to say, some sweet memories from the past . . . but although Dulcie casts her mind back as far as she possibly can, she finds a bleakish blank where those happy times ought to be. There is pain in Dulcie's face as she struggles to remember but sees nothing except moves from one flat to another, work, machinery banging in her brain, sleep, rows, up and off in those cold, cold dawns and boarded-up cardboard windows.

Life has been nothing but a struggle for Dulcie.

But there must have been some good times. *There must have been!* She twists her fingers in the neat white bedspread. It's just that Dulcie is so confused that the good times have slipped her mind.

'People are so kind, Sher. All these lovely flowers. Oh, and somebody's sent you a parcel, look.' Relieved to find something to do with her hands, Dulcie fights with the wrapping and finally manages to undo the interesting package. It takes her a while to realise what is inside.

Fifty-pound notes!

I'll be blowed.

Frowning creasily, she holds one up to the light.

How many are there?

She counts out loud. Ten . . . fifteen . . . it doesn't take long. One thousand pounds in all. Dulcie Maggs is sitting beside her daughter's bed holding one thousand pounds in her hands, more money than she's ever owned in her life although, until she reached pension age, she spent every day of it working.

'Sheralee. Unless I've cracked up completely, someone has sent us a thousand pounds.' She searches for a card, for who do they know who might do something like this? No-one. That's for certain.

Then it must be a stranger moved by their plight. Someone who has read about Jason and Sheralee in the newspapers. Some anonymous benefactor, you read about people like that but you don't ever believe . . .

She flaps the notes under Sheralee's nose, flicking through them, hoping the smell of the crisp new print might revive her. Nothing.

'Sheralee,' she encourages her senseless daughter. 'Think of the bills you can pay off. You could even afford a new cooker.'

But it's not money Sheralee needs now, it is happy memories. And no benefactor, however generous, can supply her with those.

Dulcie knows that memories don't come wrapped up in cellophane and tied with scarlet ribbons. They are more elusive than that, and expensive. And there's no place you can go and order them, no phone number where you can pay by credit card.

'Remember that time you made that coffee . . . when we were living down Wellington Road, and you nearly set the house on fire! Remember, Sheralee? Do you remember?'

Yes, Sheralee probably does, and if so she will also remember that Dulcie Maggs gave her the hardest slapping of her life, so scared that the landlord would smell the burning and evict them.

Up in the children's ward, Kirsty Maggs is faring no better.

'I want my Mum,' shouts Jason, who does not want her at all.

Kirsty smiles and tries to play with the children.

She tries to hold Jason's normal hand.

'I want my Mum.' He shrugs her off.

She stops herself shouting when Kelly, being silly, knocks the water off the bedside cabinet, and when Sandra makes a little girl cry by taking away her felt pens.

'I want my Mum.'

Time and again she bends down to replace the toys which Jason has deliberately hurled from his bed as he lies back watching her smugly.

Everyone smiles as they pass, as they peer efficiently at the little family.

But all Kirsty longs for is to get back home where she will not have to sit in this little cage of a room, pretending that everything is all right.

Pretending that she can cope.

Pretending that she is a capable mother, as she believes her own mother was.

13

One of Gerry Hardy-Brown's very worst scenarios is that one day circumstances might force him to bring his adored little family to live here.

Or if not here, somewhere equally as bad as this.

Times are precarious. Gerry has friends, mostly middle-class – architects, solicitors, designers, advertisers, all of whom were doing reasonably well running their own business or employed by worthy companies . . . and look at them now.

Caught in the trap of negative equity, mortgage arrears, walking the streets in search of work, children removed from their private schools, wives on the sherry or verging on nervous breakdowns.

And although his own hundred-and-fifty-year-old company feels safe enough at the moment, and his investments are handled wisely, these days anything goes.

So this is Bankside.

How would Jemima survive surrounded by the grot and sordid squalor of this place? And what about exquisite little Hannah, so used to playing safely in her gentle green garden? And the thought of his baby son having to fend for himself around these derelict bomb sites, broken carparks and boarded-up factories, the thought of little Felix having this as his first experience of life cuts Gerry like a knife through his heart.

A sensitive man, he is sickened by the sights that surround

him. A ship's siren dirges from somewhere out on the Sound, and to Gerry's ears it is a melancholy cry of despair.

The poor will always be with us. The poor, and their dogs. He watches as a motley hound lifts its leg against a dustbin. Two more flea-ridden strays pull at a bone in the middle of the street.

Why must it be ever thus? Disgustedly, Gerry slams the Morgan door and heads towards Montpellier Court. Looking back, it occurs to him that his car seems to be the only one with an engine. Most of the vehicles parked along this broken and desolate street are propped up on bricks, their wheels missing, or their tyres, or their bonnets are up as if their ghostly owners, still praying for miracles, are there working underneath, eternally listening for the faintest sound of a turning engine.

He climbs the steps of the grey, formidable building. At least someone has made an effort with the brightly painted doors. Number sixteen . . . he passes the inevitable graffiti as he climbs, nimbly avoiding the splashes of vomit.

Gerry presses the bell but hears nothing echoing from within. It is obviously broken. He lifts the lightweight silver handle and allows it to flop, almost soundlessly against the glossy red door. With a surge of anger, born of defeat, he lifts it and raps three times, knocking his knuckles painfully as he does so.

Nobody home.

He wonders if there is anyone next door, behind the cheery yellow. This door is badly scuffed, with score marks round the lock as if it has recently been . . .

'Yeah?'

The speaker's head is a menacing, shaven bullet, similar to the man on the Tango advert. 'I was wondering . . . '

'Who did you want, mate?' The shaved man puts his vast hand up to one of his cauliflower ears, mocking.

'I was looking for Miss Kirsty Maggs, actually.'

'We dunno anyone round 'ere,' says the man in the string

vest, with tattooes running inkily all the way down his arms. He looks like a typical sailor. A boiler man. Or a bosun's mate. Anyway, some skill that requires tremendous physical strength. Gerry, with his squash twice a week, feels trodden in like a little weed. 'We're only just in 'ere ourselves, see?'

Gerry glances at the broken door. 'And not by invitation, by the look of it.'

The man's head comes further out, lowered in a threatening manner. 'You gettin' at something, mate?'

'No, certainly not. It's nothing to do with me. But it is important that I contact your neighbour.'

'Nosy old cow bag.'

'Pardon?'

''Er next door with the overcrowding. Done nothin' but watch us all mornin'. Crouched at 'er door. As if we was spooks or sommat.'

'Well,' Gerry clears his throat. 'She was probably surprised to see the flat occupied so quickly.'

'Weren't no-one in it. What's the point in havin' homes standin' empty when there's folk . . . '

'Yes. Yes, I quite understand. And I agree with you completely.'

'Try the hospital,' calls a surprisingly cultivated voice from within, amused, as if he is party to some sort of joke lost on Gerry. And the boiler man is almost too coarse to be true. 'I heard one of the children say they were going to visit their brother in hospital. Although I don't know which hospital they meant, or where it is.'

'Okay guv?' enquires the shaven head, careful to keep the chain on the door as though he imagines Gerry might have an ulterior motive, and be reckless enough, or desperate enough, to force his way inside.

'Yes. Thank you very much for your help.'

And Gerry backs away, only to find that while he's been gone the Morgan roof has been slashed cleanly in half, from the front of the car to the back, and the badge has been wrenched off the bonnet.

Curses.

But there is no-one in sight to observe his few moments of helpless fury.

Squatters next door, dear God.

Those poor women. That poor family. How much more can they be expected to take?

And here he is like a damn fool, unduly upset about the vandalism of his car roof. If he lived here he would want to rip a few car roofs himself.

After unclipping the roof and stashing it under the back seat, Gerry heads towards the hospital, cursing his own stupidity. It will only take him ten minutes. He ought to have realised they wouldn't be home. Of course they would be visiting the fallen.

It is eleven o'clock and time for a well-earned break.

Kirsty and Dulcie meet in the hospital grounds as planned, each drained in their own way. The kiddies, happy to be outside, swarm round the biscuits.

'Wait till you see this . . .'

Dulcie cannot wait, her fingers itch to show Kirsty the fortune wrapped in brown paper.

Kirsty's first reaction is timid, 'Perhaps we should hand it to the police. I mean, maybe it's something to do with the accident . . .'

'Never you mind about the police. Somebody wanted Sheralee to have this, and have it she bloody well will. Kirsty, I'm surprised at you. You hand this in to the police and you'll never set eyes on it again!'

Kirsty sighs, 'You're right, of course.' She holds out her shaking hands and explains, 'It's just that I can't cope with any more shocks without taking leave of my sodding senses.'

Being with Jason has certainly knocked the stuffing out of her. 'Why don't we give this afternoon a miss? It's a lovely hot day. Why don't we take the kids to the paddling pool in the park, to celebrate, or something?'

Kirsty turns on her mother angrily. 'Celebrate? How *could* you, Mum? All the other kids in that ward are surrounded by visitors, a whole stream of visitors, aunts, uncles, friends, neighbours. We can't leave Jason lying there on his own as if nobody loves him.'

Oh, how she wishes they could.

Oh, how she longs to lie down in the quiet, all by herself with the curtains drawn.

And Dulcie knows very well that she cannot leave Sheralee, wrapped up in the quiet, all by herself with the curtains drawn.

'Well then, if we have to go back, how long d'you think we should stay?' She dreads hearing the answer.

'Until tea time, probably. And then, really, we ought to take the kids home and one of us ought to come back.'

What – all day and all evening with hardly a break? Dulcie starts nodding again. What is this new distressing habit? Something to do with Ativan? 'Oh, Kirsty, no!'

Kirsty gives up without a fight. 'No. You're right. Jason must understand. We just can't.'

Gerry Hardy-Brown makes his lanky and sandalled way towards the family group sitting on the grass.

No Henry Moore though, this; there is not a man among them.

'Good afternoon.' He peers at them, with miniature suns reflecting in the orbs on his spindly glasses. 'So sorry for interrupting. At a time like this.'

Kirsty looks up, shading her eyes from the sun. 'There's bad news?' What other sort of news could there be?

'Oh no, definitely not.' He hastens to wipe that terrified glint from her eye. 'My name is Gerry Hardy-Brown, editor of the

Western Express and nothing remotely to do with the hospital.'

'Kirsty!' cries Mrs Maggs in alarm. 'Never talk to the newspapers!'

'Calm down, Mum. You don't know what Mr Hardy-Brown wants to talk about yet.'

And neither does she. Kirsty cannot imagine what this lean, long, intense-looking man with the Jesus beard and the thonged sandals wants with the likes of them.

'I tried to find you at home, and the people next door informed me that you would probably be here.'

'The people next door. You must mean the squatters. How did they know where we were?' Dulcie, blanching, turns in hysteria to Kirsty. 'How the hell did they know we were here?'

He has upset them already. Jemima always complains that he is bad at handling people. 'They said they heard one of your children talking.'

Already little Billy has his arms round Gerry's trouser leg. But Gerry seems enchanted, not in the least disapproving. He squats on the grass to engage the child further, eager to make amends.

'I can see you've got kiddies of your own, Mr Hardy-Brown.'

'Oh yes, yes. A girl around about this one's age.' He pats Sandra's curly head. 'And a boy,' he looks pleased, 'slightly younger than this little chap.'

'Quite a handful,' says Kirsty, 'when you're on your own.'

'Yes, I'm sure. It must be a terrible struggle. Especially now, with your sister injured in such unhappy circumstances.'

'She's in a coma, you know.'

'Yes, Mrs Maggs. They told me. I'm so sorry. And that's part of the reason why I wanted to have a private chat with both of you. If this is an inconvenient moment – and I'm sure the last thing you want to do just now is to spare the time for someone like me – but if you feel you are able to do so I would like to arrange a meeting, sometime soon, perhaps . . . '

'Now is fine, Mr Hardy-Brown. But I don't know how you think we can help you.'

Kelly has spilt orange juice down Mr Hardy-Brown's linen jacket. Dulcie leans forward and attempts to wipe it off with a tissue. She only succeeds in making it worse. Most of the Maggs's washing has pieces of tissue in it, where the clothes have gone round the machine with their pockets still full.

'Oh, don't worry about a little thing like that,' Gerry tells her pleasantly, settling down on the grass beside them.

'It is rather awkward to know quite where to start without alarming you unduly. But I have the feeling that Sheralee's accident might not have been quite as straightforward as it appears. Let me tell you about our burglary yesterday . . . ' So Gerry Hardy-Brown launches off into a detailed explanation of his darkest suspicions, drawing exclamations of horror from Kirsty and Dulcie from time to time.

Surely Gerry should have thought twice before confiding in these limited people. A certain proportion of Her Majesty's subjects cannot cope with the truth without becoming over-excited. That is why the Government has to tell so many lies.

Kirsty's plump face falls fatly vacant. 'And so you think . . . ?'

'Never!' cries Dulcie, smacking her lips tightly together. 'Never! Who would credit it?'

'No, please understand, there is nothing conclusive about what I have told you, these are just thoughts that are niggling away in my head . . . '

'Mr Oliphant's a terrible man . . . '

'Nobody round here likes him.'

'But to go this far!'

'He wasn't to know that Sheralee wouldn't be killed! He could be done for attempted murder!'

'No, wait, Mrs Maggs, steady on, I am certainly not accusing him, I am merely uneasy . . . '

'Well, Mr Hardy-Brown, so what would you say if I showed you this?' Flamboyantly and with some triumph, Mrs Maggs uncovers the bundle of money. Pampers nappies fly out like supporters' cushions at a football match and scatter all over the grass but the notes remain secure in their pink rubber bands.

Gerry's face turns terribly serious. 'May I ask where this came from?'

Dulcie is thrilled by the effect of her gesture. 'You can ask. Anyone can ask. But I wouldn't be able to give you an answer.' Her voice turns quiet and confidential as she moves her whisper closer to the editor's ear. 'All I know is that this was handed in at the main reception some time this morning.'

'I thought it might be something to do with the guilty driver,' says Kirsty, eager as the others to take part in the sinister speculations.

Gerry thinks aloud. 'But surely anyone driven by guilt to this extent would turn themselves in? A thousand pounds! And if you believe that Sheralee probably stepped out without looking, what would an innocent driver have to fear from the law?'

'You're right. He's right, Kirsty, if you think about it. And not many people have a spare grand hanging around to stuff in a jiffy bag, to distribute to total strangers. Mr Hardy-Brown is right, it could well be a bribe. Oliphant doesn't want us making a fuss. Sheralee's accident was a warning.'

Kirsty does not yet understand. The sun has scorched her nose to an overdone prawn cracker. 'But how could we make a fuss? Make a fuss about what?'

And so Gerry has to explain about the press campaigns of the past, about the weakness of the police action in Jason's case, and about the fact that he was planning to see the Maggses, to take the whole question of security at Fingles Ponds, and other dubious points of safety affecting the public and the workforce, and open it up for debate.

'You could have taken the matter much further, Miss Maggs, if only you'd had the right advice. Even now, you must get legal aid and go for compensation. No wonder the man was worried. And Zak Oliphant warned me, very firmly, against interfering,' says Gerry Hardy-Brown, more convinced than ever now that his worst suspicions are true. 'A few hours later, what happens? Sheralee is badly injured and my house is ransacked. And now he is trying, clumsily, to buy you off with this.'

Gerry slaps at the parcel of money dismissively.

'But we're keeping it, Mr Hardy-Brown,' puts in Dulcie Maggs quickly. 'There's no question of us handing it in, wherever it came from.'

'But Mrs Maggs,' says Gerry sadly. 'It looks as if this could be tainted money.'

'I don't give a stuff how tainted it is, as long as it pays the gas bill.' Dulcie Maggs is adamant. 'And we don't know for certain. We're not sure of anything yet.'

'But the police ought to be told. This may well be important evidence.'

'Mr Hardy-Brown, don't think we're not grateful for your interest and your help. 'Cos we are, Mum, aren't we? But this is our decision, and we showed you this money in confidence. We understand what you're trying to do, and all about justice and the like, but we don't want to tell the police about this, do we, Mum?'

'No we certainly don't.'

Gerry sighs. 'Well, ladies, if you are determined to take that stance . . . '

'We are.' The two of them stick staunchly together, sitting in a nest of purple Ribena and biscuit crumbs.

'I shan't let this drop. And I should be very grateful if you would inform me should any other matters of interest arise, or if you are threatened in any way. If we can prove that this immoral man is hounding the public in this scandalous fashion, then there's no limit to the compensation he'll have to pay out in the end.'

'But what if Jason and Sheralee recover completely?' Oh dear, that's come out sounding greedy, as if Kirsty doesn't want a full recovery for her sister or her sister's son. But she has asked the question. There is no way she can take it back.

'Recover completely?' The godly editor sounds offended. 'What are you talking about? That child has lost his hand and will have to suffer all the disadvantages that is bound to entail, and his mother has gone through all sorts of pain, discomfort, terror, shock, and even if she does recover she is unlikely to get over the whole appalling experience. These sorts of accidents affect people deeply, the consequences stay with them for the rest of their lives.'

'Yes, I know . . . '

Now he is even wondering whether the slashing of his car roof was a coincidence. 'So will you promise me that? Should anything else come up to do with our discussion this afternoon, will you get in touch with me immediately? Meanwhile I will continue to hound the authorities until this business is thoroughly investigated, as it ought to have been in the first place.'

Totally in awe of him, of his sharp mind and his energy, they both agree.

So Gerry Hardy-Brown bounds away with his mettle well up, after handing Dulcie Maggs his card.

Do-gooders.

Interfering busybodies.

People may have a duty to their talents but, Gerry, hang on, is investigation really yours?

Get back to your office at once. What on earth do you think you are doing carrying out this fanatical campaign against a man whose ideals you despise?

Zak Oliphant.

A moral vacuum.

Intellectually inferior, unscrupulous, and yet a millionaire ten times over.

Are you *really* so contented with your undemanding life?

Can't you see that by following your misguided intuitions, you are going to divert the official line of inquiry, making it possible for a madman to have free access to your wife?

14

The garden of The Old Schoolhouse carries its own enchant-
ment. Not one-tenth of the size of The Grange, where Jemima's
friend Jacqueline lives, and without that formal layout –
patios, organised flowerbeds and pathways, let alone the
swimming-pool area with its raffia sunshades and Harrods
loungers – and yet the two women are as happy here, basking
in the luscious beauty of it all, as they were yesterday.

It is exactly the same for the children, who are making do
with a plastic paddling pool today, and a vast set-up of Fisher
Price farms, dolls' houses, schoolrooms and colourful
hospitals.

Hannah and Emily are lost in their innocent fantasies.

The infant, Felix, is lying in an arbour beneath the branches
of the chestnut tree, kicking, naked, on his rug. Felix is the only
one in any position to look straight up and see the face of
Fergus Johnson perched in the canopy high above him.

Perhaps that is why Felix drools and giggles every now and
then, shaking his tiny fists over something secret that amuses
him.

'He's so sweet!' exclaims Jacqueline, rubbing her shiny
tummy. 'It's only when I see him that I think carrying this bulge
around through this sort of summer is worth it.'

'It won't be long now,' says Jemima consolingly, only
knowing how glad she is that it's Jacky about to go through the
birth ordeal, and not her.

'I think you are being absolutely marvellous,' says Jacky,

examining her nails as she slumps as voluptuously as she can in one of the Hardy-Browns' shabby but tasteful Habitat deckchairs. Her heavy breasts droop. 'This is all so cosy and comfortable you would never believe that a maniac ran riot here yesterday. If I were you I'd be nothing but a haggard ruin. When you think about it.'

Jemima watches Felix with a smile on her lips, as mothers do. She has prepared a herb omelette for lunch, fighting to reclaim once more for herself her herby, spicy, garlicky, olive-oil kitchen. 'But I keep telling myself I mustn't overreact.'

'There is such a thing as too much self control.'

'And you think I've gone into a state of denial?'

'You said it, not me. You must mourn if you feel like mourning.'

'Nobody's dead, Jacky.' She looks at her friend sternly.

'No, but some pretty precious things of yours have been attacked, and lost forever. Let alone the violence involved. I'm glad I didn't see it,' says Jacqueline, half wishing she had. It was bad enough when she arrived this morning; Mrs Haddock was doing her best, working under Jemima's orders, but God knows what it must have looked like last night.

Jemima asks her, 'But you don't feel nervous now, do you, Jacky? Sitting out here in the garden? You don't believe he will come back?'

'No, I don't.' Jacky sips at her lime juice and the ice in her glass tinkles prettily. 'But I don't know what we'd do if he did.'

Jemima allows the remark to slip out as if it is unintentional. 'Gerry's got a gun upstairs.'

Now Jacqueline loves a drama. As long as it's safe. As long as she is not too closely involved. 'Oh, Jem, I think you should bring it down, and load it, just in case. Go on! Let's have a look at it!'

But first Jemima must protest. 'He only ever uses it for rabbits. He'd be furious if I unlocked it.'

'But it's a proper gun? Not just an air pistol or something?'

'Oh no. It's a shotgun. Not just any old ordinary gun, actually, it's a Purdy. Something of a family heirloom. His father gave it to him when he was eighteen.'

'But it works?'

'Of course it works.'

'I am quite surprised that Gerry didn't suggest you keep it with you, actually, under the worrying circumstances. I think you'd be quite wise to go and unlock it and bring it down. I bet he would, if he was here on his own.'

'But I'm not alone. I've got you. And Mrs Haddock's been in all morning.'

'What good could you and I do if that madman came back? Think about it, Jem. What if he tried to hurt the children?'

'Oh stop it, Jacky. Now you're making me feel nervous.' There's a sudden shadow over the innocent garden.

'Maybe you should get yourself out more. Take up good works.' Jacky is half joking, half malevolent. This is her natural way. 'Oh go and get the damn thing. Go on Jem, I can see you want to! I'll watch Felix.'

'It's you that's making me feel bad.' Jemima laughs as she goes, and the look of satisfaction on her face grows broader. 'I was perfectly okay till you arrived, you rotter.'

While Jemima is inside the house Fergus looks down and sees Jacqueline fondling her swollen breasts.

A watcher by nature and experience, Fergus has no fear of giving his position away. Many's the time he has waited and watched, outside arcade jeweller's shops, outside lonely garages, outside the Darjeeling Restaurant in Lindon Street, Wandsworth, casing the joints. Waiting until the owners hung the closed sign up and came to lock the door ready to cash up.

So Fergus is quite at home perching in the top of the tree fiddling with his knife, a position he chose when the garden was empty earlier on this morning. Access was easy, because

132

the trunk grew half in and half out of the garden wall bordering a sheltered wheat field.

No, what pains Fergus is that Jemima is so near and yet so far. What pains him is the imagined look on her face should he climb down through the branches, so far away from that fond look with which she used to caress him when he was merely a naughty boy.

Disturbed, is how she used to put it.

After the fire she spoke up for Fergus at his case conference. However, it wasn't enough to prevent him from being sent to Ryall, a special closed unit for delinquent children.

'No, you don't understand, Fergus,' she tried to explain. 'I know you came forward and owned up immediately but they're always jumpy about arson and understandably so. I mean, when you started that fire at St Thomas's, didn't it cross your mind for one moment that some of your friends might have been burnt alive?'

'They would've been, if that bastard Oliver hadn't been raiding the fridge after midnight.'

'And I don't know how you can talk about Crispin like that, after everything he did for you. He cared about you, Fergus, he really did. Crispin Oliver is one of the few genuine, caring people I know . . .'

'Bullshit,' said Fergus.

'And what about you? If you didn't think about your friends, didn't you realise that *you* couldn't have got out of that building, either?'

Fergus looked at her through narrowed eyes. 'D'you think I care if I die? And, then what would you have thought?'

'Oh Fergus, Fergus, when will you realise that I am fond of you for your own sake, not for what trouble you can get yourself into? You don't have to constantly fight for my attention. If I thought for one moment . . .'

'Fond of me? What's fond?'

'I like you, Fergus, I feel that I understand you, and I know you have been through a great deal although you consistently refuse to talk to me about it.'

'I hate that fucking word fond and I don't know why you bother to use it.'

'And you don't need to swear so stupidly to impress me either. Where have you picked up this terrible language, anyway? You've got an excellent vocabulary, Fergus, so why don't you use it?'

But he couldn't say what he wanted to say. No, shit, not even alone in his bed at night when the moon shone in through the window bars.

He couldn't say that he'd only feel safe if he could disappear inside her.

What sort of nutter would she take him for?

At Ryall they tried to force open his mind, violently, like using a can opener on a flower. Fergus saw through it all. He used to make up stories, Jeez, that used to rile them . . . and sometimes he would shiver in a corner and not speak for hours, dribbling and pretending to be mad.

They usually sent for HER in the end, when they realised that whatever they tried they couldn't get anything out of him.

They tried to make him work for points; if Fergus behaved himself he could watch one hour's television, or go for a walk on Sunday, or have Coca Cola instead of squash.

Balls. Kid's stuff. It might work on the other gits they'd got locked up in here, but it wasn't going to work on him. Twenty-five foster homes in two years and Fergus wasn't a kid any longer. He would much prefer the martyrdom of a bread-and-water diet, he would have loved to have been shackled to a cell deep under the ground, so he could prove the depths of his love.

Through suffering he could express himself.

He told himself pain was his friend. Pain would come whenever you called it.

He plucked up his courage to cut more deeply into his arm using anything at hand – rusty tin lids, broken glass, even slates that fell off the roof. So she would come and talk to him for longer. It wasn't till the scabs came off that the wounds looked like Js again.

Sometimes she brought him little gifts, like George Best's autograph, like a book about sharks.

She got him out of there in the end.

She had to.

She could see how bad he was getting and she couldn't stand the guilt. So she used her influence to get him moved, when she moved herself for promotion, to London.

Down below him the little girls' laughter jumps like the sunbeams.

'I've brought the bullets down, too.'

'Ammunition, Jem, for goodness' sake.'

'Gerry keeps them hidden, but I found them in one of his drawers, luckily, I wasn't going to waste this sunshine scrabbling around inside for hours.'

'Well done. You'll feel safer now. Loaded or not, you point that weapon at someone and they're going to take you seriously.'

'D'you think so, Jacky? And what if they're mad?'

'Even a madman understands what the barrel of a gun looks like.'

'Gerry wants to take me away. But I don't know, Jacky. I've got a feeling I should stay here and see this through.'

'You are much more frightened than you're letting on, Jem, aren't you?'

Jemima, applying more lotion to her already bronzed and slinky legs, ignores the leading question. 'And anyway, he seems to have taken up arms in another of his causes.'

'He hasn't really grown up, Jem, has he, that husband of yours? Sometimes he still behaves like an outraged student.'

'He doesn't believe that the family with the injured boy, the one at Fingles Ponds who had his hand bitten off, well, he doesn't believe that they are getting justice. He's told the police to stop wasting their time searching for a wandering lunatic and a crazed driver, and to concentrate on Oliphant instead. He's convinced himself that he is behind all this. And of course he has always loathed the man.'

Jacqueline leans over with difficulty and hands her little daughter a watering can. Emily is Jacky in miniature, blond and petite with startling sky blue eyes. Her mother's eyes flash in anger. 'Oliphant's a despicable bastard who rides rough-shod over everyone, and everyone knows that. So whatever Gerry can do to expose that toad is to be admired.'

'But he can't let things go, Jacky. You know how he is. And I worry. One day he is going to bite off more than he can chew.'

Jacqueline stretches. 'Felix is grizzling, and I'm too hot. Let's go inside for a mo and cool off while you feed him.'

'But the girls . . . ?'

'Oh, they'll be all right. We can hear them if they call, and they're very sensible together. Give me a hand, Jem, I'm stuck.'

It does not take the nimble Fergus a second to slide down his tree and over to the deckchairs where he grabs the abandoned gun and the cartridges.

Emily and Hannah, startled out of their Fisher Price world, regard him levelly with fingers in their mouths.

The jealousy Fergus feels when he stares back at Hannah, giving a fierce pretend scowl, is physical. It stabs him.

Uncertainly the child starts to giggle. This strange man must be playing, like Daddy does sometimes, and when she gets frightened Mummy tells him to stop. 'You're too rough, Gerry,' she laughs. 'Sometimes you don't realise how strong you are!'

'What's your name then?' Fergus asks her grudgingly.

Hannah simpers, hands grasped behind her back as she answers him prettily.

'That's a nice name. Well, Hannah, d'you want a present?'

'I do! I want a present.' Emily, feeling excluded, steps forward bravely.

'Here then.' And Fergus thrusts an empty lager can and a half-eaten packet of salt and vinegar crisps into the child's eager arms.

Clutching the gun he uses the tree to gain the height of the wall, and is up and over and away through the fields by the time the disappointed children find their mothers chatting in the bare, uncomfortable living room.

'Oh, Emily, put those down! Where did you get them from? They're disgusting!'

'From the man?'

'What man?'

'The man in the tree?'

Jacky throws a glance towards Jemima, but her friend is already alert, Felix abandoned at her breast.

She speaks terribly slowly. 'The man in the tree in the garden?'

Both girls nod.

'Bring those things here!'

Both girls step forward, well aware of the changed, charged atmosphere.

'What was this man like? WHAT DID HE LOOK LIKE? Did he speak to you?'

They nod in unison.

Jemima holds her breath. There are tears in her frantic eyes already. 'Dear God, what did he say?'

The little girls look at each other and burst into silly, stupid giggles.

'I'm being perfectly serious now, Hannah, that man might be the bad man who came into our house yesterday. Now, what did he say?'

Jacqueline sits bolt upright, for once unaware of her dragging lump. 'Jemima! The gun! Did you leave it out there?'

Jemima stares back at her, baffled. There is no need for an answer. She has played straight into Fergus's hands.

'Right, stay where you are, I am ringing the police right away,' Jacqueline shouts deliriously. 'You need protection. This is getting right out of line, this is bloody outrageous, what are they doing about Oliphant? Letting him go on like this? This is totally incredible!'

15

The squatter.

There he is, piping a tune, under the smell of hot curry on the balcony.

'Come away, Kirsty,' calls Mrs Maggs, battling with the children and the precious jiffy bag under her arm. 'Come away!'

> From his lodge went Hiawatha,
> Dressed for travel, armed for hunting;
> Dressed in deer-skin shirt and leggings,
> Richly wrought with quills and wampum;
> On his head his eagle feathers,
> Round his waist his belt of wampum . . .

A warrior brave if ever there was one.

Now it becomes clear why she was made to learn that particular section at school (and what the hell was wampum?) and why she had remembered it. Fate moves . . . It was fate. Every member of the class took it in turns to chant a piece of the verse but big, overweight Kirsty had been so nervous . . .

> There she stood upon the rostrum,
> School and audience before her;
> Spotty faced and grim with terror,
> Messy black shirt, button missing;
> Then she wet herself and giggled.
> 'Kirsty Maggs, please leave the platform.'

'We've got plenty left, if you want some. I'll bring it round if you like.'

'Oh,' says Kirsty, gaping, blushing. 'The kiddies don't like curry.'

'They'll like this one,' says Michael Bailey positively.

Zak Oliphant, sitting behind the gigantic teak desk in his office, protected from lesser mortals by grotesque and primitive pieces of onyx, slabs of marble, brass ink stands, computer console and gold cigarette lighter in the shape of a phoenix rising, turns pink, then puce, then a porcine purple.

He is a troubled man.

A massive rubber plant smelling of Pledge rises stiffly behind his head.

He has just come off the phone from his friend and golfing partner Inspector Derek Hooper, and he cannot believe what he has just been told.

'But surely you're not taking this seriously, Derek old man?'

'It's no longer a question of my attitude, Zak, unfortunately. Our good friend Mr Hardy-Brown is taking the matter to a higher authority and I can see myself put in a rather awkward position unless I'm careful.'

'You've lost me, Derek.'

'The man has only just this minute left my office, Zak, and I would have to describe his attitude as fanatical, fired by some magnificent spiritual purpose quite beyond me. He has got it into his head that you have been trying to muffle his newspaper, and, worse than that, the family of the boy who was mauled at Fingles Ponds the other day.'

'Muffle them? What's muffle them mean?'

'You have been issuing unacceptable threats – and he produced a couple of witnesses' names to verify that accusation – and, wait for it, Zak, you're not going to like this, but the man suggested that you organised the hit-and-run accident outside the hospital yesterday, having also arranged to scare the pants off him and his wife, and ransack his house.'

'Say again . . . '

So Inspector Derek Hooper was forced to repeat the monstrous accusations. 'And he's calling me an accomplice . . . He believes I'm being bought off, basing that allegation on the fact that, in that holy man's opinion, we did not take sufficient interest in the guard-dog incident.'

'But you attended the scene, Derek, you investigated, that wimp Cavendish gave you his report . . . Your men were swarming all over the complex like flies. What did Hardy-Brown expect you to do?'

'I think he expected us to bring charges.'

'On what count?'

'On the count of possessing dangerous animals, out of control, I suppose.'

'But damnit, they weren't out of control! They were in their own enclosure. That bastard kid stuck his hand underneath my fence, disregarding the warnings!' His eyes follow his executive toy, as a naked plastic woman disappears in a flow of bubbles.

'Well you know that, Zak, and I know that, and that arsehole Hardy-Brown knows that, but he seems to be choosing to ignore the obvious . . . '

'He'll make himself a laughing stock if he persists . . . '

'I don't think so, my friend.'

'But the other suggestions! You say he thinks I organised the hit-and-run! That I arranged the ransacking of his house! How utterly preposterous. Is he off his rocker?'

'His wife is very upset, apparently. As yet he has not gone further than making a few veiled suggestions . . . '

'I'll get that bastard for slander if he's . . . '

'This is confidential stuff, Zak. He expressed these concerns during a confidential meeting with me, and that's why I got straight on the phone. As far as I know he has not made these wild allegations anywhere else. Not yet, at any rate.'

Zak presses a button defiantly. 'I'll get straight onto him now . . . '

'No, Zak, that would not be wise.'

'But damnit, what am I supposed to do? Just sit here on my arse and let this left-wing beardie go round making his damaging attacks?'

'There's nothing you can do, yet, I'm afraid. But it looks as if we ought to bring a few chaps round here and have a look at your security system, particularly the guard dogs . . . '

'Shit, Derek, this is monstrous!'

'I realise that. I realised this would be your reaction, but think of it as a way of covering ourselves. You know these fanatical types once they get an idea in their heads, and we don't want this to go any further. All sorts of sleeping monsters might be disturbed.'

'Sleeping monsters?'

'Oh, little points of law, Zak, tax matters, health and safety regulations, planning, conditions of employment, equality nonsense . . . '

'Any one of my employees can leave as soon as they like, if they don't approve of the system. Let them find a bloody job somewhere else.' And Zak toys with the only delicate thing on his desk, a paperknife, and bends it.

'But that's the point, Zak, there aren't any jobs anywhere else, so they have to put up with conditions as they are to keep their heads above water. You know that as well as I do. Employees are in no condition to make a fuss these days.'

'Thank bloody God. Those fucking blood-sucking unions.'

'What I am saying, Zak, is that like any successful man you have your enemies. There are many people out there with axes to grind.'

'And this fucking Jesus freak Hardy-Brown could set them all off?'

'Exactly. So the best thing to do is to just lie low and let things ride, for the moment anyway. I know that's not your style, and we both know his wild accusations are right out of line, but let it just die a natural death. As it will. Believe me.'

'It seems that I bloody well have no choice,' growls Zak gloomily.

'My reputation is on the line, here, Zak. Don't forget that. I'm not too happy of being accused of turning a blind eye, of using my position, of accepting expensive presents at Christmas and holidays in Cyprus . . . '

'Okay, Derek. Okay. I get your drift. I'll sit on it.'

What Zak is sitting on is a medicated pink rubber ring and a bottom full of painful piles. And they are driving him mad this morning. He is incensed. It is blood pressure. It has to be.

Extraordinarily, the kids do like curry. They lapped it up.

Kirsty cannot believe she is sitting here, relaxing like this, the kiddies back in her own flat with a tattooed sailor, a declared Communist, and Nana.

They have transformed Sheralee's flat into something resembling a Sultan's tent with the use of a few tie-died scarves, joss sticks and candles.

It's quite a lovely flat, now the lights have been shaded. How did it always look so unkempt and barren before?

'So that's what's been happening,' she finishes, pouring her heart out to Michael with the hypnotic brown eyes. They are dark, large, soft and brilliant with long, curling lashes. She refuses a puff on a joint and gets out her own deadly rollies.

'The newspaper guy reckons this Oliphant is persecuting you?'

'He's got to be off his chump. But it's the money, see? If we could prove this Mr Oliphant deliberately hurt Sheralee, and then tried to bribe us to keep our mouths shut . . . Well, from what he said it sounded as if we could make ourselves a fortune. This thousand pounds would be peanuts.'

'You just need a few more compromising incidents, don't you?'

'Yes, I know we do. And that's why I was going to ask you . . . '

'What if Zak Oliphant sent a bunch of squatters to move in to your sister's flat and hassle you, is that what you mean?'

Kirsty giggles. 'Yes, and you've already said you're a bunch of students squatting to make a political point. Subversives . . . I don't really know what that means, but you promised you'd go when Sheralee gets out of hospital. I know that, but can't we keep that a secret?'

'We're on your side, Kirsty. That's what we're all about. It wouldn't take much to convince your friend the editor. When that Jesus guy came round, old Charlie gave him a real fright. He already believes we're a bunch of thugs.'

'But you don't look like a thug, Michael.'

Michael pulls a bulldog face. 'I can do if I try, believe me!'

Kirsty feels a sense of wonderful helplessness. Her nylon knickers are damp between her legs, drooling, a pool of desire, and she worries that she might leave a mark on Sheralee's favourite red satin cushion. Never has she seen, or come near to, or spoken so easily to, a man like this before.

Hiawatha. Her dream man since childhood. With his long dark tresses, parted in the middle, his headband, his waistcoat made out of treated skins, and his sloppy old moccasins. His features are lean and swarthy, like a real live Indian. But his well-educated voice speaks in many clever tongues which Kirsty admires tremendously, but much of which she can hardly understand.

She is very aware of her bulbous eyes, tired from strain, her rolls of fat, her unshaven armpits, nothing but a forest of coarse hair that might well be smelling by now, and her bad complexion.

But Michael, intelligence shining in his eyes, seems unaware of these handicaps. If she wasn't such a romantic fool she could almost believe he might be responding because Michael is a very 'touching' person.

A space invader.

Kirsty feels boring. 'Will they be all right, next door?'

Michael, on the floor beside her, looks surprised. 'Charlie and Jamie adore kids. Relax and leave them to it.'

'But what about Mum?'

'Mum can come in here if she wants to.'

Another weird political point? Michael is full of them.

Kirsty remembers Dulcie's last whispered warning. 'Close the door, Kirsty, you don't want to get involved with types like this.' And now the incredibly muscled Charlie and the sinister-looking Jamie are bathing the kids and putting them to bed and when Kirsty left them she couldn't remember them ever looking so happy, or behaving so well before.

Kirsty does not want to move from here. She does not want to disturb this absorbing feeling of intense sexuality. It is blissful. 'I better go and see if she's all right.'

'Okay.' And Michael Bailey gives Kirsty Maggs a sexy, knowing wink.

It is strangely silent in Kirsty's flat.

What is that silence?

Ah, it's just that the television is off.

Everything looks so organised. Clear of toys, old food, dirty mugs and nasty little dustbin bundles.

Dulcie is playing chase the ace with the shaven-headed sailor. She is so engrossed in the game that she hardly looks up when Kirsty guiltily sidles over. They are drinking Camp coffee laced with the Christmas brandy.

At Sandra's bedroom door Kirsty pauses, so astonished she steps backwards. Jamie, the baldheaded Communist with scythe and sickle emblazoned on his T-shirt, is reading the kiddies a story. All four of them. In clean pyjamas they watch and they listen with glazed eyes. She has the feeling that even Jason would have fallen beneath the spell. She wasn't aware that they had any books left complete, with all their pages.

It is all okay. She can go back. She can return to the wonder of Sheralee's flat and listen to some more mysterious music, drink some more of that bitter white wine. But first of all she goes to the bathroom and washes her face. Then straight through to the bedroom where, with very great care and a storm of desire inside her, she applies her rouge and mascara. She fiercely backcombs her hair and lacquers it over, applies her Christmas perfume, 'Allure', and rolls a liberal amount of Mum under her untended armpits.

Frowning suddenly she peers forwards into the mirror, lifts her grubby, off-white bra and, with gritted teeth, she plucks four coarse hairs from around her nipples, causing tears to rush to her eyes.

She puts a finger between her legs, sniffs, and hastily changes her knickers – just in case.

And in this way did Cleopatra prepare herself for Antony, apart from that bath of asses' milk?

The slut.

Well, hell, you never know how close things might get. But not for a moment does Kirsty believe he might want anything more than a grunt and a poke at midnight. Not for one second does Kirsty believe that she can sustain the interest of a man like this.

A rubber doll, and willing to be one, if it means bedding the most exciting, handsome man she has ever seen in her life.

Experience tells Kirsty that you can do quite a lot with memories.

She tries to lie down delicately.

'We could help you, and you could help us,' murmurs Michael Bailey, tracing a winding pattern over the top of Kirsty's left and violently throbbing breast. 'You want

146

compensation, and we want to see the downfall of this crass, arrogant bastard.'

'But why?' Kirsty gives an uncontrollable shudder. Should she get hold of his hand, of his long, sensitive fingers, and move them further down her body, or would he consider her too eager? She doesn't want to frighten him off.

The fact that his friend is sitting in the corner, smoking dope and fingering a guitar, does not seem to matter. Kirsty has already given him several anxious glances, but he is engrossed in his music, engrossed in his peaceful-looking dreams.

'Don't worry about Mark,' says Michael softly, sensing her unease as he teases her, feeling her body melt under his coaxing seduction. 'Forget about him. We drew up a list at university, some of us formed a group called Justice for the Workers, it was a long list and Zak Oliphant was on it. That's all.'

She nudges him then, and arches her pencilled, razored eyebrows. 'What are you then? Some sort of bleeding terrorist?'

All he gives her is a smile and she asks him shyly, 'And you would really be prepared to lie and . . . ?'

What else would Michael be prepared to do?

Take her next door into Sheralee's bedroom?

Or will they do it right here down amongst Sheralee's Woolies' cushions?

'I'd be prepared to say that the bastard paid us to hassle you,' says Michael, mischievously licking Kirsty's ear.

Kirsty is bewildered. Bewildered and absorbed. Wonderingly she asks, 'But what did you come here for? Why squat here? It's not a very nice place to stay.'

'What does it matter where we stay? We're only here for the race.' He reaches behind her and, with expert fingers, begins to unclip her bra.

'What race?' Kirsty, enthralled, is reaching a delicious state of delirium.

It is a sensual whisper. 'The Coast to Coast. Charlie's father has a boat this year.'

She thinks about Charlie, that lumbering, coarse-mannered sailor. 'Oh? Charlie's father? Is he helping?'

'Oh Charlie's father's not crewing,' says Michael easily. 'Charlie's father's the captain. Charlie's father owns it.'

Later, much, much later that evening, Kirsty Maggs, with Michael's support, hurries out to make an excited telephone call.

'We have the proof! I knew it! I knew it! I was right. So you see,' says Gerry Hardy-Brown, positively, to Jemima that evening, 'we are not talking about a head case, a maniac out of control, but a thug and a bully who is determined to get his own way, using whatever dastardly methods he thinks will work for him. But,' he adds, happy to be convinced, 'too cunning, too practical to allow real violence to take control. I am sure he was as sorry as anyone that the hit-and-run accident went that far.'

She knows he is wrong. Dangerously wrong. 'But Gerry, what about the gun?'

'Took it to frighten us.'

She would love to agree with her husband completely. Oh how she loves him, and his in-built, natural goodness. He is a knight, a white crusader. No wonder she gave him her bruised and battered heart.

'You're quite right. We must fight this, Gerry, and we must fight it to the bitter end. Together.'

16

We are watching the irresistible advance of a single-track mind.

Obsession in motion.

Oh, what a thoroughly distasteful person Fergus Johnson is. Who could love him?

Give her her due, Jemima tried.

All this nonsense about a hard life, the suggestion of something deep in his past that he might, or might not have forgotten.

Okay, so some people go through all kinds of shit but they don't turn out to be vicious, vengeful, vindictive monsters.

You cannot pluck somebody out of thin air and love them, and expect them to love you back. The concept is not only pathetic, but rather revolting. An almost inconceivable self-centredness.

We must not waste our sympathies on people like Fergus Johnson. He has made his own bed and he ought to be made to lie in it.

In prison, preferably.

With no namby-pamby time off for parole.

But like it or not, we have to come back to him. However loosely, we are all involved. We cannot just pretend that people like him do not exist, and ignore him. And yes, here he is with the stud in his nose, in his roadside hideaway with his Reeboks snapping on fir cones, but armed with a gun this time, a weapon that is going to make it possible for him to take some pretty hair-raising risks with the ban-dog.

As he prowls back to his den Fergus notices nothing of the dusky summer's glory. The air is heavy with the resinous scents of the pines and the crushed sap of the bracken. The evening is hot and already every fragment of sky is twinkling with stars. He notices none of this. Here in this desolate place he can be alone with his sickness, and he creeps to it as a dog creeps behind a hedge in order to lick its wounds.

As he'd known it would be, the dog is waiting for him, motionless, expressionless, as if it is carved out of stone.

He burns.

She took him home to meet Mummy and Daddy, oh yes she did.

It was his thirteenth birthday.

A weekend treat, she called it, and went to great lengths to get permission before she collected him from Ryall and accompanied him to his next approved place of residence – a foster home in Wimbledon, but not just any old foster home: Fergus was headed for rather a unique experience.

The trouble people go to to pander to losers like Fergus. The money we are forced to spend, a waste of human energy, surely, let alone scarce resources.

He had never been near a house like that, save when the Burchalls took him to some decrepit Elizabethan manor and he'd been bored to death and only interested in buying something from the crappy old gift shop.

Mummy and Daddy lived in a brown and white house like this, clung with creeper, nestling into the ancient earth as if it had grown there like the stones and the flowers.

The wooden house looked not only old, but scored and scorched with age. It was more like a ship than a house, the *Mary Rose*, black beams and slanting passages. The windows peered out through a foaming sea of wisteria, all flung open to embrace the garden. Broad steps, bordered with urns, led from the mossy, cobbled drive and up to the gnarled front door.

He was sure it was full of ghosts.

Jeez. Swimming pool. Tennis court. Paddock.

The green of it all was overwhelming.

'Come on, Fergie, Mummy'll be sitting in the courtyard, she obviously hasn't heard us yet. Let's go and surprise her.'

In her flowery dress with her big straw hat, skipping, God, Jemima was worse than a kid.

The courtyard rang with the blending of hundreds of voices and was decked with the discarded playthings of the gentry – copies of *The Times*, Panama hats, striped towels, sun specs and glasses with ice and lemons and straws.

Fergus paused, startled. 'Why didn't you tell me there'd be lots of people here? I thought it was just your mother and father?'

'Don't worry, Fergie,' Jemima encouraged him brightly, 'I never thought to say. There're always masses of people around. That's just how we live and I'm afraid I took it for granted that you'd know that.'

A multitude of frosty eyes looked up and stared at him.

'Mima!' squawked the scrawny woman with the bracelets all up her arm like snakes. 'Darling! Come, come come . . . and just in time for lunch, how marvellous!'

How could anyone BE so affected and get away with it? Ugh! Fergus watched grumpily as Jemima flew into her mother's arms.

The woman gave him a haughty look over her daughter's shoulder and said, 'And this must be Fergus. Welcome to Greenways, Fergus,' and she flapped her waterproof-looking hand.

Fergus stood where he was, and scowled.

'Fergus is a little bit nervous, Mummy.' But her traitorous eyes were laughing.

'Well, naturally he would be,' said Mummy, eyeing the

others meaningfully, reminding them where he came from. The little nonentity. They had probably never seen a genuine delinquent before.

And then, shit, Jemima tried to introduce him, instead of just ignoring his misery and letting him gather his wits. He clenched his fists behind his back. He hated her seeing him like this, so out of his depth, turned into something worse and weaker . . .

Mummy wound towards him, the elegant bitch, saying, 'What would you like to drink before lunch, m'dear, some fresh orange juice? How about some of Tilly's home-made lemonade?' As if she was doing him a favour or something.

Everyone was listening to see how he spoke . . . he *knew* they were . . . he could feel it.

'Okay.'

'But which, dear?' she insisted, and her silly hand hovered between two jugs.

'Any. I don't care. I'm not even thirsty.'

'Look, Fergus,' boomed Jemima's father, bobbing down suddenly, and pointing towards the sky. 'A kestrel!'

Fergus followed his hand, saw the bird, and remained unimpressed.

'D'you like birds, Fergus?'

What the hell sort of question was that?

'Don't mind them, I suppose.'

'When I was your age I had a whole collection of birds' eggs, definitely not on now of course, not with all these disappearing species. No,' he guffawed loudly, speeding unwittingly towards a trap, 'Nowadays I suppose the local bobby would come along and carry me off to prison!'

There was almost a gasp from the gathered assembly.

'No, sir, you'd need to do summat a bloody sight worse than that. You'd probably just get a warning.'

'Ah, well, that's a damn relief then, eh?' said Jemima's father – Daddy, wearing a hideous bright green shirt and a pair of old khaki shorts. Pompous arsehole.

'We thought we'd eat out here as it's a special occasion, Tilly's brought the doors out. It's warm enough, isn't it?'

Silly cow. It was boiling. Far too hot. They'd've been better in the shade.

Shit, all this and they couldn't afford a proper table. Fergus looked and saw two dirty old doors laid together on trestles, and some maid was covering them with a snowy white cloth. Obviously too bloody mean to pay out for garden furniture.

Everyone – and there must have been nearly twenty – appeared to be the best of friends and never ran out of things to say, right through the meal. Fergus ate very little, watching hard to see which knife and fork he should use.

They tried to bring him out to begin with, but even the woman with speckled breasts who sat beside him gave up when she realised he was not prepared to entertain her.

Jemima frowned at him every so often, but he looked down at his food and ignored her.

Fergus squirmed. She should never have brought him here. He wished he had not come.

They stared when he asked for sugar for his peach.

And then – *that maid type of woman brought on a birthday cake*!

And they all started singing 'Happy Birthday To You' – as if they were mates of his, *as if they really knew him*! As if they were sorry for him because they knew he had nowhere else to go on his birthday.

Fergus blinked, his furious face growing redder and redder.

Shit, and they'd bought him presents. He had to sit there and unwrap them while they all shouted things like, 'Jolly good, Fergus,' and 'that's the spirit!'

He looked up secretly at Jemima, shooting hatred from under his lashes. She mouthed, 'Please,' and she looked so sad, so hopeful, so sorry, that he suddenly determined to do the best he could in front of her friends and relations.

Shit, what the fuck anyway. He was stuck here, wasn't he? Might as well perform.

A Walkman from Jemima ... exactly the kind that he'd asked for, and a kite – can you believe it? – a box kite from everyone else. It took some time to figure out what the sodding thing was and, across the table, Jemima had the grace to look apologetic.

And off they all went that afternoon, because it was Fergus's birthday, and flew the kite in the parkland which was part of Mummy and Daddy's estate.

There were deer browsing under the trees.

He did his best in order to please her.

He ran with the wind like a little boy.

He shouted as the kite rose up into all the immensity of the sky.

It was like a party all the time. Theirs was an unflagging vigour. They never stopped, these people. They never watched the telly, or came indoors much before dark.

'Swimming, Fergus old chap?'

He said he had no swimming things – but really he could not swim. He had never been taught. 'Oh that's all right dear, keep your pants on or go in the altogether, we frequently do.' He flopped about in the shallows aware of his grey and scrawny body.

'Tennis, Fergus?'

Fergus could not play tennis. He stood and watched the others. He pretended to enjoy being ballboy.

'Coming for a ride?'

Fergus was afraid of horses. He had never been near a horse in his life. As soon as he approached Jemima's mare it laid back its ears and bit him.

But Jemima was good at everything.

Teddy took time with him, you knew where you were with Jemima's dad. He took him round the point-to-point course and showed him how they built the jumps and Fergus could feel relaxed with him as they chatted, man to man. He didn't use a walking stick, he used an old golf club and went round thwacking the bushes as if he was angry about something. He talked to Fergus, serious conversations about sacred stones, and he shared Fergus's love of tomato-ketchup sandwiches.

Jemima looked happy to see Fergus setting off with her father.

Like a son, thought Fergus.

He liked Daddy – 'Call me Teddy, none of this sir rigmarole' – with his florid face, his collection of fishing flies, his leather elbows, his dogs and his knitting.

It was like the Garden of Eden, and Fergus knew why people would want to live here forever.

It was the highest, most sumptuous bed he had ever slept in. 'Don't you like sleeping with your window open, Fergus?' And Mummy sounded thoroughly disgusted.

But Fergus wasn't used to opening windows. Fergus's windows were always barred, so it never crossed his mind.

And so that memorable weekend wore on, taking longer and longer to pass and Fergus felt all the weariness of trying too hard, but buoyed up by the belief that he was succeeding. They even went to evensong and Daddy lent Fergus a tie.

Fergus was careful to curb his hostility and everyone was jolly and pleasant and terribly, terribly kind.

For once he had done well – he knew he had – and Jemima would be proud of him.

Christ, it was easy, piece of shit.

It was just as they were leaving, as Fergus was lifting the latch on the heavy oak front door, carrying Jemima's weekend case, when he heard Daddy bidding goodbye to the daughter he referred to as 'sweet', in the hall.

There was no way Daddy could ever speak quietly. That was one of the many things about him which Fergus had come to admire.

'Cheerio, sweet, take care, marvellous to see you, but I don't really think we want sorts like that here again, rather awful. And Tilly says he pissed the bed in spite of the pot in the cupboard . . .'

Alone again, there was no longer any door by which to leave or enter.

Rubbing his stinging eyes, Fergus regards the ban-dog intently.

Cast in blue shadow, boy and dog seem to burn with the moon.

If anything the dog looks bigger, more threatening this evening.

He leans towards it, it is almost a bow towards a superior, bending from the waist.

'Not yet, you fucking freak, not yet, but later, when it gets really dark and when I have something in my hand that can blow your frigging brains out.'

17

Jemima lies in a melancholy suspense, with the photograph of Mummy and Daddy beside her because she finds their cheerful and positive faces reassuring. She needs to be reassured just now. She and the children are back in Clara's house again, Gerry having insisted that although they are determined to fight this menace together, their pact definitely does not include the children.

Clara's house smells of the elderly, of unused rooms and of bruised and broken roses.

Since Daddy died last year Jemima does not go home so often, but this is not because she preferred Daddy to Mummy – oh no, how could she make such painful comparisons – the reason is the horrors of the journey. Hannah is not a good traveller.

This is the excuse she makes – in fact, before she was married, she used her childhood home as an oasis, an escape from the barrenness of the city. She came to drink from the deep, sweet waters of normality.

She is so relieved that Daddy saw Hannah before he died, that he knew his only child was settled and contented. He thought the world of Jemima, his proud progeny, his sweet, sweet daughter, and though he bore it stoically he disapproved of her job from the outset, 'particularly the element it brings you into contact with, sweet'.

'Oh Daddy, don't be such a frightful snob. What would you like me to do with my life, something silly and frivolous?'

*

We all approve of Jemima the victim, but wasn't Jemima a snob? Born and bred to be one? As certainly as the horses were bred to be fleet-footed, or gentle-natured, in Daddy's stables?

Brought up to believe that she ought to put something back in the system that had granted her such privilege, Jemima set forth to do good work in the world that lay beyond the dark. Jemima's wasn't so much a rebellion as a need to explore her deepest dreads – Pigling Bland setting off to make his fortune with one eye directed on the market – before she came back to roost, disillusioned by life and well defended to fulfil her destiny.

And who can honestly blame her?

If she had stayed out there in the void any longer she would have been obliterated by the lying and the cheating and the misery.

This is probably why she chose safe, gentle, sweet Gerry, no dark moods or fiery emotions to disturb the shafts of sunlight peeping through her dimpled schoolroom windows.

Everyone likes sensible, steady, cultured Gerry.

Everyone came to the wedding and, deep in one of England's shires, the bees buzzed with the wedding bells all day long.

But now the past is surging in to overwhelm the present.

Fergus has outwitted her because she underestimated him as usual. Fergus has the gun she needs to defend herself when he comes, with his knife, to attack. But no need to worry, she will easily persuade dear Gerry to bring her another one.

Her bravest hour. She does not pause to question her motives. She is assailed with a dreadful longing to get this ordeal over with. Fergus is coming, and the knowledge, now it is here after so many years, is almost a relief. There will be no more peace till it's over. She has to obliterate her past before she gets on with the rest of her life.

Thank God for Gerry and his noble campaigning, thank God for Oliphant and his stubborn will – two conceited men with horns locked in combat, and without them it is possible that Fergus might be apprehended.

Jemima does not want that.

So Jemima Hardy-Brown, victim-in-waiting, lies sleepless but almost happy, listening to the breathing of her children. She is not afraid for her children. She can handle Fergus, has always handled Fergus, and knows that he cannot hurt her. No, the real question is – can she bring herself to do what she knows she must?

The lights shine bright in the Oliphant's house – or ranch.

'And there's not a damn thing I can bloody well do about it.'

Kimberley Oliphant sits listening to Zak who is too disturbed by the day's events to sleep. He sits excitedly, bolt upright against his pillows with his pyjama jacket open, and the tie round his waist will not meet.

Quite simply, the powerlessness of his position is destroying him.

Kimberley, who took a couple of Mogadon earlier, fights against the very drowsiness she longed for.

'It'll pass, Zak, everything always passes.'

But she cannot feel any sympathy for her husband. He is not a man who asks for sympathy or even understands the meaning of the word, and if he suspected that she felt anything bordering on pity Zak would be disgusted.

'Shit sticks,' he replies ominously, 'and there's a muck-spreader of it being directed at me by that left-wing wanker, Hardy-Brown. I mean what sort of goddamn name is that . . . ?'

'Lies, Zak, they can't hurt you with their lies.' Night cream packed with rejuvenating powers lies slickly on her face. She can never confide in Zak now. It has gone too far for that.

Zak sits forward. 'And I just damn well wish, Kimberley, that you'd take more of a lively interest in my problems and not just lie there in that dull-witted way mumbling platitudes. I don't think you realise how serious all this is. I mean, somebody paid that fucking family one thousand pounds, or Hardy-Brown is lying to Hooper. It's all very well to say they're unwilling to come forward and present the evidence but hell,' and Zak slaps his forehead, 'well, what are they trying to do to me?'

'That editor's jealous of you darling, that's all. He never leaves you alone. Everyone is. They're just jealous.'

'Humph,' and Zak sounds gratified. Perhaps he is ready to turn out his light, but no . . .

'Just let one of those bastards make one of their scandalous accusations out in the open, or print something, goddamn it, and I'll take them to the fucking cleaners. Or better still . . . ' and he wrinkles up his angry eyes, 'I'll send someone round to sort the buggers out properly.'

'And then you really *would* be in trouble!'

How could poor Kimberley have dreamed that her impulsive generosity would backfire on her husband in this way? During their frantic evening she was tempted to confess many times, but self-interest warned her against it. Under the circumstances, desperate to undermine Hardy-Brown, Zak would revel in flaunting the truth before that self-righteous man and probably demand a public apology.

Anything to push his enemy's nose in the dirt, but quite unable to understand what a court case, trial and conviction would do to his wife's reputation.

She can hear him arguing with her now. 'Christ, Kimberley, so it was you, and it's only a matter of a fine and a ban. The woman's not dead yet, is she? And even if she was, we'd get you a driver . . . Mrs Bowles's daughter wants a job and she's just passed her test. She'd do the job for pocket money . . . '

'But Zak, that's not the point!'

'Well damnit, what is the point if it's not clearing my name and dumping Hardy-Brown in the shit?'

It is not within Zak's capability to imagine how essential it is for Kimberley to be properly accepted into the group of neighbours who go to the new country club off Albany Place. Oh it's easy for Zak, outwardly a pillar of society because of his generous and thoughtfully directed donations – chairman of this, vice-president of that, chamber of trade, school governor.

He sometimes jokes that he'll end up a knight of the realm if he plays his cards right. Zak's jokes have an uncanny habit of coming true.

But what of his wife?

You see, Kimberley has reached an important turning point in her life. No longer able to command instant admiration because of her flirtatious manner, and her beauty, hanging onto her husband's arm like a scented poodle and attending all his fancy functions, she is now forty-nine years old – though no-one would know it – and only known by first name terms at the hairdresser's.

Women friends were never her style.

Women did not trust her.

Kimberley is concerned with her image. Life is not over at forty, but hell's bells . . . what about fifty, for God's sake?

The thought both frightens and appals her.

So, after carefully noting who else was on the list, she has recently put her name down to help with the fundraising for deprived children's holidays.

A conviction for drunken driving would not help her new social image – that of cultured, caring, yet charismatic older woman. She must be halfway there already, well look, she already pays for and protects three mistreated, ungrateful donkeys.

Cultured and caring like Suzie Benson, like Christie Soames, like Harriet Calder . . . all living in the same cul-de-sac as Kimberley, but all appearing to have the most interesting lives. Fulfilled. And all members of that snooty Albany Country Club, with a waiting list as long as your arm.

Zak would sneer at her pretensions. Zak would call her a silly cow. Why the hell did she want to bother with arseholes like that? I'll get you in tomorrow if you want to join.

And he would get out his wallet and wave it.

But Kimberley wants to be proposed and seconded like everyone else.

If she is totally honest, she would rather join by herself, without Zak.

Once, when these women walked past, she saw them sniggering at the stone eagles flanking her gate.

At the time she was unaccountably distressed.

And sometimes, when she is sitting outside, alone under her parasol, she hears those women roaring with laughter together over sherry in Suzie Benson's garden.

No, Kimberley's going to keep her secret.

Zak will triumph without her help.

Zak always does.

Well look, now she is wide awake and he is snoring.

Kirsty Maggs never knew fucking could be like this. Or go on so long. Or be so two-sided.

Whenever she has done it before she has lain there with her legs apart, watching her feet bang about in the air, trying not to think about tea for tomorrow.

Whenever she has done it before it has been for payment . . . payment for the easing of loneliness, payment for a curry down at the Taj Mahal, payment for an evening of free rum'n'cokes, payment for the cinema.

Recently, with the kids and that, she hasn't really fancied it. She would rather stay in and watch the telly and get an early night. It is easier to pay for the telly, a stamp every week down at the post office and she is round there anyway for her giro.

'I'm frigid,' she told Sheralee.

'Huh, and you've only just sussed it. I've been frigid for years.'

'And it messes up the sheets – pubes and spunk in the bed and that stench dripping out in the morning – and you always feel you ought to use clean ones.'

'Since Sam left for that over-developed bitch I haven't even missed it, and sometimes I go for three weeks without changing the sheets at all. And that awful temper men have, sulking all day like a bloody great kid if you aren't in the mood.'

'I reckon, if you fancy it, you're better off with one of those vibrators. Cleaner. And you can put it exactly where you want it. Barbara Kiery had one, got it at one of those parties. Runs on a tiny little battery. She showed me hers but I didn't want to touch it, you know . . .'

'I'm celibate,' said Kirsty thoughtfully. 'Lots of the best people are celibate, you know.'

'But not Alan Bennett,' muses Sheralee. 'Everyone thought he was, and then he went and surprised them all. Perhaps you'll do the same.'

'Who's Alan Bennett when he's at home?' her sister replies.

Phew.

Here we go again.

With her face flat on the floor, kneeling, squatting, or the right way up, she groans under the heat of his mouth.

It could be the antenatal clinic.

'Let me look. Let me lick you,' and she moans as he seizes her anew. Michael Bailey is a very experienced young man.

Even the tones of Michael's voice stroke her back, her legs and her breasts, tenderly, steadily, voluptuously. She does not care what he is saying but she wants him to go on talking.

She draws her legs up towards her chest. From between them her parted lips gape at him like a call-girl's smile as he eases her into a better position. Nothing is denied to him. She opens herself for him, leading with her middle finger, eager to be found wet and waiting. She pushes her chewing gum hard against her teeth, frightened that he will see it and disapprove, afraid that the peppermint smell might put him off and stop him.

She moans and closes her eyes.

Do it again. Oh yes, oh yes, do it again!

How glad she is that she plucked those few ugly hairs from her nipples. She smiles again as he kneels across her, taking hold of her wrists with one hand and keeping them there above her head as he teases her tingling tits.

She is overpowered by her own musky smell of Allure. Not BO, thank Christ.

She could get to like this sado-masochism thing, bondage, leather and shackles and so forth, she is sure she could, if only she properly understood it. Pain and joy mingled together – *oh God*.

Perhaps she ought to struggle harder. Is that what he wants?

Michael, a bit of a sexual athlete, knows very well what he wants.

As he pushes himself deep inside her a sensation of incredible warmth and delight fills her body. Lumpy, luscious Kirsty, naked as a jay bird and a handful for any young man, yields to a carnal intensity the like of which she had not known possible.

Kirsty tries to catch her breath. 'I love you, I love you,' she thrashes and moans through lucky lips. 'I want to be your squaw.'

'Don't use that word, Kirsty,' he pauses, 'never say that. The Indians never used it, only the white man. It's the Indian word for vagina and a terrible insult.'

'Oh Jesus I'm sorry . . . '

'And I love you, too,' whispers Michael, smiling, lowering himself, working deeper.

Does he mean it?

Can miracles really happen?

She loses all sense of herself and becomes a primitive

creature, Michael's creature, as he grinds on, grimacing, heedless and inexhaustible. She is the vast and endless range and he is a wild shaggy buffalo.

Hang on a minute!

What the hell are we doing watching them like this? Are we no better than men in macs, browsing amongst the top shelves, peeping toms who ought to know better? Good lord. This is Kirsty's business and we certainly ought not to be watching.

All we need to know is that Kirsty is totally and utterly happy in the flickering, golden candlelight. Don't let's worry about whether Michael Bailey is genuine, or if he might hurt her, or about his long-term political intentions.

Is nobody sleeping tonight?

Breathing deeply, but not so deeply as Kirsty Maggs, Fergus Johnson works on the wire with a stolen pair of clippers. Furtive lest he be heard, yet he is impatient to finish. Rust flakes onto the moonlit undergrowth. Every now and again the blade flashes pure electric blue. The Purdy is loaded and standing against the fence, near at hand so that as soon as the ban-dog is free he can grab it, in case the bastard attacks him.

For the first time he smells the creature before him, and it's a strong, stale smell. You cannot tell his mood from his face, but his eyes are steady, alert and watching. A kind of mutual respect seems to have developed between them, as if they can recognise something familiar, each in the other, tormented by their needs.

There are a thousand and one things Fergus would like to say to Jemima, but now he doubts he will have the chance.

For an hour and a half he works, until his limbs and his back ache from the strain of holding the same position. The red raw wound in his arm burns. Rage strengthens his hand. The fire of obsession blazes his eyes.

His destiny is entwined with Jemima's.

Where has he gone wrong? What could he have done to change things? She has forgotten that he is alive.

If he had been rich, famous, successful, handsome . . .

What does it feel like to kill a person?

He curses under his breath. *I hated everyone in the world except you!*

His baseball cap falls off his head but Fergus works steadily on.

Behind him, on the road, the cars pass spires and towers, fields, hills and rivers . . . families on holiday, all-night lorry drivers, travelling salesmen looking for somewhere to rest for the night. The odd police car looking for speeders. Even their dipped headlights do not reach the verge outside Fingles Ponds, the verge where the grass is high and the white cow parsley lies like spindrift. Nobody sees, not even the leathery, swooping bats. Blind to the place where Fergus labours with sweat standing out on his forehead.

Freedom. Will the dog show gratitude? Will he welcome it?

How can anyone tell?

'Nearly there, you evil bastard. Get back! Nearly there.'

And Fergus wedges the shotgun firmly under his arm as, with his other hand, he eases back the tattered wire.

18

The ban-dog left America under a cloud, but at least he left it in one piece. For a while there, he was in danger of being destroyed.

'The trouble is, chief,' said Ed Maloney, waving a fistful of bucks as he and Cyrus Fitzgerald hung over the ice-hot metal fence rail at the back of the Texaca Truck Plaza, staring at the blood and guts and broken ice left in the ring. 'Trouble is no jerk's gonna want to put his animal up against yours no more, not with the kind of record this mean sonofabitch crazy's got, for Chrissake.'

The last storm had already slammed a couple of trees down on the hillside.

Against the cold the men wore their hunting caps with the ear flaps down, and their hands were protected by thick gloves. A mountain wind gusted up the scattered snow and whipped it onto their hunched backs, and its breath was cold as death. They watched the fumes from the losers' Chevvys and trucks belch whitely in the frozen air, and the crunch of the chains made cracking sounds on the ground as they drove away, great grilles grinning.

'Goddamnit, Cy, they know when they're beat, there's no dough to be made from a red-hot favourite. I guess they figure there's not much sense of excitement if you're gonna end up with just a red bleeding mess whining in the back of your auto. Art's new bitch was nothing more than a slab of raw meat with its leg bones showing through. If you don't watch it you're gonna bite off the hand that feeds you.'

'No big deal, Ed. How 'bout we dope the fucker a coupla times?'

'Naw, these guys'd be wise to that kinda crap. You're not dealing with a bunch of fat-arsed Ivy League bastards. They're gettin madder 'n madder. They'll not come back, Cy, if you don't withdraw him. They're not that dumb.'

'Okay, okay, take it easy.' But Cy was pretty depressed. All that expertise, all that work. 'Can't you see I'm trying to think,' he snarled to his neighbour and buddy.

'I dunno, Cy. Nobody wins,' sniffed Ed.

What the hell. Cy's proudest achievement. Jute. Not a bad name either . . . more subtle than Satan, but sharp sounding, like a bite. There's only one time in your life you come across an instinctive fighter like that, and if you can't grab an opportunity with two hands what are you meant to fucking well do, after all, this is the U.S. of A.

Behind them, in his padlocked and bolted ramshackle shed, Jute the ban-dog lay torn and panting on the frozen floor of sand and dirt. A half-inch layer of ice covered the water bucket.

Cy stamped his feet on the snowy ground. What a bummer. So you breed the best, the meanest, the most vicious, wickedest killer on four fucking legs in the whole of goddamn America – and then you find yourself with your head slammed up against a brick wall. Greedy bastards, all of them. Cy scratched the back of his pants with his heavily mittened hand. Shit. Hardly fair, considerin'.

Damnit, Cy should've acted earlier. He had let his love of money dull his cunning wits, he had really gone and fucked up. More and more, just recently, that fighting ring had been reduced to nothing but a butcher's slab – terrorised dogs rolling their eyes in pain, caterwaulin' 'n screamin', and the cursing and raging of the men reduced to disgruntled whispers as foam from the ban-dog's mouth sprayed the air. They finished the wounded off with a hammer. Busted guts were shovelled up and tipped into buckets. Sawdust sprinkled over the pain.

A circus for certain slaughter.

That dog Jute was still a sort of mystery to Cy. He wasn't scared of the critter, it wasn't that. But the fucker wasn't scared of him neither, no respect, too goddamn morose and his eyes were filled with hatred. If he turned his back on that sly black sonofabitch Cy, fast though he was with his hands and feet, wiry as a metal spring, knew the fucker'd have him. That thought made Cy's blood run cold. The smartarse dog did exactly what he was told or he got the chain 'cross his back, and Cy never handled him without a pole with a clip attached to his collar. Like an ornery bull. He never got within touching distance, shee-it. Once, only once mind, Cy had been forced to bring the whole weight of the chain down on the bugger's head, blood 'n brains spouted out of the wound like a fountain and Cy feared he'd gone and blinded the brute.

Hell, ain't nobody asks for trouble.

Ed sidled up to Cy. 'Maybe some smartarse from up country . . . ?'

'Naw. Everybody into fighting knows that dog of mine.' Now he had good cause to regret the fact of which he was most proud. When you have truckers as your clients, word tends to spread. Cy scratched his bristled chin, and leather rasped against stubble. 'Unless there's a market over the border.'

Cy was thinking of Mexico then. He'd never dreamed he'd accept an offer from Great fuckin' Britain. Some clown with dollars for eyes set on running a breeding programme, heard of the brute from a driver of his. They'd be registering with the Kennel Club next. Cy was reluctant to sell, but tempted by the price. Because when it boiled down to it, if he wanted to stay on the fighting circuit what goddamn choice did the sucker have? Any permanent alternative would be nothing but a waste of a friggin' bullet.

Fergus Johnson points the barrel of the shotgun straight at the ban-dog's head, just stopping short of nudging him with it as he steps through the tangled hole in the wire, hardly requiring to exercise the great muscles cut in his shoulders.

Voice still with terror. 'Steady boy. Steady.'

Fergus can hear his own heart beating, and he hopes it's not true that dogs sense fear.

Shit. Now it's through, nearer than ever, it looks double the size. Its back reaches Fergus's waist. No point in bothering with a rope or a chain, this bleeder would pull you over in no time.

Slowly, not slackening his grip on the gun, Fergus opens the bag full of offal he picked up behind Safeways, on his way to Middlehempston this morning. Half the bag is bloodied water. He tips it onto the grass and watches the ban-dog's slight flicker of movement.

Turning, so it faces Fergus, it lowers its massive muzzle and starts licking at the slops of raw meat. Its eyes, rolled back in its head, do not move from Fergus who steps back in some satisfaction.

Cautiously, Fergus bends and makes a temporary repair to the fence with eager and fumbling fingers. His body shivers and his head aches with fear that almost blinds him. He does not want anything else coming through to join them. Are there any more in there? One of these buggers at a time is enough.

Staring behind him all the while, Fergus sets slowly off along the verge, keeping well to the shadows, keeping close to the fence. He slaps the back of his thighs in a hopeful gesture of encouragement.

Just let the bugger step out of line and Fergus will blow its brains out.

But the dog, licking its lips free of the feast, shows no signs of aggression. Not much interest either. It seems to be trying to work out what Fergus is doing.

Twenty yards on Fergus stops and whistles.

No reaction, none at all.

Fergus calls softly, 'Come on you bastard, come on . . . '

Nothing. It stands squarely, motionless, watching, could even be preparing to spring.

Bloody hopeless.

Fergus vaguely recollects some batty woman on telly, can't remember her name, her with the short jerseys and the sagging breasts, on a programme about training dogs. You had to admire her. Christ, she knew all about it. She could bring the most vicious to heel with a bright call and a tug on a chain, but Fergus dare not get that close.

He raises his voice a fraction.

'Come!' He feels like some bleeding nutter.

The dog flicks back its ears for a second, alarmed, and the sweat pricks under Fergus's arms before it starts walking in Fergus's direction. Its eyes are black holes under the shadow of its brows. Christ, it moves with the power and silence of a padding lion. But it stops before it reaches Fergus, on guard again.

Okay. Okay. So you want to feel your way around a bit.

Fergus walks on with his neck twisted behind him, a little further this time before he stops and issues the same high-pitched command. For a second time the dog moves forward, towards him, sussing out its chances, perhaps. It does not seem too impressed by its freedom, or the big outdoors. Perhaps it doesn't realise it's free, but supposes there's another fence somewhere and it's going to come up against it in a minute.

Or perhaps it has never known freedom before and does not know what to do with it.

After an hour and a half of manoeuvring like this Fergus and the dog have been right round the perimeter fence and are back to the start again.

Slightly more at ease with the brute – but only slightly, he won't let go of his gun – Fergus bends to pick up a fir cone. He shows it to the dog, getting as near to those jaws as he dares, finger almost depressing the trigger.

Then he throws it.

The dog stares at him vacantly.

Fergus repeats the process.

The dog does not move.

Its eyes whisk. A thought forms in them like a cloud, and then slowly dissolves. Then there's a long, dragging silence while Fergus stands there, unsure, anxious. At length Fergus grins. 'Okay, okay, so you're not straight out of a circus. Just checking.'

Fergus takes his time, he raises his arm to the sky, the leather sleeve of his jacket crackles and this time there's no mistaking the dog's reaction. Its hackles rise. It sinks to the ground in one fluid motion, baring its teeth, coiled for a spring with something that could be fear in its eyes. But no, it's a hard glitter, nothing so messily human as fear.

Like a soldier drilling, Fergus brings the threatening arm cracking back to his side. He dares to shout, 'Lie down!' as he levels the gun at the creature's head.

The dog rises, growling. Fergus freezes, and waits.

As soon as he can pluck up the courage he repeats his Nazi salute, with exactly the same response from the dog.

'Lie down!' shouts Fergus once more, the sweat of terror slippery like milk on his hands.

But at least he is getting a positive reaction. The fucker doesn't just slink off, bored with the game. At least, terrifying though it might be, it is giving Fergus its fullest attention. Restless, eager for something though not knowing what, it might co-operate if it knew what Fergus wanted. What he does not want at this stage is to try its patience too far, too soon, that's all.

Fergus's attempts are punctuated by frequent swigs from a lager can. When he has finished he squeezes, buckling the metal before throwing it down carelessly and pulling the top off another. He has all the time in the world. You cannot hurry something like this. So far this operation is working better than he dreamed. He was quite prepared to shoot the bugger, quite prepared for the possibility that its first response would be to attack. Nobody knows Fergus is here. Nobody knows the ban-dog is free. Well before the eight o'clock curfew Fergus plans to have it back inside the fence . . . if he can. But surely the promise of food will be reason enough for the ban-dog to return with no hassle.

So wounded. There is no light in the ban-dog's eye.

It is purely by accident, and two hours later, that Fergus stumbles upon the correct word of command.

The trigger word.

The word for which the ban-dog has been trained to listen and wait.

It happens when Fergus, exhausted and fed up by his efforts to get the thing to lie down, picks up an innocent branch and shouts, 'Go!'

Aghast by the speed of the response, Fergus presses against the fence and stands, petrified, as the slow-moving shape turns into a racing demon, covering the ground at the speed of sound, leaping on the branch and tearing and shearing its great incisors into it, stripping it of its bark in an instant, tossing it into the air and catching it with its massive jaws and grinding. Till the thing is just shavings. Pencil sharpenings on the grass.

As if some mad rage has been released from inside it. Something unendurable has been let go. A savagery that cares for nothing . . .

Fergus, recovering slowly, tries it with an old lager can, and it works.

Obey his command it may, but the animal stays as remote from Fergus as it was at the beginning.

The truth takes time to dawn on Fergus.

Jesus Christ. It has neither brain nor will of its own. The thing is a machine, programmed to respond to certain commands, and it's just a matter of finding them. All that crap he tried earlier on. What did he think he was going to do, train this fucking killing-machine in a few short weeks? He, a jerk who knows nothing about dogs save for the funny old biddy on telly.

Fergus's lips twitch before he grins and then laughs gleefully. His thoughts are racing ahead of him.

Fuck, a conscienceless automaton.

Fergus is mightily impressed.

How can a living thing get like this?

A tawny owl hoots from the row of pines. Other than that it is a world of silence, just Fergus and the dog, breathing.

Fergus allows himself a smoke and, for just one foolish moment, he thinks of the possibility of returning to London with a dog like this beside him, for one light-hearted second he forgets, comes out of the darkness and his face shines, almost happy. He can see it all, imagine – a dog unable to do anything except obey his every command. Holy shit, wouldn't that be wicked? He thinks of the faces of his mates, so jaunty and confident . . . and his enemies . . . and the birds nudging and giggling . . . he feels a natural boyish desire to swagger into his local pub with this at his heels, pleased with his new, dignified image of himself . . .

Bewildered and empty.

His hands shake.

His body jerks as the iron door of obsession bangs down.

Her beautiful hair is shot with gold.

So wounded. Perhaps Fergus's eyes are so dull because of the lack of life's tears.

Tears only travel as far as Fergus's throat. Even when he was little he made sure they never got to his eyes.

19

Can you remember a summer like this? Week after week. Month after month the sun keeps on shining, the grass is dusty dry, and every day you can safely set off without an umbrella.

Stoic campers who have risked another ruined holiday in this country smile smugly as they draw back their tent flaps and prepare their breakfasts outside.

People can wash their curtains.

Murders and suicides are up, breaking all previous records.

The dry beds of reservoirs crack and little fishes sizzle. There is an officially declared drought.

The Oliphants and the Hardy-Browns and their ilk can leave their garden furniture out without fear of it getting soaked, even the sun beds, the deck chairs and the umbrellas.

Dulcie Maggs perches disapprovingly on the front left-hand seat of a fluorescent-pink double-decker bus on her morning visit to the hospital.

It looks like a baby's cot covered in lurid daisy stencils.

A bright pink bus, an unhealthy colour – you would think it would stand for chaos and yet, in the last few days, into her life has come order and comfort.

Has she gone mad? She is forced to pose this serious question.

They have slipped much further into this worrying business than they ought to have slipped, and Dulcie should know better. And Kirsty, if you please, she had always thought Kirsty a bit dim-witted to be perfectly honest, Kirsty encouraging that hippy boy to tell a pack of lies in the hope of getting massive compensation.

Perhaps Kirsty is not quite so dull as she seems. Directly ahead, in the driver's seat, muscles expanding in tune with the wheel and well in control, is her friend and fellow tippler of last night, Charlie the tattooed sailor – though not really a sailor, as Kirsty tries to explain.

'That's just his persona, Mum, he's a student, just finished a law degree, and taking a year off. They all are.'

'Persona? A year off? A year off what?'

'No need to look, Mum, if you're that nervous,' calls Charlie, seeing the older woman's gritted teeth and rolling eyes as they round a sharpish bend. 'Here, have a Fisherman's Friend.'

She used to be so frightened of people. Only yesterday she was frightened of people. So what is happening to her now? She snaps, 'Keep both hands on that wheel please, Charlie. I can look after myself.'

And then she falls uneasily silent. Heavens, she hopes she does not see anyone she knows.

That is unlikely.

She hardly goes out any more, and has lost contact with the few friends she did have years ago.

There was never much time for friendship in Dulcie Maggs's life.

The kids, the state of high excitement which is normally impossible to contain, are somewhere on the top deck being entertained by the bald-headed, stooping Communist, Jamie. He is better than any nanny, or mother, for that matter. Kirsty and Michael are in the back seat canoodling.

It is disgusting.

They cannot keep their hands off each other and Dulcie is glad she does not know what went on between them last night.

She did pop round to Sheralee's flat to see what was happening after she was ready for bed in dressing gown and slippers. After dark. She was tired, a little tipsy, and could not wait up for Kirsty any longer. She got as far as the little hall, tapped softly, and peeped through the rippled windows, but backed away when she saw the strange, subdued lighting and heard the mystical music. It sounded as if they were holding some strange religious ceremony. She knew she would not like it so, feeling isolated and threatened, she backed away quietly.

God knows where anyone slept.

In the past few days normality has been turned upside down, and Dulcie hopes Kirsty is not getting too emotionally involved.

The bus was parked in a reserved area of an Admiralty car-park, safely secured against thieves and vandals overnight. Dulcie was shocked when she first saw it but what could they do . . . they had already accepted a lift by then.

'You'll never get us all in,' giggled Kirsty, before she saw the kind of vehicle they were intending to use.

'Don't just stand there, climb in!' And Charlie picked Dulcie up, no mean feat, shopping bag and all.

Kirsty, showing off this morning in that over-tight skirt that shows half her arse, had trouble mounting the step. Little tramp.

But when all's said and done, what do *they* look like?

Charlie going about in the string vest of a navvy, with thick blue working jeans and the shaven, threatening head of a missile. Jamie the Communist, as gaunt and shrunk as Charlie is stretched, with wide fanatical eyes, and last but not least these two hippy types in their flowing garments, and the one fiddling about with Kirsty is animal, like some rabid, primitive being.

Still, give them their due, they insisted on taking the kiddies off for the day, down to see the sailing ships . . .

'But you must keep your eye on them every second, they're

only babies, and they don't understand about water.' But then Dulcie turned to Kirsty and whispered, 'Is this wise? After all, we hardly know them. They could be members of one of those sects.'

'Frankly, Mum, I couldn't give a toss who they are, if it means we can have one day, one bloody blissful wonderful day, without the kids.'

And so it is that they are dropped off at the hospital – like having your own private bus service, like the Queen – and when they come to wave goodbye the kiddies aren't even watching.

Oh deep joy!

Sheralee Maggs is compos mentis.

'Oh Sheralee, thank God and thank the lord Jesus! I had visions of having to make the awful decision . . . '

Kirsty stops her mother quickly. 'No, Mum! Not now! And you have to be a damn sight worse than Sheralee to have your machine turned off.'

'Quite,' says the nurse crisply. 'We're all very pleased with Sheralee, aren't we dear? She woke up in the night as calmly as you please and demanded a cup of tea! Asked all about little Jason. Gave the night staff a right start . . . '

'So all my talking was a waste of time,' says Dulcie, happily stroking her daughter's hand, a thing she has not done since she was four years old. 'All those memories!'

'I don't remember a thing, I wondered what I was doing here when I woke up,' says Sheralee brightly, looking almost delicate and only slightly paler than normal, which could well be the reflection of the starched hospital sheets.

Dulcie lowers her voice, 'You're the victim of a particularly nasty hit-and-run . . . '

'Yes, Mum, they told me. And I know I'm very lucky . . . '

'No. You are certainly not lucky at all and you must never say that. It should never have happened. And it wouldn't have happened if certain people had managed not to behave any better than wild beasts.'

And so they explain to a baffled Sheralee all the extra-ordinary suspicions of Gerry Hardy-Brown – the parcel of blood money, the attack on The Old Schoolhouse – 'and he even believes the slashing of his roof was more than a mere coincidence.'

'What?' Sheralee attempts to sit up much too soon, and winces. 'Since when has anyone been able to park outside Montpellier Court and get away with it?'

'Yes, well.' Kirsty dismisses her sister's scorn and warms to her subject. It is okay to talk freely, the three of them are safely alone, the nurse has left the room. Her whisper is conspiratorial. 'And now we've got a real chance to sting that bastard for enough lolly to see us through for the rest of our bloody lives.'

'How come?'

Poor Sheralee, faced with such sudden drama, is uncertain that she has come round at all, and believes this to be one more stage of coma. She will probably come round properly in a minute.

'Compensation.'

'For Jason's hand?'

'Not only for Jason's hand, Sher. Mr Hardy-Brown says that if we were willing to come forward with the bribe, we'd probably get him for your accident as well.'

Sheralee's brain is revving up through the gears. 'And risk losing the money? The police'd never let us keep it.'

'Ah, but now we've got someone who's willing to make a statement that that man Oliphant paid a group of students to squat in your flat!'

'Hang on, Kirsty. Hang on. What are you saying? That they're going to lie? For us?'

'Sheralee . . . Sheralee, it won't be us that's lying . . . and we won't even need to go to court. Mr Hardy-Brown says that statement will be enough to get that man to settle . . . '

'No, Kirsty, they'd be lying, but we'd be in collusion. We'd never get away with it.'

'Oh. So there's one law for them, and another for us, is that it, Sher? D'you think that bastard Oliphant hasn't lied in the past . . . '

Dulcie Maggs butts in. The discussion is getting too heated and Sheralee is obviously not ready to see sense yet. Her recovery is going to take time and she really does not need an argument with her sister at this point in her progress.

'We must go and see Jason and tell him the wonderful, wonderful news about his mum. And maybe, just maybe, they might agree to let you two meet, now you're so much better!

Sheralee falls back heavily against her pillows. 'Better not, Mum. Not yet. I'm very wobbly on my pins, and they wouldn't let Jason into this ward.'

'But they could wheel you up to the kiddies' ward . . . '

'Mum, just don't interfere. Just leave it as it is for now, will you? I don't want to overdo it.'

Mrs Maggs kisses her eldest daughter, and departs with her bags, her bundle of comics, and Kirsty, to call upon her grandchild.

'Won't be long, dear. See you in a minute!'

The terrible Jason is up and out of bed and playing at one of the activity tables. You can hear his strident voice from the door. He ignores his family when they arrive, as usual, and picks an argument with his playmate.

'Leave him, Mrs Maggs, just leave him! He is behaving like this for attention, and it would be better if you left him to his own devices,' says sister in her knowing voice, restraining the flustered Nana.

The experts have had the pleasure of Jason's company for three days now, and are getting to know him quite well.

So Dulcie stands back, and pretends to be sorting out his

locker, and lo and behold, by the time she turns round, Jason is playing happily again.

'You see, dear,' explains the sister, 'with such young siblings at such a close age, Jason has established the habit of using bad behaviour to make himself feel important. We see this so often here. A few more hugs when he IS behaving himself might well do the trick.'

'Nosey old cow,' sniffs Dulcie, behind the sister's back. 'What does she know about kids? I bet she's not even married!'

'Neither am I, Mum,' Kirsty reminds her.

'Exactly, and look at you.'

Trying to unravel this logic but failing, Kirsty approaches Jason with the fire-engine he requested yesterday. It cost almost a fiver. Part of next week's rent will have to wait. He takes one cool look and ignores it, preferring the colourful building blocks.

Kirsty tries not to be hurt. 'What are you making, Jason?'

It is left to his friend to answer politely, 'A railway station.'

'Oh yes, of course, I can see that now.'

'No you can't,' says Jason, pushing his aunt roughly away.

Dulcie should love this little grandchild of hers. She should not feel this terrible urge to hurt him. 'I just don't see the point in us being here,' wails Dulcie, folding his dirty pyjamas and sniffing. 'He's far happier without us.'

'Aha, that's just a brave act he likes to put on, don't you, Jason,' says the sister, passing professionally, with a bedpan under paper wraps.

'Huh. Three days and they reckon they know more about our kiddies than we do, isn't it just the way,' tuts Kirsty. 'But they don't have to put up with the hassle day and night . . . '

Dulcie turns to Kirsty and whispers fiercely, 'It'd all be different with a few thousand stashed away in the bank!'

Kirsty turns to stare at her mother. 'Christ, Mum, you sound like a gangster.'

'Well perhaps I am at heart,' says Mrs Maggs flatly.

For Kirsty, the whole of last night and the start of this day have been different from any other.

She cannot wait to be back in her new lover's arms.

He said, 'I'll come with you to the hospital if you like.'

'You'd hate it there.'

'I don't mind where I am. I just enjoy being with you.'

Such a simple thing to say and Kirsty repeats it over and over again in her head as she sits around in the children's ward, not even worrying about the screams and the wails and the casualties moving around on stretchers. *I just enjoy being with you. I just enjoy being with you.* Kirsty has gone to another plane where nothing can really reach her.

'You don't mean that,' she replied at once. 'You're just saying it.'

Michael looked troubled. He raised one of his hunter's hands and stroked her backcombed hair with his arrow finger. 'Why would I say it if I didn't mean it?'

'Dunno.'

'Dunno,' he teased her, sulking like a child between his locks of flowing black hair.

'I suppose I just can't believe you could really mean it. Someone like you. Rich. Handsome. Brainy. Different. Someone like you, wanting to be with someone like me.'

'And don't you think I might feel some of those things too, about you?'

She hung her head. She pouted. 'Why would you? I'm fat, for a start.'

'Okay, so I like fat women.'

'And I'm older.'

'I'm twenty-two. What are you then? Thirty?'

'Twenty-one.'

'Well then,' Michael declared, 'You're wrong then, aren't you?'

'But I *feel* so much older. I look so much older. And I'm boring.'

'If I didn't care,' said Michael seriously, 'why would I bother to lie on your account . . . '

'Because it's all just a game to you, and people like you, really, isn't it? It's a bit of a laugh. Not very important.' She was perilously close to tears. 'And for all I know this is something to do with your weird political theories . . . '

And then he had kissed her, laughed at her, and pulled her out to the bus.

He will go away. Someone like that. Why would he hang around here when he has so much else in his life? Loving family. Friends. Brilliant future. But whatever happens, Kirsty tells herself, from now on and for ever she will spend time putting together the pieces of the most wonderful dreams.

Like the second-hand jigsaws she was given to do as a child.

You had to follow the lid. It was only the lid that gave you that heart-breaking glimpse of the finished picture. You never managed to do it yourself.

The editor is coming to see the Maggses at the hospital at lunch time. Kirsty phoned from the reception area to tell him more about the squatters. 'So it looks as if you were right all along, Mr Hardy-Brown,' she lied.

She could sense his satisfied smile. He is so ready to believe anything bad about Oliphant.

'And these people are willing to come to see my solicitor with me . . . ?'

'Yes, perfectly happy.'

'Did they tell you how much Oliphant paid them?'

'One hundred pounds each.'

'And do they still have the money?'

'No, they've spent it.'

'One thing puzzles me. You say they're university students. How did Zak Oliphant contact them in the first place?'

Kirsty was primed with a reasonable answer. 'Apparently there was a notice up on the students' union board, you know the sort of thing – easy pickings. They were skint, so they answered it.'

'But you gave me the impression that these lads were all fairly well-heeled, so why would they stoop to this sort of unsavoury crime?'

'Oh, they didn't know it was a crime, Mr Hardy-Brown. Oliphant told them he owned this empty flat, and he wanted them in it to keep an unwelcome tenant out.'

Suspicion sharpened his voice. 'But Miss Maggs, surely Montpellier Court is owned by the council?'

'Some people have bought their own flats, and are subletting them. I think they must be mad, but they're going so cheap it's a snip . . . '

There was a pause. A tissue of lies. Had Kirsty got it right? They had rehearsed it enough times, over and over again in the flat, all of them together. She knew the arguments off by heart but had she sounded convincing?

'I see. Tell you what. Why don't we have a brief meeting round there at lunch time – same time, same place . . . '

'You want to convince us to hand over that money, don't you? That's what you're after?'

'Well I must say it would make a great deal of difference to our case . . . '

'But you know we can't do that, Mr Hardy-Brown. We daren't. That sort of money means a lot to people like us.'

'I know. I know. And Oliphant knew it, too. But just let's have another little chat, and we can arrange for me to meet these neighbours of yours. Before we go any further I must make sure I have got this whole thing sewn up as tightly as I can. And I'd like to spend a few minutes with your sister, Miss Maggs, if that would be possible, now she has come round.'

So Kirsty had to agree.

She may be thick as a plank, she may only have Communications Studies and Art GCSEs – D is a pass, isn't it? – but Kirsty understands exactly what she is doing now.

Michael has explained how it will work.

'A settlement out of court' is what they are after. 'Putting the frighteners on that man Oliphant' is how Michael puts it. 'You'll get your money, well-deserved, and pressure can be brought to bear to change some of the scandalous practices going on at Fingles Ponds.'

'You'd think there'd be an easier way. I mean, the country has laws, and inspectors to make sure they are carried out, doesn't it?' asked Kirsty.

'Balls,' said Michael. 'Those laws mean absolutely nothing these days. Not when you get tyrants like Zak Oliphant with his fingers in so many pies. Nobody dares stand up to him. He paid you a thousand pounds, knowing full well that you were in no position to refuse it. And there's a threat implied in that, Kirsty, don't forget. No, if there was another way, don't you think a good-thinking man like Gerry Hardy-Brown would be taking it?'

Kirsty felt slow and silly. Why did she ever bother to argue? 'Yes, yes, I see what you mean, Michael. I suppose they would, wouldn't they?'

'And it's our duty, as decent citizens, to do all we can to help him. Even if it does mean a little toying with the actuality.'

Michael Bailey was quite right. Of course.

20

The following morning the *Western Express* comes out with an editorial which condemns any local companies who are using the economic situation in order to exploit their workers:

Paying below minimum wages;
Refusing to provide contracts of employment;
No paid holiday;
Compulsory weekend working;
Compulsory overtime;
Unsafe and unhygienic working conditions;
Dismissal without notice;
No equal pay for women.
And so forth.

The article does not specifically name Fingles Ponds or Zak Oliphant, but everyone knows who they are getting at, and the editor invites all those people with complaints, old and new, to contact him forthwith, confidentially, on the appropriate number.

'But Gerry,' cries Jemima when, as is his new habit, he comes home at lunch time, 'you're deliberately goading this man. Where is all this leading? You haven't proof enough to come right into the open and accuse him, there's not enough to take him to court, so you make all these dangerous allegations and you know what he's like . . . '

'Jemima.' He comes across the empty, echoing room and soothes her.

The professional cleaners are in. Jemima discovered she could not possibly start afresh unless all contamination from Fergus's visit was steamed and scrubbed from the ceilings, corners and cornices of every single room in the house. 'It's the thought of what the eye can't see that's got right under my skin,' she pleaded. 'I know I'm being ridiculous, but pander to me, Gerry.'

So he did.

'Please try and understand, Jem, this scandalous situation is something I ought to have highlighted years ago. But I didn't; to my eternal shame, I did nothing. And so now the monster has managed not only to survive, but with his four huge, wildly successful complexes, he's breeding as well.'

Jemima pushes him off. She won't be consoled, not yet. While he is convincing her he is reassuring himself. 'And what if he comes back? And what if he hurts the children?'

Gerry sighs, for how many times have they been through this, in the middle of the night, first thing in the morning, bed time, tea time . . . even in the bathroom.

'We are dealing with a paid lawbreaker, some rascally crook, hired by Oliphant to do his dirty business for him. Now remember that, Jemima, whatever happens here is over in the cold light of day . . . unemotionally, practically if you like . . . '

She interrupts him hysterically, 'Gerry! Do you honestly think that what you're saying is making me feel any better?'

'Well it should! It should make you feel a great deal better. To think that we are refusing to be bowed by such a diabolical man, to think that I have started the ball rolling with that editorial today, and that hundreds of unfortunate victims of his are now going to come forward making it possible . . . '

'I'm sorry, Gerry, I really am sorry for being so ignoble and pathetic, but I really don't care about your high-falutin' ideals. All I'm worried about – and damnit, you should be, too – is the safety of my children!'

'I've told you before, Jemima. Take them away. Go home to

Greenways for a couple of weeks until this whole thing dies down. I really wish you would.'

Now she is sobbing, but see how easily he will convince her to stay in the end. 'No, Gerry, you don't. You would prefer that I hold out against something you perceive as unprincipled and evil, that I, too, should be brave enough to withstand . . . '

'But I don't . . . '

'Well I'm not! I'm not brave enough. And I don't particularly care about employment laws and contracts and enforced overtime. Frankly, Gerry,' and she stands up and faces him, 'I don't give a shit!'

'You don't mean that.'

Jemima runs a frantic hand through her soft, beautifully cut and highlighted hair. 'Gerry, don't you know anything at all about me? I do. I *do* mean it. I say I care, but deep inside me, I don't! There! I've said it! All I honestly care about is you, me, Hannah and Felix!'

Gerry's long arms hang limply by his sides. His voice is calm and controlled. 'In that case, you should do as I suggest, you should take the children and go.'

'And leave you here in your Jesus mode, waiting for the inevitable crucifixion, like a martyr!'

'If that's what you think about me, yes.'

Jemima, having said far too much, hangs her head, and gives a mighty sigh that shudders through the whole of her neat, sophisticated body. She asks him, 'You honestly feel, and you can say with your hand on your heart, that you believe we are in no danger?'

Gerry summons all his convictions together and makes a pile of them in his promise, 'Yes. That's how I feel. Contemptible bastard though he is, I do not believe Zak Oliphant would consider hurting you, or the children.'

'And the hit-and-run?'

'Meant to be a frightener, but Sheralee Maggs was too bewildered by her own terrible worries, and stepped out when she should have stepped back. Jem, don't you see, he merely intended to give the woman a shock!'

'Oh? And what if his man, or men, come here with their orders, and things manage to get out of hand? What if they get carried away, for example . . . I mean, Oliphant's not going to be too happy with this, is he?' And she slaps at the paper as if it's a wasp, knowing very well she is in no danger from a stranger.

'Oh, Jem, Jem,' he says sadly. 'Nothing I say is going to convince you when you're feeling like this, is it?'

She flares, 'Oh, it's the silly little woman syndrome now, is it? What do you mean, when I'm feeling like this?'

And so their conversation goes on. Getting nowhere.

But Jemima Hardy-Brown means precisely what she says. She was speaking the truth when she said she didn't really care.

Oh, the shameful creature, she pretends to care all right . . . about the things she knows she is supposed to care about. All the old chestnuts which Gerry reads about daily in his worthy newspaper, the *Guardian*. She would never say so, but deep inside she prefers the *Daily Mail*, which she gets to read sometimes at the hairdresser's.

She was a closet supporter of Margaret Thatcher.

She is a closet supporter of the monarchy, and the House of Lords, although she is prepared to argue, gently, against them.

She secretly believes that some people are born to rule, some are born to be led, and some are born to be losers.

Genes most probably.

Jemima was telling the truth when she confessed to her best friend, Jacqueline, that she is becoming more and more like her mother.

She didn't start out like this of course, who does? It is time and experience which have moulded her.

Gerry, so honourable and so politically sound, would die if he knew.

She prays he will never find out, because she loves Gerry more than she has ever loved anyone on earth. She would do anything rather than lose him.

And if he believes he is right – that his persecution is a controlled and limited thing – then he can also believe that he has convinced her to stay in Middlehempston and take her chances.

But Jemima has no intention of leaving.

There are men in the house all the time now, cleaning, measuring, estimating, decorating. There is no time she is ever alone, and if she feels uneasy she can go next door, or pop Felix in the pram and make the ten-minute walk to Jacqueline's house.

Gerry believes she is safe.

Gerry believes passionately in what he is doing.

And if Gerry believes passionately, then it is right that Jemima should be seen to be standing solidly by his side.

'Oh, Gerry, I'm sorry, it's just . . . '

'I know, Jem, I know . . . '

'I wouldn't dream of leaving you at a time like this.'

'Whatever you decide, Jem, you know that it will be right.'

Oh look how he admires her, and values her, and considers her as noble as he is.

Isn't Jemima ashamed to be standing before him like this, allowing him to take her in his arms and plant an almost reverent kiss on her saintly forehead? Is she not ashamed when she signs the petitions he brings home – Free the Manchester Four, the Blackpool Six, the Colchester Two – when she firmly believes they were probably guilty anyway, by virtue of being Irish and in the wrong place at the time: what are the police supposed to do, massage their feet as they sit in the interrogation room, mix them exotic cocktails? But sign the petitions she does, with an independent flourish.

Does Jemima not even blush when she dips into her purse

and buys raffle tickets to support the suffering miners, when she secretly believes they ought to be glad to come up from their underground worlds . . . hell, they made enough fuss about their conditions before their jobs were threatened. And there is no market for coal, and anyway, it is a filthy fuel. Jemima would never dream of burning that ugly, dirty black stuff in her living room fireplace . . . it would mark the canopy, and make the room smell foul. There's nothing sweeter than boughs of applewood.

And her Aga runs on gas.

Unmarried mothers ought to be put into hostels and the long-term unemployed should, for their own good, be conscripted.

Jemima was always Daddy's true daughter.

'I feel so much safer when you are here,' she looks up and tells Gerry, meekly. 'Sometimes I let my imagination get out of control, that's the trouble. And then you come, and everything's okay again.'

'I know. I know. And that's natural. So far it is you who has borne the brunt of these disgraceful attacks. I'd probably feel like you if I'd been the one to suffer directly.'

'Forgive me, Gerry? If that Maggs family can be brave, and hold out against Oliphant, then I certainly can.'

Gerry's response is simple, and slightly naive. 'There is nothing to forgive.'

That afternoon he accepts a phone call from the infuriated Oliphant.

'What's your game then, Hardy-Brown?'

'It is no game, Mr Oliphant.'

'You realise you're coming close to a big fat injunction?'

'If you are confident that you are not infringing the rules, then why should you take my editorial so personally?'

'Is this phone bugged?'

'Oh come now, Mr Oliphant. You might consider yourself to be a big operator, but don't let's get completely paranoid about all this. You only have to pay a reasonable amount of compensation to the Maggses, make certain adjustments to your working practices . . . '

'This is blackmail, Hardy-Brown. And as such, indefensible.'

'If you say so.'

'You know bloody well that I had nothing to do with that accident, that I didn't pay to shut those women up, that I wouldn't dirty my hands or waste my hard-earned money on organising a blasted attack on your putrid little house . . . '

Gerry clears his throat. 'How about squatters?'

'Squatters?' roars Oliphant.

'Yes, how about paying a few students to move next door to the Maggses and put further pressure on them to keep quiet?'

Zak Oliphant blusters, 'Hogwash! And you call me paranoid, you crazy fucker. You want to look in your own mirror! Have you gone off your goddamn head?'

'Please don't waste my time with more of your childish ranting. Certain matters have come to light . . . '

'You fool! You pissing idiot! You stupid, scheming, devious bastard . . . '

'Have you no control of your language, Mr Oliphant? This is all quite unacceptable.'

'Damn well right it is! Come out . . . Come out, you whinging toady, take off those bloody sandals of yours and come out and accuse me of some of this shit in public . . . '

'I might have to, Mr Oliphant, if you don't change your unscrupulous ways. And if I'm not mistaken, I might soon acquire quite a few more interesting points to put to the Crown Prosecution Service by the time the response to my editorial comes in. People who have been too afraid, up until now, to come forward. People you have used. You are a bully,

Mr Oliphant, a bully, a cheat, a fraud . . . So why are you waiting? The ball is in your court now.'

'What's in this for you, Hardy-Brown – or John the fucking Baptist, which is it? What drives you, that's what I'd bloody well like to know?'

'You wouldn't understand it, I'm afraid, but it's not as rare as you think. It's something called basic human decency . . . '

'Oh you fucking poser, oh you self-righteous, petty-minded prat! Giving yourself these pretentious airs, who do you fucking well think you are? Who d'you think runs one of the most successful businesses in this fart-arsed part of the woods with more than a thousand employees, built up from nothing . . . '

'It is not difficult to make money out of the exploitation of other human beings. Slavery was quite profitable, I believe, in its heyday. As was child prostitution.'

'Good God, you really *are* mad!'

'Well, let us just wait and see what happens. But I tell you this, Mr Oliphant: if you should even think about sending anyone else round to my house to threaten my wife or my children, or any member of the Maggs family, I will personally make sure that you never operate a business in this country again – no, not even a dry cleaner's – that you are broken, exposed for what you are, taken for every penny you own, and, if it is remotely possible, that you spend a large proportion of the next ten years behind bars!'

'You crazy shithead!' roars Zak Oliphant, in tears of rage, as he slams down the phone.

21

'Now then, Hump.'

If Hump's slick of grey hair wasn't stuck to his head by dirt and time, it would be up in a frozen point by now, like a startled horn.

Nobody ever comes here at night.

This is an age-old understanding between Hump and his boss. Hump does the job he is paid to do, and he does it well, and if anyone starts interfering he gets all upset and messed up in his head, 'all over the place and how am I supposed to concentrate when somebody's nosing around in my private business?'

Up until now Hump's solitary preferences have generally been respected.

'Whadyawant?'

'I'm at the main gate, Hump, and I would like to be allowed to enter my own bloody premises and have a word with my chief security man. If that's all right with you.'

There was only one security man, but it pleased Hump, better than a rise, to have the 'chief' put on his job description.

Hump worked for Zak Oliphant's father, in the days when the Melrose Fingles Ponds, and old Mr Oliphant's first venture, was merely a humble storeshed which sold army surplus boots, jackets, haversacks and socks, mostly catering for big-footed working men, walkers and local farmers.

Sticky tables and cigarette butts.

Pieces of engine and oil cans, galvanised piping and torn pieces of oily rag, helped to create the atmosphere.

A masculine place selling hairy, hardy, homespun masculine products.

Zak's father, sensing an opening, set himself up with a stall at all the various race meetings, markets, fairs and fêtes, and managed to secure a bit of a name for his cheap but hard-wearing products. He photocopied some brochures, just straightforward A4 pages folded in half down the middle – and generally stained by the time they were posted off – with some crude drawings which depicted his most popular wares.

Most of his brochures had 'Pay by recipient' stamped on them when they arrived at their destinations. The rest escaped the eye of the busy Post Office completely.

This mail-order venture took off around about the time of the sixties when the kids started buying his boots and jackets considering them fashionable, and so he decided to expand his store. He took out a loan and concentrated on the basic stuff country people needed; cheap kitchen-ware, glasses, pans and the like.

Like a tinker.

His turnover was tremendous. His profit margins lip-licking. He cut a little here and he diddled a little there until he realised exactly what could be achieved with the cunning fiddling of the books, bulk buying from dubious sources, large storage facilities well off the beaten track, and a watchful eye for a sucker.

Hump, a sour and mean-minded man, was his first employee and just the job. He never did say much about his past, save that his stooped back was the result of a cave-in when he was a boy in a South Wales colliery.

But his general pallor, hatred of closed doors, and attitude suggested that, between that time and this, the man might well have been detained somewhere at Her Majesty's pleasure.

Zak's father wasn't much bothered.

Hump lived on the site even then, hardly ever moving off, with just a paraffin stove and an old lloyd loom chair to sleep in, and a disreputable van. The eventual success of Fingles Ponds had much to do with Hump's ferocious attitude and sheer hard work. A better man might have promoted Hump to partner when it became apparent just how successful his new enterprises were going to be. But by then his son, Zacharias, was keen to get a grip on the reins and anyway, Hump was always too busy grumbling and hating to notice.

'Hang on, Boss, I'll call in the dogs.'

Hump whistles, and begins banging the sides of the feeding bucket. One, Two, Three and Four come in immediately like paddle boats on a pond, salivating and snarling, but no sign of the ban-dog.

Hump bangs again, more irritably this time. Where is the cursed bugger? Got his nose stuck down a rabbit hole, most likely.

Zak parps his horn and calls crossly into the speaker, 'Goddamn it, Hump, what d'you expect me to do? Sit here on my arse for the whole sodding evening?' Zak is at the end of his tether, driven to action by the manifestation of a pure and a futile fury.

Kimberley cannot, or will not take him seriously.

Behaving strangely of late – could be the change – she seems more interested in making peg-dolls for some damnfool fundraising effort. Hideous things, and who the hell would buy them? 'Why don't you pay them off, Zak, like they're asking you to? Compensate the Maggs boy, you must be able to get it back on your insurance. And how much would it cost you to change a few silly old rules at work . . . '

'But you don't understand, Kimberley. They're making all sorts of ludicrous allegations against me.'

'Since when have you cared about what anyone said?'

'They're blackening my name in the whole vicinity.'

'I thought it was black already. This would be your chance, Zak, to redeem yourself in the eyes of decent society.' He is only being so stubborn because he detests Hardy-Brown.

'Fuck society!'

And Kimberley sighed.

And his blasted solicitor, Cyril, wasn't much more forthcoming. 'We cannot act, Zak, unless Hardy-Brown comes out and says what he's thinking. While he couches all this in vague insinuations which could apply to anyone, our hands are tied.'

'But he's directing all his vitriolic spleen towards me! It has to be me. And well you know it, Cyril.'

'I hope not, Zak!' For he has heard the rumours.

'Well, no, of course not the criminal accusations – wouldn't touch that sort of hanky-panky with a barge pole. But you know full well who he's getting at in that damn editorial about working conditions.'

'You've answered your own question, Zak old man. How can we make a challenge for libel when everything he suggests is perfectly true?'

No. No bloody help from that expensive quarter, but no doubt Cyril will put a bill in anyway.

And now here he is, driven from his home by a sewing machine and indifference, tapping his feet and drumming his fingers, kept hanging about outside his own bloody premises.

'Hang about, Boss, with a bit of luck I'll 'ave 'em in in a minute.'

'Well make sure that you do!'

Hump calls and bangs again, to no avail. There is nothing else for it. He chains up the alsatians grimly, and shuffles over to open the main gate, eyes peering from side to side, heart beating angrily.

'Great Gawd in 'eaven,' he mutters to himself. 'I'll sort the varmint when I see 'im.'

'Ah, Hump.' Inside at last, Zak climbs clumsily out of his bright red Jaguar, clutching the door frame, heaving out his legs, his Maxwellian, well-fed body following.

'Nothing wrong, boss?'

'No, Hump, nothing wrong. Just wanted a word.'

And Hump coughs and looks up at the stars. 'Nice night?'

Zak seems surprised that anyone, particularly Hump, would notice it. 'Yep, I suppose it is.'

But Zak is past formalities or niceties, never mind that he has not set eyes on his security man for over a year. He must get on. 'Now, there's been quite a bit of trouble following that accident with one of your dogs on Tuesday.'

'Unfortunate business, that.'

Zak nods and rubs his fat hands together. The gold rings, and his bracelet, spark in the moonlight. 'Most unfortunate. And the incident has unleashed all sorts of other sleeping monsters.'

Hump is confused. Is Mr Oliphant calling his dogs sleeping monsters?

'And it seems that the police in their wisdom, not satisfied with their original report, will be coming round in the morning, Hump, to inspect your whole set-up.'

Hump hawks. 'Waste of fucking time.'

'That may well be. But we must make absolutely certain that they don't find any cause to bring a case against us. Now,' and Zak looks around, 'where were your dogs when that damn kid got his hand bitten off?'

'In here, Boss, chained up, 'zactly like they are now.' Hump sweats more profusely than usual. Where is that sodding hound?

Zak gingerly makes his way through the iron door and into the square of Fingles Ponds that belongs to Hump. What a mess. His hut is more of a tumble-down shack than a decent, upright shed, and a tattered rug is thrown over an earthen floor, trodden in long ago until the colour resembles that of old mud and brown roses. God, how does the man survive this spartan existence in the winter?

Zak eyes the four alsatians, who stare back at him suspiciously.

'And now show me the hole in the fence, Hump.'

'Right over 'ere. I showed 'im to Mr Caruthers hisself when 'e came round that afternoon.'

'But you have blocked it up, since?'

'Course I 'ave.'

'So how could any one of these alsatians who are chained up over here, now, how could they have reached that fence and bitten off that lad's hand?'

Hump scratches his filthy head. 'Doan ask me, Boss.'

Zak stares hard at Hump. 'But something bit off his hand.'

'Must 'ave. If 'e says so.'

'Hump. It is a fact that some animal chewed off the lad's hand, it was never a matter for speculation.'

How stupid can one man be?

'And there are no other dogs on the premises? No dog which might have been inadvertently let loose at the time?'

'Naw. Just these four.'

Zak peers around him. He confronts Hump, man to man, pinning him with his sharp piggy eyes. 'You're lying, Hump.'

Hump's face reddens. 'No, Boss, I ain't.'

'The facts, and common sense, say that you are.'

'I can't help what facts say.'

'You bloody fool. The police will be round here tomorrow and tear your story to shreds. And then we'll all be in the shit, thanks to that pissing Jesus wanker . . .'

'Boss?' Hump, cringing like a slave, pricks up his ears. This sounds better, more along his lines. What Jesus wanker? Someone to hate? Someone to blame? A way to get himself off the hook?

'. . . making up all sorts of absurd allegations about me paying people to go round and frighten him off. Threatening to take matters further. I tell you, Hump, that man is mad as a bleeding hatter. Should be locked away. Pity I didn't carry out a few of those lunatic suggestions of his, might have done me a damn sight more good than sitting around on my arse waiting for the next attack.'

'That'd sort him,' whinges Hump.

'What?'

'That'd shut his gob for 'im.'

Bloody fool. What does the hawking Hump know about life in the world outside this stinking, Godforsaken chicken house? People like Hump have it easy. Sitting around here by night, drinking, sleeping it off by day. Contemplating the mysteries of life. None of the pressures that are slowly and surely killing Zak, pushing out his piles, pushing up his blood pressure, squeezing his heart to death.

For a fleeting moment Zak envies Hump.

'I know all about warning folks off,' says Hump, astonishingly, in his sly and fawning fashion. 'I used to work for the big boys . . . years ago of course, when that sort of thing were more fashionable than 'tis now.'

'What the hell are you mumbling on about?'

'Bookies, money-lenders, landlords having trouble with tenants, oh yes,' Hump's sodden eyes shine as if they have lit upon some tender memory as he goes on artfully. 'Anyone who wanted to bring pressure to bear in those days down the East End, they got in touch with old Hump here. They knew Hump was reliable, see. Hump had the knack.' Hump attempts a smile and Zak stares in horrible fascination. 'Yep. Pincers they used to call me. For my way of prisin' an' weedlin' an' squeezin'.'

Pincers? Zak, repelled, cannot help asking. 'And then what happened?'

'I moved on, didn't I? Worked out it were better to work for myself. Had ambition in them days, see. Set myself up in a big way, all sorts of different rackets goin' on. But then, an' isn't it always the way, some jealous bastard coughs and you're in the slammer before you know it with all your mates cursin' you on the opposite side of the court room . . . ' Hump stops to wipe his eyes.

This must be the longest speech Zak has ever heard Hump utter. He is shocked.

'I never knew that, Hump.'

Hump wipes his nose with the back of his bony hand. He twists his tortoise head and looks up at Zak. 'Oh yers. I doan make a habit of talking about myself, like some.'

'Pincers, eh?'

Hump chuckles. 'Pincers by name . . . '

And Zak wonders if his father knew, and if his father employed Hump for just those foul purposes during the hard times when he was establishing the business. There must have been customers slow in paying . . .

'Bit rusty now, I suppose, Hump?'

'Naw, it's like riding a bicycle, you never forget. I always reckoned meself to be rather like one of those Desmond Morris what-do-they-call 'ems – had 'im on telly in the nick – with a knowledge of human behaviour, you know, basic human nature.'

Yes, muses Zak, intrigued, very basic indeed most probably.

Hump offers Zak a cup of tea, so they sit on the bench and wait for his kettle to boil while Hump subserviently spoons condensed milk into chipped enamel mugs. He is still on edge – for where is the ban-dog? – but he feels he has his master's attention and, with a bit of coaxing, he might be able to edge himself into a more favourable position.

Already he has an idea.

'It doesn't take much to put a stop to these little games,' says Hump knowingly, pouring the boiling water, with a rag wrapped round the hot metal of the kettle handle. 'Not when you know how, it don't. These days they've lost the skills, it's all pick-axe handles and knives, but in my day it was art, we didn't need any of that crap.'

'Really?' The tea is scalding, and has burnt a passage all the way down to Zak's chest. 'Christ, Hump . . . '

'A visit from me'd sort out the bleeder.'

Zak is silent, contemplating the circling, hypnotic bug in his cup, feeling himself being led into a crafty trap.

'I daresay you're right, Hump. But that's the last thing I need, to be involved in a trick like that. I am already in it up to here. The slightest mistake would finish me. I could lose everything. But then again, if this man continues with his holy war against me, I could be finished anyway.'

Obviously Zak has worked out the pros and cons to his best advantage. He cannot risk a court case. There would be too much evidence against him. The working conditions at Fingles Ponds, brought out into the light of day, would create a national scandal.

He would have to settle out of court and kowtow to that self-righteous prat Hardy-Brown. The thought of this slays him, but nevertheless it would be cheaper. Paying off the Maggses would be no problem, although it would hurt Zak's wallet, but changing the working practices at his four Fingles Ponds sites would be a different kettle of fish.

He happily pays the necessary fine for opening on a Sunday, but Zak's profit margins are small. He knows full well he is as successful as he is because he pays slave wages, because he hires and fires at will, because he puts none of the profits back into improving conditions at the workplace, and pensions schemes are nothing but a source of ready capital.

And apart from all this, once he is seen to be down, all sorts of vultures will gather for the pickings – the planning department for one. And how long could he expect to keep Inspector Hooper's loyalty? A few crates of champagne and a few holidays in Cyprus don't go very far when your job is on the line.

Sharp-eyed accountants would pry into his books.

If he improved working conditions, and stuck to all the employment laws, Zak might as well give up, take the money and get out.

He would die before he contemplated that.

He wonders if Hump has anything in mind? He wonders if Hump, a sixty-year-old pisshead with scrambled brains, can be trusted?

Hell no. He must be insane even to contemplate such a ludicrous plan. The times Hump has been talking about were years ago, when Hump was a younger, and presumably less distasteful, specimen than he is today.

But Hump has different ideas. Ideas of his own, designed to edge himself into the boss's good books, to prove his lifelong loyalty to father and son, and to make up for the trouble he's caused.

All it needs from him is a bit of initiative. Of course Oliphant can't ask him, he's a gent now, isn't he? It is up to Hump to decide what has to be done, just as he did in Zak's father's day.

'Yep,' says Hump, fiddling with the disgusting piece of newspaper around his paraffin ring. Zak watches him warily, as you might watch a bug going across your carpet. Can it be there for hygienic purposes, or does Hump only use it for rolling up dangerous flares to light his fag, as he is doing now?

Hump says no more, but winks offensively, and repeats himself, 'Yep.' His security man is clearly off his head, talking to himself, not even aware of his presence any longer.

Probably won't even remember he has been visited tonight.

Because Zak never comes here.

Nobody does.

I mean, why would they?

22

The fat is in the fire.

That old security guy catches Fergus on the hop as he and the ban-dog explore the tatty stretch of woodland that borders the southern perimeter fence of Fingles Ponds.

They are up here when they hear the whistle followed by the banging bucket.

It is one of those dreary, ramshackle woods, which, because of its unfortunate position, catches the litter which drifts from the site, wrapping itself round the trees, blowing in streamers against the clutching bellbine, and rolling its cans along the dismayed and uneven earth.

But in this dark and abandoned place – scheduled by Zak to be used as an infill site if he can squeeze enough money out of the council – there still lives an assortment of motley wildlife – rabbits with little imagination and even less ambition, skulking cats on the rampage, grey squirrels at war with each other, and the odd mangy badger.

Some wag once said they had spotted the Beast of Dartmoor coming out of the shadows – a panther-like creature, black and slinky – and naturally Zak had milked the publicity for all it was worth, but although various beast experts arrived within the next few weeks with their cameras and their tracking gear, the excitement soon fizzled out.

Fergus had gleefully set the ban-dog on an assortment of the small, wretched residents of the wood, marvelling at its quickness and skill. The grey cat flew into the air with a yowl, only coming down with its back between the ban-dog's jaws, and the crunch had been something else. The badger put up more of a fight and for just one moment Fergus was worried, because the ban-dog clearly did not know the nature of the beast it was facing.

It watched for a while with malignant eyes. It soon took the initiative, and had the badger scratching and snarling, backing away towards its lair with its head snapped upwards, but the dog cut off its escape route and from then on it was virtually all over.

The dog, weaving, lunging, caught the badger behind its neck and lifted it clean off the ground before banging it down, again and again, weakening the creature, breaking its sturdy bones as the flesh tore and grey fur covered the ground like feathers spattered with globules of blood while the badger grimaced in agony.

The dog's gleaming black hide shone with malevolence as it dragged the leg of the badger backwards, snapping it clean from its body.

Fergus watched, hugging himself, a wide grin on his face. He sighed as he felt himself grow hard.

'*He is too damaged,*' he heard Jemima tell Margery Block. '*If I were you I would not allow him alone with the dog, certainly not with the baby.*'

'I don't believe that, Jemima, I cannot believe you. You are talking about a boy who is completely unknown to me! I would trust Fergus with anyone, I wouldn't consider it possible that he could actually hurt a living thing!'

And Margery Block was no sentimental cow. She was built like a block an' all.

Mad Marge, with her vast, untidy body in her vast untidy house, who took in the sick and the weary, the barmy and the bad, the dregs and the losers, the lost and the lonely, and wherever her smile rested there was room for hope and trust and love to be born.

'I have known Fergus since he was eight years old,' said Jemima, sadly. 'You only have to look at his case notes to see what sort of trouble he has been involved in, and the results of his devious games and manipulations. So far I have managed to protect him from the worst excesses of the law and of course, apart from his short stay in Ryall which was disastrous, he has always been too young for a custodial sentence. And as you know, since he's been with you it has been either another warning, probation, conditional discharges or supervision orders, and I am just warning you, Marge, not to take anything he says to heart.'

Marge sighed. 'All that, back at the beginning. Fergus was testing us, Jemima. He had to do that. They all do. They've been let down so many times. And sometimes, whatever we do, we fail them. And I have seen Fergus at his worst. But I have to listen to what you are saying because I know that nobody could have done more for Fergus than you have, and he understands this very well.' Marge ran wild fingers through her outstandingly messy hair. 'I'm particularly sorry to hear what you are saying just now. Fergus has started talking to me, just lately, all sorts of things which I know he's never told anyone else.'

'Real things? Or products of Fergus's morbid imagination?'

'Does it really matter?'

'Well, no . . . I suppose . . . '

'There is always *some* truth in everything anyone says . . . '

'Hah, just like there is always some good . . . '

'Well, I may be unfashionable . . . '

'You're marvellous, Marge, and you know it. Nobody would have put up with Fergus for four years . . . '

Jemima laughed but Marge was serious. 'We mustn't forget that Fergus has also put up with me.'

He had hated Marge Block at the beginning, hated her transparent goodness, and the fact that he couldn't use it, as he had learnt to do with so many other stupid cows pratting about in the system.

There were no flies on Marge.

And her anger infuriated him. What right had she to tell him exactly what she thought . . . to fly at him, and smack him across his head, completely out of order. To cry, and let him know in no uncertain terms that SHE had feelings, too. And that he was hurting them. That she had rights, just as he had. And that if he wanted any bloody tea he would have to get it himself. As far as she was concerned she'd be happier if he starved.

So Fergus stopped eating. Made a big show of it. Arriving at the table and sulking, fingering his food so that nobody else could have it. That crazy slag, Marge, took no fucking notice. She didn't make any effort to encourage him, even making him dishes of cooked cheese, which she knew he detested.

One day he started teasing Tess, her ugly, huge-bodied, small-headed collie bitch with the soft brown eyes. He knew that Marge adored her.

Fergus wasn't hurting her, not really. He was only lying on the rug beside her, seeing how far he could bend her leg back before she yelped.

Mad, bad Marge Block flew across the room and kicked him with her heavy, unfashionable boot. She roared, 'It's me you're angry at, you snivelling little coward. And if you want to bend somebody's leg back, here, have a go at mine.' And with that she lifted her terrible smock and exposed an ugly ham-bone of a leg, right up to her thighs she did, waving it round at him, mocking him, laughing at him, furious with him.

'Now, you bloody well better make it up with that animal, and take her out for a good long walk while you sort your nasty little head out.'

'I don't take dogs for walks.'

'You take this one, or you'll be sleeping rough tonight.'

Outside it was beginning to snow.

The house, from without, looked beckoning and friendly,

casting a rosy warmth on the road with all the lights burning, none of the curtains drawn, and the smell of stew wafting up from the kitchen basement.

Fergus tugged at Tess's lead and she followed him mildly along, believing that he would not try to hurt her again . . . Stupid bitch, to trust like that. Fergus got round the corner and knelt beside her with evil intentions in his heart. She looked at him steadily with her dumb brown eyes. He let go the lead and ran his hands down her legs. She just stood there and let him, gently wagging her tail . . . well, she couldn't do much else, could she, Fergus was bigger and stronger than her and she was old, grey round the muzzle.

Stupid old bitch.

Why would he bother? They called him Dogboy in the papers, and Fergus was proud of his name.

Fergus dragged on the lead and she followed him, waving her tufted, unkempt tail, and sniffing her way happily along through the overcast Wimbledon suburbs.

Marge and he never said any more about that.

There was no need really.

And whenever Fergus got into trouble, whenever the police brought him back, there was a cup of hot cocoa waiting and a couple of fags beside the saucer.

But when he nicked that fiver from the tin in the kitchen, she went berserk, she threatened him with boiling porridge and she would have thrown it, she would have . . . but she never threatened him with leaving her house.

That time he had to paint the ceiling in the breakfast room before she would allow him one penny of pocket money.

'But you have to give it to me. It's paid for by the taxpayer. I'll tell Jemima. That money's not yours. It's nothing to do with you.'

'Bollocks, you bad bugger,' said Marge, bundling him into her outsize overall and equipping him with some rock-hard brushes.

When he first arrived, it was embarrassing. In her speech of greeting she came straight out with it. 'If you've got a bed-wetting problem there's a laundry downstairs – the instructions are on the wall, it's not difficult to work the machine – and while you're about your own sheets you can go round and ask if there's any others. There's bound to be.'

And it was true. That's the way it happened. Many mornings there was a knock on Fergus's door, and a boy or a girl shouted loud as you like, 'Sheets! Chuck'em out.'

Dogboy was dry in a fortnight.

You could do what you liked to your own room. You could stay inside it, lock the door, and never come out as far as Marge was concerned. You didn't have to speak to anyone, or come down for your meals, not if you didn't want to.

You had to ask if you wanted to go to school.

School was thought of as something special, with a great fuss made about it, and a good deal of attention going on those who decided to try it.

But, to Marge's dismay, not many stuck it for long.

Fergus didn't bother. He got on okay with the kids, quite stupid, mostly, Fergus was wiser than them, but a few of the guys, like Duncan and Nobby, they were pretty neat.

You were neat, too, if you hung around with Duncan and Nobby.

To start with Fergus decided to paint his walls black – even the gloss – but nobody took any notice and it soon peeled and got shabby looking. The next time, Fergus asked Marge for money to go down the DIY and she gave it to him without asking what he was planning to do. He chose red and yellow in the end. But it was hard to cover the black, and some of it still showed through. He stuck posters over the bad bits.

'This is better, Fergus,' said Marge, when next she came visiting. 'Although I like black too. But this idea of yours is so much more spacious, somehow.'

*

210

He used to like being invited into Marge's little sitting room of an evening, her by the fire, and Tess lying there at her feet.

'My womb,' Marge called it. 'Where I curl up, be warm and feel safe.'

'I feel that way about my room,' said Fergus.

'Everyone needs a private place, with a key,' said Marge.

'Like your head.'

Marge laughed. 'Yes, where you're safe from nosey parkers.' She got out a brown paper bag, and tipped a load of chestnuts onto the rug.

'But I like people, I feel glad when Duncan or Nobs come into my room. I like them to see how I've got it.'

'But not your head?'

'No, I wouldn't like anyone to see what was in there. Not people I like, anyway.'

'They wouldn't like you any more if they knew what you were thinking? Is that it?'

Fergus concentrated on cutting into the chestnuts, making his slices deep and accurate. 'That's right.'

'Or, perhaps, if they knew what you know, about some of the things that happened to you when you were very small.'

'I suppose.'

'You must have been pretty bad, Fergus, to make even your mother do those unkind things to you.'

'I suppose.'

'You can't have loved her enough. You must have done something wrong.'

'Yep.'

'Even when you were a tiny baby, unable to walk, or to speak, or to smile, or to laugh, or to . . . '

'I do want to talk to you, Marge.'

'But not now, eh? It's too soon, isn't it? Was it wrong of me to ask you?'

'Why do you want to know?'

'I don't, particularly, Fergus.' She leaned forward and poked the fire. She looked like some dishevelled old whore with a beautiful face pushed through all the pain. She laid a row of chestnuts on the little black rail, and poured some salt on a piece of newspaper, for dipping. 'But you want to know, Fergus, don't you?'

Jemima told Margery Block that Fergus could not be trusted.

She watched him with the dog, Tess, and she watched him with Janice Curtis's newborn baby.

Everything was suddenly spoiled.

Everything was different.

He would have liked to have told Marge that Jemima was wrong, but that would be construed as another manipulative game of his, pitting one expert against another.

There was nothing Fergus could do but watch the destruction happen.

When Fergus hears the whistle from the quiet site below, followed by the familiar banging, he stands to attention and watches for the ban-dog's reaction.

What is the old guy doing, banging at this time of night?

There is nothing Fergus can possibly do. He has no command for stay – although the word 'come' sometimes brings a delayed reaction. He watches as the dog pricks up his ears, sniffs, and turns its hot eyes upon Fergus.

Fergus shrugs.

If the ban-dog obeys the old man's command it is doubtful that it can push its way through the fence without Fergus's help. It might force itself through, of course, slashing its sides on the lethal pieces of wire that stand out, jagged with rust, around the sides of the hole.

Or it might stand at the fence barking, and create an uproar.

Either way, its nightly escapades will soon be discovered.

The game is up.

The ban-dog stands there, perfectly still, waiting, staring straight at Fergus.

Jeez, the thing is looking to him for guidance!

Is it possible that it now sees Fergus – the provider of some slight entertainment, and the odd piece of obnoxious liver – as its friend and master?

It bloody looks like it.

Fergus does not know how to feel. Gratified, he supposes. Although he cannot believe that there's such a thing as loyalty in this creature's maddened brain.

But even a machine like a computer, Fergus knows, needs a key word and is controlled by its operator.

Fergus is going to have to play this by ear.

Two hours later the ban-dog and Fergus return to the hole in the fence, only to find that during their absence it has been most efficiently clamped back together with over a hundred staples.

Of the sinister old watchman there is no sign.

23

Where is the sodding bleeder?

All hell is about to break loose.

But what alternative does Hump have?

If the fuzz are planning to come round tomorrow then what is the point of traipsing round searching for that wicked varmint? It is pretty goddamn fortunate that the bugger chose to rip its way out tonight, what with the Boss's sudden visit, and the warning.

Though how it chewed its way through that lot beggars belief. There must have been a fault there somewhere.

Hump, sweating and swearing, with staples like bristles clamped between his lips, a pair of pliers and thick gloves, makes perfectly sure that the dog will be unable to chew its way back, certainly for the next few days at any rate.

The gods must be smiling on Hump tonight.

If the ban-dog does turn up, Hump can deny any knowledge of it, but the idea of that evil black swine running free somewhere out there is enough to make even Hump's stringy flesh crawl.

Perhaps he should call the police himself and maybe report a sighting. He could say he had seen the Beast of Dartmoor, and protect himself against suspicion.

But that would bring the press crawling around, and under the circumstances, Hump does not think his boss would be entirely happy with that.

So Hump does nothing, always the safest response, but lives

with the hope that the dog will remain prowling around the vicinity, sleeping by day as it's trained to do, and tomorrow night, when it is safe, he will go out in search of it.

Bloody hell, the bastard cost him five thousand smackers. This thought hurts Hump most of all. He won't miss the dog – hardly good company at the best of times – which has caused him nothing but sodding trouble. It is bound to come back. After all, when you think about it, where else has the vicious bugger to go?

Hump has more than his missing talisman on his mind at the moment. It is many years since Hump has required himself to do anything more than drink and sleep.

His addled brain struggles to remember the few small details Oliphant let slip – a school house, he'd said sarcastically, 'typical, to live in a village like Middlehempston for a start, and in an old schoolhouse, how bloody predictable that man is.' And if Mr Oliphant's adversary is not dealt with soon, it sounds pretty much as if Hump, and everyone else at Fingles Ponds, will be out of a job pretty damn smartly.

After he has mended the fence, Hump pours a gallon of petrol into his foul and musty van.

Middlehempston is only two miles away, and there's no point dithering around, waiting for the right moment.

Hump prefers to move at dawn.

In Hump's experience, dawn is the time when folks are at their most vulnerable. More people die, and are born, at dawn than any other time. He can easily be back before the eight o'clock deadline, and the animals will just have to put up with shit-high straw tomorrow. Serves 'em right, thinks Hump, rooting through a pile of rank bedding for his van key, teach 'em to appreciate what he does for the jammy bastards.

The alsatians are safely chained up and looking evilly at him for curtailing their few hours of freedom. He will re-set the alarm after he has passed through the gates.

When Hump has finished with the oil and water, he moves several crates from the driving seat – the passenger seat is long gone, the space full of rotting rubbish – turns the key, and the van, which has never failed him yet, coughs into spluttering life. In his back trouser pocket are his precious savings of three hundred pounds without which he will never leave the site. Hump is not an advocate of banks.

Hump roars his black fumey way towards the village of Middlehempston, and The Old Schoolhouse, which he is sure will not be difficult to find.

In his alarm, Fergus retreats to the derelict wood, the ban-dog at his heels.

This latest development means he will have to move earlier than he had planned. He won't be able to keep himself hidden up here, not with this bloody great beast beside him. He is trapped. For how can he make the journey to Safeways and leave this fucking sod on its own? And he cannot imagine this creature's reaction if it is left to go hungry for long.

Fergus returns to the slaughtered badger, takes out his army knife, rolls up his sleeves and skins it. He cuts up the pieces of raw meat while the ban-dog stands by, watching.

'Half for today, half for tomorrow,' says Fergus, wondering how, without bread, he is going to keep himself alive. Perhaps he might have to . . . ? He stares at the carcass. No, you'd have to be desperate to tuck into this filthy mess. But one minute later he is totally unable to prevent the ban-dog from strolling forward, ignoring all efforts at intervention, and gobbling up every scrap, every slop of black blood until there is nothing left, not even the shreds on its vicious fangs, not even the scum on its muzzle.

'Okay you bastard . . . ' But at least, now, it will last through tomorrow.

But Fergus, it is tomorrow already.

Look at the sky. It is almost dawn.

*

The Hardy-Browns are back sensibly in their own beds again. But the landing light is on, there are extra chains on the doors, and the children have been moved in with their parents.

There is even a lock on the bedroom door, the freshly decorated bedroom, back to its original sweet, cottagey look ... patchwork quilt donated by the local Women's Institute (it was destined for the village fête raffle) as a gesture of support.

Jemima wept when Mrs Vaughan-Hughes called to present it, along with a bunch of fresh flowers.

'Just wanted you to know, dear, that all the good folk of Middlehempston are standing right behind you.'

The Scouts volunteered to do the bedroom, to Jemima's initial concern, but she need not have worried. Tony Scobel, the scout master, knew exactly what he was doing and in two days it was back to rights again.

The rug that sits on the varnished floorboards, replacing the old one which had to be burnt, was donated by Dotty Willow – she had no room for it in her own house but wanted Jemima to have it because it belonged to her mother, recently passed over. People are so kind.

So beneath the pine four-poster bed pink roses settle sweetly amid a pastel blue pile.

Jemima sleeps soundly, wrapped in Gerry's protecting arms.

Gerry sleeps soundly, uplifted by the support of his wife, and his worthy cause.

Hannah sleeps soundly, with her pretty little thumb fallen limply from her rosebud mouth.

Felix does not sleep soundly.

Felix has violent wind.

Hump Bass also has wind, but he does not let it build up inside him as poor little Felix is forced to do.

Hump Bass farts loud and crudely as he arrives at the turn-off to Middlehempston and runs his van behind a stand of trees. Great clumps of mud fall from the battered mudguards as the van frees itself from the weight of past excursions.

Hump carries a torch, and nothing else. Only his racked breathing can be heard as he creeps along the verge towards the dark and sleeping village. No lights here, save for the wrought-iron lanterns hanging under the porches.

No pavements.

No common concessions to the twentieth century.

After all, few people actually walk anywhere round about here. You would be really stuck if you didn't have a car because the local shop-cum-post office has long closed down, and there is one bus every two days into Melrose.

Most people round here take their estates and fill up once a week at Safeways.

Hump moves steadily on, casting his crafty eyes this way and that, on the look out for trouble . . . an insomniac dog-walker, perhaps, or some barmy milkman getting his rounds done early.

The Old Schoolhouse stands out immediately. Hump recognises it at once, for this is exactly the sort of school he attended way back when he was a boy buried in his little Welsh valley. One large schoolroom divided into two by a door on runners, and, for morning assembly the two classes would get together.

Hump, an obvious no-hoper, left when he was eleven. He ought to have gone on the bus to the senior school in Cardiff, but he couldn't afford the fare, and anyway, as his Mammy said, it would have been a waste of time and money.

'No, cariad,' she told him in her soft Welsh lilt, slapping him round his bad ear. 'You get up on that tip and start working for your keep.'

After the cave-in he was labelled disabled, and never worked (legally) again, not until old Mr Oliphant employed him after they let him out of Wandsworth.

Stingy old bastard.

But Hump cannot complain.

He would if he could but he just does not know how. Because who the hell would be bothered to listen?

He stands, gawps and listens for a moment, before moving like a crooked shadow up the path towards The Old Schoolhouse door. He even remembers the name of his old headmistress, Miss sodding Blodwyn Evans, the bitch, the cow, the hard-faced cunt.

Hump pulls out his wrinkled penis and points it towards the letterbox.

Gerry nudges Jemima.

Jemima nudges Gerry.

They scratch and yawn simultaneously.

'Felix is grizzling.'

'He'll be screaming in a minute.'

'Shush, don't wake Hannah.'

'No need to do that. Felix will wake Hannah.'

'I'll do it.'

'No, you stay here. I'll do it.'

'You did it last night.'

'Doesn't matter. I don't mind. It's nearly light outside anyway.'

Felix has always been bottlefed at night because this makes it possible for Jemima and Gerry to share the broken nights. But needless to say, during the day he is breast-fed.

Gerry Hardy-Brown, responsible father, staggers into a state of near wakefulness. He sniffs, ruffles his hair, slings his paisley dressing gown on over his crisp cotton nightshirt, and goes towards the window for a much needed gulp of fresh air.

He looks down into his garden and sees the most repulsive looking old man staggering towards the schoolhouse door with his trousers half undone.

'Jesus!'

Gerry clutches his dressing gown round him, wrestling with

the cord on his way downstairs. He calls as he goes, 'Jemima! Get up! Ring the police! Wake up the children and stay exactly where you are. I think we've got him at last!'

As Gerry rushes towards his front door he wonders, 'or is it just some old drunken tramp?'

Flying across the half-decorated hall he pauses in horror as he sees the stream of yellow urine spurting through the letterbox.

'My God!'

Gerry wrenches open the door to discover Hump Bass, with a half eaten roll-up hanging to his lip, both hands between his legs as he aims the stream of acrid liquid, which is now not passing through the letterbox at all, but straight onto Gerry Hardy-Brown's calfskin slippers.

'You filthy swine! What the hell . . . ?'

But Hump has started so he must finish.

Gerry slops towards him, hardly able to bring himself to touch such a repellent person, catches Hump by the scruff of the neck, turns him round so that all that vile, steaming ammonia is directed at the roses, and stands there listening as the piss hits the soil.

Jemima looks out, confused, from her wisteria-tangled window.

'What is it?'

'It's the scum that's been round here pestering us for the last blasted time . . . Have you rung the law?'

Not Fergus? Oh God, no, let it not be Fergus. But if not Fergus, then who? And why? 'Of course!' Jemima stares, horrified, at the sight below her, for what sort of creature is that? Ugh. He is like a monster out of a nightmare come stumbling into the picture. Surely Gerry's stupid calculations cannot be true?

'And are the children all right?'

'Hannah's still asleep and I've turned Felix over on his tummy. Keep hold of him, Gerry! Don't let him go!'

'Oh don't worry! There's no fear of that!'

Hump, having finished, wriggles in a hopeless attempt to button up his flies and replace his still dripping penis.

'No need to call the law, boss. I didn't mean nothin',' worms Hump.

'Oh shut up,' says Gerry caustically.

'I were just havin' a pee, that's all . . . '

'Through our letterbox! Well naturally, where else would you choose to relieve yourself while passing through a village on a midsummer night?'

'Let me go, boss, let me go, you're 'urtin' me!'

'Not likely, you revolting beast!'

'Let me go, an' I'll never come back! I swear it!'

'Please don't waste any more of your highly unpleasant breath. I'm going to get to the bottom of this tonight, with your help. I'm going to find out just how much you've been paid to come here and threaten me and my family . . . '

'Doan know what yer on about.'

'No, I'm sure you don't. But let's see what the police have to say about your behaviour.'

Within ten minutes the police arrive – they respond to cries of help from such places as Middlehempston, after all, these are the people who pay their wages. These are the people who create real havoc if they do not feel themselves to be properly protected.

The hapless Hump is whisked away to face the wrath of the law.

Gerry Hardy-Brown and Jemima sit in the shell of their living room amidst the bracing smell of turpentine, and tell their story to Constable Gordon Wakely.

'But could he be the man up the tree? Didn't the little girls give a very different description at the time? A younger man, I believe.'

Yes, thinks Jemima, sipping her cup of herbal tea. They gave a description so accurate that two three-year-old girls ought to be proud. But Gerry sips his coffee and stands before his empty fireplace, a man pleased to be well in control of his own domain.

'You cannot possibly depend on the testimony of three-year-old children. Children who had been badly frightened by the ordeal at the time.'

'But the damage done to this house under one week ago was quite considerable. And I'm just wondering, Sir, if an old man like that would have the stamina.'

'I bet he jolly well would, if the money was right,' chips in Jemima, angelic tonight in her virginal cotton with her eyes shining over-brightly. If the truth clicks and the police start delving more deeply, up on their computer will come Fergus – just when he is drawing so close.

Gerry leans forward, eyes sharp. 'I only want you to establish the connection between this appalling incident tonight and that man Zak Oliphant. There is absolutely no doubt in my mind that this is just one more exercise organised by that terrible man to threaten myself and my family. I have had enough, quite frankly, Constable, and now I expect the police to start taking my accusations seriously.'

'I understand, sir . . .'

'Good. And it's time you did. We have been through hell, Jemima and I. Take a good look around you. Do you imagine we always live like this? We are still suffering from the violence of that evil man, who seems to think he can get away with anything. Now why is that, Constable?' and Gerry stands back and crosses his bare ankles. His stinking slippers have gone in the dustbin. 'Why is that? You tell me. I would be most interested to know. Could it possibly be because Mr Oliphant and your Chief Inspector happen to play golf together, happen to take holidays together, and just happen, by the strangest coincidence, to be members of the same masonic lodge?'

Constable Wakely pats the hat on his crumpled knee. 'I do take your point there, sir . . . '

'Good.'

'And I assure you that this will be investigated most thoroughly.'

'Good.'

'I will interview this man myself, tonight. And if there is the slightest evidence that he has been paid to come here and carry out this disgusting . . . '

'Good. That is all I need to know. And from now on, I presume, my wife and I can go to sleep in perfect safety.'

'I am sure you can, sir.'

'Without all the chains of Fort Knox dangling from our doors?'

'I am certain . . . '

'And without going in fear through the daytime, lest someone is moved to stick his penis, or any other part of his anatomy, through some handy crevice and onto our private premises?'

'Leave it to me, sir.'

And the long, lean constable almost hits his head on a beam as he makes his hasty way out.

And so the net tightens round poor old Oliphant. How smoothly the pieces can be made to fit when there is someone like intellectual Gerry blindly fighting for right, with his good wife standing staunchly behind him. And Jemima Hardy-Brown smiles a satisfied smile.

24

Jason is home, hooray!

Jason is home, and Zak Oliphant has been arrested in what Kimberley dramatically describes as 'a dawn raid'.

It is all so tremendously exciting it is difficult to know where to go . . . which door to peep through first.

Would you believe it, only last week little Jason was bleeding, near to death, and yet, thanks to the skills of doctors, surgeons and nurses, here he is home again, with his stump plastered securely, and instructions to take things carefully.

Years ago he would have been flat on his back for two months. He would have become institutionalised, a situation which might well have calmed him down.

But naturally he has to go back to the hospital every three days, for all the necessary check-ups.

Without Michael, Charlie, Mark and Jamie, the Maggses would have found it impossible to cope. They would probably have requested that Jason remain in hospital at least until his mother was better, because of the inadequate conditions and lack of appropriate care at home.

But now here he is, with his little eyes gleaming, back at home and ruling the roost, sitting on the sofa with the channel changer in his good hand, making sure to switch over as soon as he can see that the other kids are really enjoying the cartoon.

And the volume control is almost on full.

Kirsty and Dulcie have taken on some of that stooping,

careworn attitude again. You can see it in the way they stand, talk, move, smoke, as they hide away in the kitchen.

Could it be that the last joyful week was merely a dream?

Jason's discarded toys, offered kindly to him by the other kiddies, have been hurled across the floor along with the crayons, prised-open Kinder Eggs, two toffee-apple sticks and Kelly's favourite blue elephant.

And worse, far worse, the police have just this minute left number 16 and gone round next door.

What a start!

What a start to a morning!

'So what do we do now?' Kirsty asks her Mum, dreading the answer.

'We'll have to hand back the money, and make a statement.'

'Go to court, you mean?'

'That's what they said. Jesus Christ, you can't trust any bleeder when it boils down to it, can you? And I thought that man Hardy-Brown was on our side!'

'He thinks he still is on our side. But he's got the power to decide what to do and in his great wisdom, encouraged by the law, they are now ready to take Zak Oliphant to court. Well,' says Kirsty, her heart in her mouth, 'Michael won't like this. Michael was prepared to swear they'd been bribed to squat, but not in an open court of law. A solicitor's office is very different.'

'They'll clear off now, probably, those know-all buggers,' says Dulcie. She sees her daughter's miserable face. 'You daft cow! So what the hell did you think would happen . . . all lovey dovey, romantic crap my arse. He'll blame you for this, that's for sure. I'd think you'd be wiser by now, my girl. If you don't know men and what they're after by now . . . '

'Stop it, Mum, please don't. Please don't make it worse than it is.'

'Huh,' says Dulcie, rolling her knowing eyes to the place in the ceiling where the damp has come through and hangs like a mushrooming curtain of mould. 'And don't say I didn't warn you.'

Kirsty tries to ignore the screams from the sitting room, she just can't cope with that now. 'I thought he was different,' she says, the age-old story, and Dulcie Maggs is so tired of it all she can hardly bring herself to respond.

'You fool! You fool! You stupid fool! And I hope you took precautions.'

'He did.'

'Oh? Well! That's a first.'

'I told you Michael was different.'

'They'll scarper, that's what they'll do, or I'll eat my hat and the police will probably come after us for aiding and abetting a fraud. We'll be left with the mess.'

'Perhaps they'll be prepared to go to court. After all – we are.'

'Kirsty, do come to your senses. We're going to court because we have no option. We can't disappear. Do a bunk just like that. We're stuck right here as firmly as shit to a nappy. And anyway, we're going to court to tell the truth. We did receive that parcel of money . . . '

'Yep, but there's not a lot of it left.'

'Can we help it that we happened to owe on the club and the rent and then there's the gas that had to be paid?'

'The judge won't look at it like that. He'll want that money back.'

'Well he'll have to take a running sodding jump then, won't he?'

Yes, he will blame her. Michael will hate her now. And Kirsty thinks of what she has so briefly had, and of all she's about to lose.

No-one believed Hump Bass. There was no satisfactory explanation for the three hundred pounds in his pocket.

Kimberley Oliphant, alone once again in her house, reminds

herself that prison visiting is a worthy cause, and no doubt some of the more sophisticated residents of the cul-de-sac are involved in the scheme, but she doubts if many will have relatives in the establishments they visit.

What will become of her now?

It was terrible. The most appalling shock.

It was round about nine-thirty when the police burst through the door – well, they did ring the bell, and it was to the chimes of *Greensleeves* that they outlined their merciless intentions.

Zak was on the point of leaving for work when they strode into the kitchen and confronted him.

Asked him his name.

Cautioned him.

Led him away.

And then descended on the house in their droves, rifling through his desks, chests of drawers, boxes of papers, no stone was left unturned . . . they even grubbed about under the sink, although Kimberley tried to tell them there was nothing there but a bucket, a bag of clothes pegs and a couple of scrubbing brushes.

Now she looks out of her window pitifully.

Two police cars stand in the drive, prominently positioned so that all the world can see them.

Perhaps Suzie Benson, Christine Soames and Harriet Calder think the Oliphants have been burgled. After all, for what other reason would squad cars be lurking in the cul-de-sac?

She touches her boxful of peg dolls, useless now. For who would want a box of peg dolls made by a criminal's wife? They weren't much good anyhow, as Zak said when she showed him her finished work so proudly, 'looks as if the bloody cat's brought them in.'

And how much must she blame herself for this sudden attack on her husband? How much are they basing their accusations on the fact that the Maggses received a thousand pounds from an unknown donor? And the charge of attempted murder – surely the most damaging of all the accusations and the only one she is certain that Zak is innocent of – can be laid squarely at her own miserable feet.

What should Kimberley do?

Confess?

What's the point of that?

They wouldn't release him.

They are holding him on many more charges than that.

Perhaps they will give him bail, and he can at least come home. She will try to make things up to him by cooking a special meal the minute she hears any positive news.

'What the hell's going on here?'

Jamie the shrivelled Communist is astonished to see and to hear the mayhem in the Maggses' flat.

All the kids are crying and upset, and there's this cretinous child perched like a sultan on the settee and casting a primitive malevolence like an incense all around him.

'You must be Jason.'

The children flock towards Jamie their saviour with hope in their darting eyes. Jason turns the volume up and totally ignores his visitor.

Jamie walks towards the wall and unplugs the television deliberately.

'Hey,' shouts Jason, 'turn that back on! NANA! NANA!'

'No,' says Jamie, 'I'm too busy.'

'I'll bash you . . . '

'Okay then Jason.' And Jamie replaces the limp armchair cushions, takes up a comfortable position, and begins to play with the wooden figures he carved for the children yesterday.

'I want them!'

Sandra reluctantly turns to obey, gathering up three of the small, basic carvings, but Jamie takes her arm and gently restrains her.

'Not yet, Sandy, we need those for the story.'

'But Jason . . . ' her face registers childish fear.

'Jason can wait.'

'But Jason won't wait,' says Kelly, who knows. 'And Jason's had something really horrible happen.'

'I know all about that,' says Jamie reasonably, returning to his story. 'And when we've finished we're going to put this room back just as it was before, so we've got room to move around. Where's your Mum?'

'She's in the kitchen with Nana. That's where they normally are, in the kitchen.'

Cyril the solicitor sits at the police station, waiting for an interview with his most trying client.

'I am sorry sir, but Mr Oliphant is being so obstreperous that we don't feel this is the time to allow him his rights . . . '

'I beg your pardon, Officer?' The solicitor is understandably miffed.

'If you would like to follow me, sir.'

'And where is Inspector Hooper this morning?'

'Inspector Hooper has been temporarily suspended from his duties pending further enquiries, sir.'

As they draw closer to the cells the sounds of obscenities rise up fuming, like goal fever in the old Main Bridewells.

'I hope you have not placed my client in a cell!'

'There was no other way to confine him, I'm afraid, sir. He refused to remain in an interview room, became abusive to the desk sergeant, threatened the interviewing detective, and in the end we had to charge him with resisting arrest.'

'My God, the fool!'

Cyril peers through the hole in the door and there he sees Zak Oliphant with his head lowered like an angry bull, red eyes staring from their sockets, his jacket sleeves rolled up and his teeth grinding in his head.

'You pissing sodding bastards you . . . '

This is not good. Not good at all. 'Come on,' says Cyril, 'I'll wait a few moments upstairs to see if he calms down before I attempt to go in there.'

'We have Mr Bass next door,' explains the officer. 'And unfortunately I think Mr Oliphant realises that. I fear that most of his fury is directed at his old employee . . . '

'The man you took into custody last night, I presume?'

'Yes, the man who swears he was acting alone. The ruffian with three hundred pounds in his pocket.'

'Hardy-Brown'll be well chuffed by all this.'

'Indeed, this is the proof he has been waiting for. Mr Hardy-Brown, in my opinion, is behaving in a most admirable manner,' says the police officer primly, 'considering.'

'What's happened, Jamie, where's Michael?'

Jamie pauses in his programme of child entertainment and looks up at the harassed Kirsty.

'He's next door. The police have just gone. They want him to make a statement. We've all got to go down to the cop shop this afternoon.'

'We have, too. I'm really, really sorry. If we hadn't been so greedy there'd have been no need for the lies. It's my fault. Any trouble you lot get into now is my fault.'

'We wouldn't have gone along with it if we hadn't wanted to. Nobody was to know that the thing would spiral, we all believed there would be an out of court settlement, under the circumstances. Go and talk to him, Kirsty.'

Kirsty dare not do that in case . . .

'But what's going to happen now, Jamie? What are we going to do?'

'Well, there's not a lot we can do, is there, when you think about it?'

'But what about the story?'

'We'll have to withdraw it.'

'No! You'll get into so much shit!'

'We'd get into more if we let the police sniff around, checking it out. They'd soon find out that whole idea was concocted. The main thing is that Oliphant has been nailed without our help. At last the bugger's going to get his due come-uppance . . . why don't you go and find Michael, Kirsty, he's the one you should . . . '

Without any warning Jason hurls his shoe and hits Kirsty directly on her cheek. She flinches, and at once a red mark shines on her face, taking the place of the pallor.

No strength left, no will to go on, Kirsty starts to cry, great blubbering tears which gather round her nose and the mucus there, dripping down her chin . . .

'Don't you dare! Don't you ever dare to do that again!'

Jamie, up and across the room in a jiffy, has Jason's good arm in a wrist lock.

'Get off me! Get off me, I hate you! I can do what I like!'

'No, Jason,' Jamie's voice is calm and sober. 'No you certainly cannot do what you like.'

The children gawp, open mouthed, at the scene.

'Oh yes I can. I haven't got any hand! The dog chewed my hand!'

'Well that's just bad luck Jason, and no reason for you to behave like this to your aunt who is only . . . '

'Who are you? You're not my Dad. Why should I take any notice of you?'

'This is why you're going to take notice of me, Jason, if for no other reason, this is why.'

And Jamie swiftly rolls up his right trouser leg, pulls down a peculiar long sock, and unhitches his false leg. He takes it off, with all his weight upon the other, and hands it, with all its straps, to Jason. 'Now then, Jason,' says Jamie drily, 'if you want to hit someone, why don't you hit me with that, and see what happens to you, sonny?'

Jason's eyes are big and wide as he stares, first at Jamie's pinched and angry face, then down at the well-sealed stump, and then over to the marvellous, heavy device which rests in his own chubby little hand.

Silenced for the first time in his life by something bigger than him, and shivering with shock, Jason Maggs hugs the leg and gapes stupidly on.

25

This is nothing to laugh about.

'Mrs Oliphant, can you explain that fresh dent on your car?'

She is wide-eyed with terror. 'Fresh dent, Officer?'

'Can you explain the withdrawal of one thousand pounds, cash, from your current account on Tuesday of last week?'

Silence as, beneath the rouge, Kimberley's tango smile fades and behind it her face turns ashen.

'And although you have denied that you were anywhere near the hospital on the day in question, can you confirm that you did, in fact, attend the radiology department and keep an appointment with a Mr Rodney Tremain, the consultant there?'

How toe-curlingly mortifying. What is happening to her aim for an interesting and useful, for *a more spiritual side* to her life? Kimberley's brain races to find a way out of the trap. Who would have thought they would rummage through her affairs with a fine toothcomb like this . . . why didn't they just accept that Zak did it . . . after all, he did everything else, didn't he?

Kimberley has a dizzy spell. She raises a frail hand feebly to her forehead.

Now what is going to happen?

Up until now she has assumed the manners of a middle-class English lady, speaking down to the officers, putting them in their place now and then, as you would with any blue-collar worker who came, uninvited, into your home. She likes putting on airs and graces in a girlish, flirtatious sort of way, and she quite enjoyed having the police around, sensing how much they admired her status in life, and all her expensive possessions like her Winston Churchill plate and her collectable baby dolls . . . until now, that is.

Now she feels like a prefect who's been caught with her knickers down and a cucumber in her hand in the gym.

Kimberley clears her throat and turns red, two signs which convince the inspector, watching narrowly, that she is guilty as hell.

'The dent in my car can easily be explained, Officer. A branch fell on it; as you must well know, it's happening all the time, the trees in the hedgerows are dying through lack of water.'

'Well,' says the inspector with a knowing sniff, 'we can soon verify that.'

They do not know anything. They are just trying to frighten her. Kimberley swallows down a sickly blob of terror as she determines to carry on with her bold bluff.

'And I frequently remove large sums from my bank account. I went on a shopping spree and blew the lot.'

'Have you, by any chance, the dated receipts?'

'I don't bother to go round collecting receipts,' says Kimberley frostily, thrusting out her tempting chest.

'Well maybe we could have a look at some of the purchases you made on that day, and the store labels, so we could compare records with the retailers in question?'

Kimberley is lost for an answer.

Bastard. Bastard. Bastard. If she was ten years younger she would probably be able to influence this cold, menacing man, draw him to the bedroom with a beckoning finger maybe. Kimberley has never experienced the level of hatred which she is feeling for this ignorant little turd with the watching eyes, the grey suit and the coat over his arm. A coat – in this weather!

and how awful, to think that the police have been making enquiries behind her back.

What will they think of her at the bank?

'And I may say that I did go to the hospital, but frankly I was a little embarrassed, it was a personal problem you understand, with no bearing on anything, and I was never anywhere near the road where Sheralee Maggs was knocked down.'

'Which road was that then, Mrs Oliphant?'

'They showed it in the paper,' she rushes stupidly on.

'No, Mrs Oliphant, I am afraid they did not.'

'They did, they did, they appealed for witnesses, I saw it!'

'They did not mention the name of the road . . . '

'Oh well, of course, I just assumed it would be the main road beside the carparks,' Kimberley bridles.

'Assumptions like that can be dangerous things, Mrs Oliphant.' The inspector carries on, while Kimberley, listening, goes redder and redder and weaker and weaker as he reinforces the horror, 'And you were perfectly prepared to allow your husband to carry the can for your offence. What sort of a wife are you, Mrs Oliphant?'

He dislikes her intensely! Kimberley stares at him, trying to collect her wits. And it does look like that, yes. Kimberley squirms in her seat. This is how everyone is going to see it. Hard-faced wife, allowing a charge of attempted murder to be brought against her husband in order to get herself off the hook. They will not understand that Kimberley, as Zak's little lambkin, is unable to stand the terrible pressures of life, and that Zak, so strong, so able, would shrug it off and probably get away with it.

And he IS getting away with it.

Kimberley has been nailed.

The inspector does no more but starts reciting the formalities . . . caution . . . taken down in writing . . . used in evidence . . . My God, anyone would think that Kimberley Oliphant is no better than a common criminal!

The papers!

The local news!

Exposure to the world and no hiding place!

If Zak was here he would protect her, but she has been abandoned in her hour of need.

Maybe if she went round to the Maggses' and apologised. Maybe that would look good in court, they like to see signs of remorse. They tend to give lighter sentences if they know that you are sorry.

That worm inside Kimberley, the flaw her hateful mother pointed out – you are nothing but a spoiled, self-centred, lazy whore – has emerged at last. Not in the form of cancer after all, but in the wriggling form of society's cold shoulder and Kimberley sees the flaw in herself, not as a crack from chin to elbow, but a crazy network of black lines, hideously wrinkled, and rendering the marble unstable as dust.

Kimberley jumps up from her chair and strides to and fro on her spiked heels. She bats her stiffened, spidery lashes, she bends so the top of her breasts bulge from the scooped neckline of her summer dress.

'I beg you not to take this any further, Inspector.'

No reaction but silent scorn.

Helplessly shrugging, her heart sinks to the terrible emptiness of despair. She will end up in Holloway jail after all, being visited by her neighbours, probably in some special wing because everyone will hate her for knocking down the mother of a handicapped child and trying to blame the crime on her husband.

When the inspector has gone Kimberley goes outside and stands, shaking, in the garden. She shivers as she hears the laughter of Suzie Benson, Christine Soames and Harriet Calder, blowing through the lilies in the ornamental pond and ruffling the water.

With an anguish only bearable because it is too much to suffer at once, Kirsty Maggs states flatly, 'But I can't come with you, you know I can't, and that's why you asked me, Michael, isn't it?'

He takes no notice of her doubts. 'But you've got your passport, Dulcie says your Uncle Kenny got you all passports when he took you to Benidorm and ever since then your Mum's kept them up, and added the children's names as they came along.'

'He wasn't a real uncle,' Kirsty admits, 'just one of Mum's boyfriends. And Mum added the children's names because she always hoped we would emigrate to Australia. You know, a kind of silly dream of hers. She's got all the brochures. She went to see them at Australia House, once, but they didn't want factory workers or cleaners.'

'So I'm asking you again, why can't you come?' In his eyes she imagines she sees mockery and disdain for her cowardice.

There he sits, plucking his guitar as if his suggestion is perfectly reasonable, totally calm and self-contained, agonising her with his hard, virile, powerful beauty. Oh, and he is beautiful. He is spectacular, beyond any dream she has ever had. Oh, the thought of being left behind in the great adventure of life and love leaves Kirsty stunned and sick. She gets a horrified glimpse of her dead life at Montpellier Court, her days trailing, one after the other like leaves at her feet, without him. 'Because I can't leave Sheralee stuck there in the hospital. And I can't trail round the world with Jason, not with his hand!'

He knows all this. It is so obvious he wants to travel alone, of course he does. Why would he want a tramp like her tagging along, holding him back, dragging her two demanding children? They plan to cross to Africa when they have finished with Europe and Asia – Kathmandu, The Silk Road – journeying to the Skeleton Coast. She can see it all in her mind's eye like she's seen it on telly, agonisingly vivid when you know you can never go.

They could be gone for one year, two years or three,

vaccinations and visas picked up along the way, the details don't seem to worry these sons of rich and powerful fathers.

It is extraordinary, pampered and paid for, yet all they seem to care about is not turning out like them.

If Kirsty's heart wasn't breaking she knows she would find the concept violently exciting . . . almost too exciting, certainly for losers like herself. It is cruel, really, but since she met Michael she has been given a new vision, turning the old to a dirty haze, like her windows. Maybe she does not want to see out. Maybe that's why she never cleans them. Kirsty has not known Michael long, but long enough for his passion and energy to rouse her from a comatose state.

Which is the dream? Which the reality?

How she would love to abandon everything – Jason, Sheralee, Mum, and say sod it, sod everything, let's go. But that is not possible. They are part of her family and she loves them. And even worse than that, she can imagine the look on Michael's face should she agree to go with him: embarrassed, disappointed, squirming painfully on the hook.

But Michael does not let up. Why must he be so outrageous, persistent, tormenting and tantalising her like this? 'Sheralee could discharge herself . . . '

'What? Go against doctor's orders . . .?'

'Why not, damn you? Why must you insist on this outmoded reverence for authority? They say there's nothing the matter with Sheralee that rest and time won't cure. And there are hospitals on the other side of the Channel, you know, Kirsty. Contrary to what's put about, we really are not the best in Europe! All Jason needs is for his hand to heal, and a little expert attention now and again.'

'They'd chase us, catch us and drag us back!'

He continues to stare at her while he strums his magic music with his rousing fingers. '*What on earth for*? D'you really think they'd bother, for a weedy little contempt of court? And you haven't done anything wrong anyway!'

'But you haven't got anything planned! How would you cross the Channel . . ? '

'When your father is a vice-admiral, Kirsty, it's amazing what you can do.'

'You hypocrite! You bloody hypocrite! And you're the one who is campaigning against privilege and power . . . '

Michael laughs lightly. 'But I'm not about to look a gift horse in the mouth while things are as they are. I'm not that stupid.'

Oh, oh, it is so hard to be in love.

She can't let him go without her! Kirsty makes a pretence at tidying the room. Frantically she darts about, shoving chairs aside, pumping cushions, boxing toys, emptying ashtrays before a particular tiredness assails her.

'When are you going?' Kirsty has to know. But even asking the question sends a chill down her arms and back like a bucket of cold water, ending with an uncontrollable shudder. She has to know how long she has got.

'I'm not going anywhere without you.'

'Don't be silly, Michael. The likes of me isn't for you and you know it.'

But he reaches out to touch her arm and her body inclines helplessly towards him as he repeats the amazing statement. 'I'm not going anywhere without you.'

'I am in terrible trouble,' says the stranger at the door, tears streaming down her cheeks and little sobs breaking spasmodically through her crusted make-up. She twists a scented violet handkerchief in her hands.

'I think you must have the wrong house, I'm so sorry,' says Dulcie, uneasy and unused to visitors.

What a time! Can't she sense the tension in the house?

Kimberley frowns, catching her lower lip with her teeth, finally raising her head and facing Dulcie directly.

'You don't know me . . . '

'No,' says Dulcie, 'I'm afraid I don't think I do.'

'Are you Mrs Maggs?'

'Yes,' Dulcie is guarded. More trouble? How can they handle any more trouble than what's going on at the moment? Dear God, there must be a limit.

'I'm the person who knocked over your daughter.' And with this confession off her chest Kimberley breaks into a lather of tears. Swaying. Sobbing. Making a spectacle of herself in a state of utter collapse at the Maggses' door.

'You better come in whoever you are. You can't stand out here in this state.'

What sort of people would live in a slum like this? Kimberley has never seen anything like it. At once she adopts her superior tone. 'How kind.'

'Sit down.'

She looks at the shiny arms on the sofa, stiff with old dirt. She looks at the stains on the cushions. She nods at the primitive man on the floor and the fat slag who stands there holding his hand. How incredible, the way some people live. She asks, 'Anywhere?'

'Of course, anywhere . . . what d'you expect me to do, pull up a chair?'

'So sorry.'

'Hang on,' says Dulcie, knowing her type, she has cleaned for many a Kimberley Oliphant in her day and is ready for any nonsense. 'I'll make you a cup of tea.'

'I had to come round,' Kimberley gushes again, addressing the astonished Kirsty. 'My conscience just wouldn't allow me to stand back any longer. I was the one who knocked your poor, poor sister over, and I was the person who sent the money.'

Michael Bailey sits up straight. 'It wasn't Zak Oliphant at all?'

'No,' Kimberley sniffs so violently that she jerks her dangling rhinestone earrings. 'It wasn't my husband.'

He frowns at her with distaste. 'You're that foul man's wife?'

'I am indeed. Yes, I am. And at the time of the accident I was round at the hospital myself, having the news broken to me that I had cancer. Is it surprising that my mind was temporarily off my driving, and I didn't see your sister? I was so frightened – can you understand me – so terrified of my illness, and my husband's reaction, that my judgement was affected. But I couldn't bear it. I felt so anguished about your sister that I had to send the money. How I would have loved to have walked to her bedside and given it personally. Look, I had to meet you . . . '

Michael Bailey regards her steadily. A woman in a powder-blue jersey suit, with a reinforced bust and reinforced hips and a reinforced face . . . almost begging for mercy.

'I understand,' says Kirsty, worn and battered, lumbering over, quick to respond to a fellow human ensconced in such obvious grief. 'You poor thing, when I think what you must have been through . . . '

'Nothing compared with your own ghastly experiences, my dear, absolutely nothing.'

'But cancer!' Kirsty can hardly bear to utter the word. She does not ask where. Nobody likes to ask where if the sufferer does not volunteer it, not because of the personal element, but because there is a perception that some cancers, like lung and stomach, are far more lethal than say, breast or cervix.

'Yes,' cries Kimberley softly. 'My time is limited. Every day, every minute, every hour is important to me now. You learn, you see, my dear, to jump at happiness when you have the chance, because it's not often that happiness flutters your way, soft as the butterflies in the garden.'

And self-pity causes Kimberley to break out in a fresh bout of weeping. 'The thought of spending my last few months wrapped up in a frightful court case . . . '

'No!' shouts Kirsty. 'No, that would be too terrible! That

can't be allowed to happen, can it, Michael?'

Michael is smiling at Kirsty fondly.

Kirsty wobbles with forgiveness. 'Don't you worry, Mrs Oliphant. I'm sure that Sheralee, once she knows about this, will drop all the charges . . . '

'It's not up to Sheralee, Kirsty,' Michael puts her straight. 'It's a police matter now.'

'But surely they'd listen if Sheralee insisted . . . '

'I doubt it.'

'Well, don't just sit there, Michael, don't just sit there smiling so hatefully, what can we do to help? What can we do . . . when you think . . . and this woman gave us a thousand pounds of her own bleeding money . . . '

Kimberley winces. 'I didn't expect you to help me,' she says faintly, fluttering her embroidered handkerchief, 'please don't think that's why I came to see you. I came because I wanted desperately to apologise and try to make things right. And I'd also be grateful if you kept my confidence to yourself. I don't want people to know about my condition. I would rather deal with it by myself . . . '

'But Mrs Oliphant, the authorities ought to know, it would be a way of mitigating your circumstances or whatever they call it, they'd treat you far more leniently if they understood the reasons . . . '

'No, my dear. I thank you for your genuine concern, but I think not. And now I must go . . . '

'What about your cup of tea?' puts in Dulcie, returning to the sitting room with a tray bearing tea and a saucer of biscuits in the way of Mrs Overall.

'I won't impose on you any further. I am just glad the whole business is now out in the open, relieved to know that your poor sister is recovering so well, and only sorry that the tragedy happened in the first place.'

'Please stay,' begs the humbled Kirsty.

'No, no. But remember what I told you, my dear. Live for the moment. Life is precious, no more so when you are on the brink of losing it, believe me.'

And with that the wicked Kimberley Oliphant closes the door behind her.

She must get out of this dump. Surely that sofa is filled with microscopic growing things that are catching.

Hah, that ought to do the trick.

With the Maggses' attitude of forgiveness and concern influencing the courtroom, surely her sojourn in Holloway will be many years shorter.

Live for the moment.

Kirsty has tears in her eyes.

'My mind's made up. I am coming with you, Michael, so there, whether you want me or not.'

26

Blessed relief, they are gradually getting back to normal. Gerry Hardy-Brown, the champion, shines in his wife's emerald-green eyes for the public-spirited man he is, and the gritty fighter.

Without his strength behind her Jemima knows she could not have endured the waiting.

Now it's all over, as far as Gerry is concerned, and he is still happily embroiled in the aftermath, interviewing the very few respondents to his call for information; liaising with the police, hob-nobbing with the accountants. Heaven knows what will come out now that bully is no longer there to protect his back.

He applied for bail but the police contested it.

But Jemima is not even vaguely interested in the fate of Zak Oliphant, or the nasty little man who pissed through her door last night, and lied his head off down at the police station.

What is going on? So many misunderstandings. If she didn't know better Jemima would be tempted to believe that somebody else had it in for them.

But she does know better.

Jemima lives in The Old Schoolhouse and attends the sweet peas in her garden. She does not want to know about people like that, and lives like that, on the other side of the tracks. No, all she wants to do is fling her doors and windows wide, walk across the fields to pick the poppies and cornflowers and breathe in the smell of newly mown hay.

All she wants to do is go round to Jacqueline's house with

the children, spend the occasional night at the theatre with Gerry, go to the local hunt ball in the autumn, read books and give fresh and healthy dinner parties – lots of roots and nutty salads with herbs grown in her vegetable garden.

And there is nothing remotely wrong with that.

Sounds like quite a reasonable life.

She is not hurting anyone.

She is minding her own business.

And Jemima is a marvellous mother, born to it, one could almost say.

Everyone who meets her is warmed by her, and charmed by her natural friendly manner.

But first she must deal with Fergus.

Gerry acts as though a weight has dropped from his shoulders at last.

'If we'd run away we might never have caught him, and Zak Oliphant would still be sitting there in his offices at Fingles Ponds conducting his nefarious businesses. Now, thanks to the Lord and that disgusting fellow, it's all over. End of an era. And I believe they are already considering Oliphant's membership of the golf club.'

'People are so shallow,' laughs Jemima lightly. 'It's true, you soon find out who your friends are when you are in trouble. Look at us, Gerry, how kind everyone was. How they all rallied round!'

And Gerry looks at his wife most lovingly. 'At least you can start leaving the door unlocked again, and let Hannah run free in the garden.'

Oh, and Jemima raises her brown, freckled arms to the sky. She turns around against the blue like a ballet dancer, or a daisy on the grass trying to follow the sun. 'Oh yes, and enjoy what's left of this lovely, lovely summer!'

She shouts, as though to blot out the echoes of her distress.

*

When she'd first started her training in Bolton it was nineteen seventy-six. She started straight from university . . . training on the job was thought to be the answer.

Fergus was her first case.

Before she went on her first visit, escorted by a senior worker, she was given his file to read.

This child's mother, recently deceased, was educationally sub-normal, hardly able to cope with her own life, let alone her child's.

Nora Johnson was well known to all the charities and the authorities in the city. They kept a close eye on her, and were only sorry when she went and got herself pregnant. It would have been far better if the woman had had the baby aborted or adopted, but she insisted on keeping it.

'I want something of my own to love,' she mumbled dully.

Fergus was on the 'at risk' register by the time he was six months old, and forever being admitted to hospital for various bumps and bruises – it was impossible to be certain whether his injuries were the result of Nora's deliberate mis-behaviour, or just a case of general neglect, caused by her cack-handed, clumsy ways.

By the time he was two he had had two arms broken, and eight ribs cracked.

Jemima was horrified. 'But why didn't they move him, for goodness' sake, why did they take the risk and leave him with that woman?'

'They loved each other, Jemima, in their own way. And really, Nora was a very good and caring mother, most of the time. She was inadequate, that's all. And he didn't come to any real harm, after all, he is eight years old and there's nothing much outwardly wrong with the boy.'

'But the man – this Roland Carter – what a sinister sounding person he is. It's a good thing he doesn't want Fergus, else we'd have to recommend he be moved. He's been convicted for sexual offences . . . and what is he doing co-habiting with a sub-normal woman?'

'You can't judge people on their past behaviour, Jemima. As far as we know, since he took up with Nora, Roland Carter has mended his ways. And he's kept down his job as furniture salesman with Faraways.'

'But why did he want to live with Nora in the first place? Didn't anyone think that was odd?'

'We made discreet enquiries, we kept a close watch on the pair, and other than that there was really nothing that could be done. We can't go throwing our weight around and forbidding people to fall in love.'

'Huh! Fall in love? Surely people like Nora Johnson are incapable of falling in love!'

The supervisor looked at Jemima oddly. 'I am uneasy with some of your attitudes, Jemima. What chance do you think children stand in children's homes? Why do you consider them superior to a child's natural environment?'

'Well I don't. Not really. Not unless it's quite obvious that the child is being harmed.'

'And you would suggest that Fergus has been harmed?'

'By the look of this case report, yes, I certainly would. What Fergus wants is a nice, comfortable, steady foster home, people with the right values . . . '

'Well let's go and meet the lad and see what we can do.' And the tweedy Miss Bird swept Jemima before her, and squeezed her into her Morris Minor.

Horrors.

How can you be instantly repelled by a stranger – and a child at that?

Was it a defensive reaction Jemima felt when, following Miss Bird through the dark, narrow front door, treading the brown, flaky lino, she met the child with the needy eyes, the bad hair-cut, the snotty nose, the unhealthy pallor, the poorly fitting clothes?

The child's hands were stiff and bony and red, his eyes were dull, his teeth were broken, his skin was sallow and his skinny blue legs were covered with scabs.

And how much more abhorrent that he should step forward and take her hand, trusting her to have the skills to understand and help him.

As if he had no idea how she felt.

When he came closer she saw that he had nits in his hair. Pale brown nits, crawling, jumping . . .

Unclean!

Her first instinct was to run out, to race from this grimy, neglected house in this narrow, soulless street shadowed by the factory wall, to heave her horror onto the dog-piddled pavement, to flee from the child and what it stood for and to shout at Miss Bird – Why didn't you tell me? Why didn't you tell me it would be as distressing as this?

It was distasteful.

It was pitiful.

It smelled.

It was indecent.

Jemima licked her lips and sat down on a hard brown chair.

The child came and buried itself on her knee.

She tried to recoil, but could not. She was stuck to the dirty leatherette. Drawing a deep and nervous breath she automatically circled the stiff little body in her arms.

She was distantly sorry for him, but he revolted her. Her heart was hard, she could feel no real pity. The jump between the two lives was too sudden and too great. She had no experience of this. Jemima had had no real idea . . .

Everything about him revolted her. With Miss Bird standing, arms akimbo, watching from the unwashed hearth, Jemima knew that she over-reacted, compensating for her hateful feelings.

'Well now, Fergus,' she started off expressionlessly while the child picked at his fingernails and she was afraid that the silence would widen and eventually engulf them both. He rubbed his eyes, he pretended to cry as he huddled there, as if it was a performance he had noticed and knew that he ought to copy at a time like this, *but there were no tears*.

He was a child like no other she had ever known or imagined.

She tried to slacken the tension and moved her head closer to his, as near as she could without being physically sick, only to hear him whisper pitifully, 'Are you going to die, Miss?'

She looked nervously at Miss Bird who nodded. 'No, Fergus, I'm not going to die. Between us, you and I are going to work together to find you a home where you are going to be very happy. Now come on, give me one of those gorgeous smiles.'

This was the way she was used to addressing the estate children when they came to the house for their presents at Christmas, and it seemed to work well enough.

She tried to ignore his moving hair.

She tried to pretend his pants were not damp.

He fidgeted constantly.

'What shall I call you?' asked Fergus cloyingly.

'Call me Jem,' she said, so afraid that the wrong expresssion would find its way to her face, 'which is what my best friends call me.'

From the dirty hearth Mrs Bird nodded approvingly.

And Fergus repeated the name, over and over, 'Jem, Jem, Jem,' sounding it out in his mouth, smearing his lips with his sticky fingers as if he was enjoying it.

While Jemima felt herself crumbling as if there was nothing solid inside her.

Over the years Jemima struggled to overcome her shameful prejudice. Oh how she struggled.

And the more she struggled the more Fergus came to adore her.

Gradually, by sheer will power, Jemima managed to come to terms with the distressing incidents she was forced to confront day by day, but try as she might, she never managed to conquer that initial horror she felt towards Fergus.

She tried to alter her emotions using logical argument.

It wasn't the child's fault, she knew that. Fergus Johnson was no better, nor worse than the vast majority of cases she had to deal with.

Although he was troublesome, and they went through that abuse episode at the Burchalls', most of the time he was surly but biddable, his most outrageous behaviour – like the fire – caused by his constant craving for her attention. (She was never totally convinced about the outcome of that incident with the Burchalls. Certainly the doctor's findings could have applied to abuse Fergus had suffered earlier in his life, or then again, it was not beyond Fergus to cause his own injuries deliberately.)

He was ever a clever and manipulative boy.

Jemima knew full well that, because of her unprofessional feelings, let alone Fergus's growing obsession, she ought to have been firm and handed him over to a colleague. An experienced social worker would have done that right from the start. But if Jemima had capitulated and followed that route she would have failed – not so much Fergus, but herself, giving in to such appalling emotional blocks.

She hated herself for her lack of genuine feelings.

She hated herself for being flawed by her lifetime of privilege.

She hated herself for being so proud and so stubborn that she could not even go and talk about her failure, even to her understanding supervisors.

Guilt, guilt, guilt, guilt.

'You don't care about me.'

'Of course I care, Fergus. I care more than you'll ever know.'

Oh dear god, blessed with a childlike intuition, did the boy sense the truth?

She musn't let him read her thoughts. He was so needy of her. She must not hurt him!

'You'd be happier if I was dead!'

'Fergus, you are hurting me, please don't say those things when you know they are just not true!'

'You'll go away and leave me just like all the others.'

'Fergus, I will never leave you, I have told you that again and again!'

But she should not have promised him that. She was behaving in a most unprofessional, emotional manner, and she knew it.

'If you really cared about me you'd take me home with you and introduce me to your family. You say you care, but you don't bother with me when you're off duty!'

So she took Fergus home with her, and look what happened then! That weekend was a total disaster.

So was just about everything she tried to do to make it up to Fergus.

Except for his time with Margery Block – the most expensive and the most successful carer in the whole of London. Expensive because Margery Block insisted her children should regularly visit the theatres and galleries, experience holidays and trips, take full part in schemes and courses. Nothing was too good for her precious charges, no specialist help too costly, no effort, financial or otherwise, too great.

What was the matter with Jemima, why did she find it so intolerable when she saw that somebody else could naturally love the boy she detested, and receive his love back?

And when she realised that, for the first time in his life, Fergus was actually making progress?

Well, up until that time Jemima had managed to pretend that he was unlovable, and therefore she could not be blamed.

But Margery Block was a different matter.

That fat, ungainly woman, with no idea of dress or taste or acceptable expectations, gave her wholehearted love to Fergus, and Fergus returned her love.

He was not too damaged, as Jemima made herself believe and had written in her copious notes, to give love naturally.

She was proved horribly wrong.

Look at all she had done for him, and yet what did she receive in return – a weird, obsessional love stuffed with manipulative behaviour and game-play.

Fergus was only giving back that which he was receiving, and this knowledge was too much for Jemima to take.

'It is time Fergus was encouraged to stand on his own two feet, Marge . . . '

'Oh surely it's far too early for that, Jemima. He's only just beginning to find himself here with me. Do let him stay!'

'I have gone to enormous lengths to find a suitable bedsit . . . '

'But the child is only sixteen. He needs a good home, and care!'

Jemima smiled coldly, 'Do I sense a slightly over-emotional involvement on your part, Marge . . . ?'

'Bollocks! You know my opinion on that! There has to be bloody emotional involvement else what the hell is it all about?'

'You know the official view on that as well as I do.'

Marge wheedled, fighting her corner, 'You care about Fergus, Jemima. You, of all people, must understand what he needs.'

'Yes, Marge, I am afraid I do. And I know Fergus can twist a good-hearted woman like you round his little finger with his eyes closed. He has been doing it all his life, and is quite expert at it. No, Fergus is ready to take responsibility for himself, to enjoy a taste of freedom, and to put all the benefits you have given him in the last few years to good use.'

'I'll be sorry to see him go, I can't deny it. And I have to repeat that I feel he is not yet ready and could be too easily influenced by others . . . '

'I am in charge of this case, Marge, and I must follow my own professional instincts. I am sure you understand that.'

'I understand, Jemima,' said Marge very gently. She looked away and stared into her cosy little fire. 'But I wonder if I like what I see.'

27

Fergus is poised for his mission.

He is fit, alert, dedicated and carelessly desperate.

He is as near to commanding the ban-dog as he is ever going to get.

He finds it strange that nobody has come searching . . . Last night the old watchman guy left the premises after he had stapled up the hole in the fence, and Fergus took deep cover, afraid that he might be roaming the area, casting his headlights to right and left, calling for his dog and banging his bucket.

Fergus doubts if he could have controlled the ban-dog in those challenging circumstances. But the battered old van drove off into the night and so far it has not returned. As far as Fergus can tell the alsatians have remained chained up ever since. The store opened for business at nine o'clock as usual and the familiar heavy queues of cars began to build up.

Fergus remained in his woodland shelter in case the hole in the fence was reported and nosy employees came sniffing around.

Now it is late afternoon and hotter than it was this morning, and here in his wood, where the air is wet and torpid like a weight, there is almost perfect silence. It is like a conspiracy – save for the hum of the cars on the road below. Not many birds choose this place for singing their songs.

Now and again, when Fergus moves his eyes to the ban-dog, his stomach gives a sickening lurch as he takes in the size of it and the power of those muscles under that sleek and gleaming hide. It never lies still for long, but is up, pacing restlessly like a bear in a zoo, sneaking its eyes surreptitiously round as if about to break out.

But there is nowhere to break from.

Unless the bastard feels trapped in its head, just as Fergus does.

Christ – he had been so soft, so helpless, so unguarded.

And she, so beautiful and gentle, so willing to accept him for what he was.

Fuck that.

Sometimes it runs its tongue round its mouth as if it is savouring something it has just devoured, or is about to . . . and at times like these Fergus is suddenly overcome with terror, because he is close to so malignant a thing. He keeps his gun close beside him, watching the deadly eyes, but then the ban-dog will quieten down, lift its great paw and scratch at its massive black head.

Making itself almost normal.

When all's said and done Fergus is helpless, with no control over the creature's actions, its emotions, or their eventual fate. He knows this when he sees the ban-dog hunting, nostrils flaring and blowing spume, eyes rolling wildly, consumed by a monstrous excitement infinitely beyond anything Fergus has ever experienced until now – now that he is ready to kill.

As the car splutters to a halt below him and the three distant figures get out, at first Fergus takes little notice. Someone has broken down. They will walk along the hard shoulder to phone for help, or use one of the ones at Fingles Ponds. There is no earthly reason why they might follow the fence round and head for this sloping, litter-strewn, unwelcoming wood.

Fergus gets up from his misshapen stump, feeling some strange sense of dread and not yet knowing why. He views the approaching family with some apprehension at first, then with abruptly rising panic. He wants to run forward and wave his arms – 'Keep away from here, you bastards, you stupid fucking arseholes! What the hell's the matter with you? Get back! Get back!'

His heart beats faster as he checks on the ban-dog and sees it has not yet noticed the three stumbling figures – a man, a woman and a child. But it won't be long before it does see, and before it sees it will hear.

It was just like the time they were in that house in Thornton Avenue . . . nothing much there except a video and a CD player, never knew why they were in there really, something to do, and Fergus was in desperate need of something to do since he moved into 41B, Blackhall Row, West Hampstead.

What a dump.

He had never experienced such utter loneliness in his life before.

It made high-pitched sounds in your head and if you played your music loud in order to keep the whistling out the Paki next door'd knock with a hammer and crack the plaster.

Mad bastard.

He kept the telly on all night, for company.

He couldn't sleep unless he could feel it vibrate on the bedside table.

There was a fish 'n' chip shop below him and sometimes the smell of the food drove him mad with hunger as he heated up his lonely tin of tomatoes on toast. But food never satisfied the emptiness inside him, his gnawing hunger.

Jemima had got him a job washing up at a café across the green, but it didn't pay much.

He didn't like going back to Marge's, not when she'd let him be sent away even though she told him, 'It was Jemima's decision, not mine. And you are her responsibility, Fergus, while I am only following orders.' And then she looked at him directly and said, 'Fergus, there's nothing wrong with you, and you remember that. Whatever happens, please remember that.'

High praise from Marge, but what was the point of praise?

Anyway, it had been different there since Jemima warned Marge to keep him away from the dog and the baby. He thought Marge looked at him differently after that.

And he didn't have the money to go out drinking, or to the Odeon, all he could do was hang around with his mates and go into town now and then. It was humiliating, not having money, and having to queue up once a fortnight with the rest of the scum.

He used to hang around the social services in Wandsworth and wait for Jemima to come back.

She was always pleased to see him. She would always give him the odd pound, or money for the cinema, and he always got a cup of coffee no matter that that hatchet-faced secretary stared at him as if he was nothing but a piece of shit.

Sometimes she let him spend the odd evening at her flat.

She'd got it really nice.

All Habitat-type stuff, sturdy and tasteful with lots of green plants and rush matting, like you see in magazines. He would take a video round, and she'd go and fetch a Chinese, and send him packing at around ten o'clock.

'You never let me stay the night in the spare bedroom.'

'Of course I don't, Fergus, you've got your own home now. You have got to learn to be a little bit less dependent . . . ' and she'd laugh, knowing how much he worshipped her, knowing how much he loved to be near her.

But this time he was in an upstairs bedroom in the house in Thornton Avenue when he saw the owners draw up outside.

It wasn't so much that he wanted to warn Duncan and Nobby, it was more that he wanted to knock on the window and warn the owners to drive away and come back later.

'Get back! Get back you stupid bastards! What the hell are you bloody well doing?'

For a video, for a third rate CD from Dixons, was it pissing well worth it?

But of course Fergus did not shout, he stamped on the floor instead and Duncan yelled up, 'Okay, mate, nearly finished,' and Fergus pulled back the curtains a fraction, hoping they would see the light, but they didn't. The woman was pissed. The man was shouting and dropped his keys.

But not so loud as he shouted when he stepped inside and Duncan got him with his own three iron.

Jesus effing Christ. The blood.

'You fucking wanker, you've killed him.'

The woman sat down on the sofa affair, or was it called a chaise longue, and trembled all over like a pink party jelly. She was sober enough now.

'Balls. I only tapped the bugger.'

'I heard his fucking skull crack. Let's get out.'

'What, and leave her?'

'We can't . . . '

'We fucking well can.'

'Don't hurt me, don't hurt me, I beg you,' shrieked the woman. 'Take whatever you like,' and she struggled to wrench the ring off her big fat finger.

'Tie her up,' shouted Nobby. 'Quick. Before the fuzz come round again.'

'Stick her face up.'

'Oh no, please no, I suffer terribly from asthma . . . '

'You should try an' lose some of that weight of yours then, darlin' . . . '

'I'll suffocate. There's no way I'd survive. Please just go! Go, and I swear on my life I'll say nothing . . . '

'Oh yeah, you and who else's flying pigs.' And Nobby found some parcel tape in the guy's repro desk and whammed it all over the woman's face, used it to tie her hands to the back of the chair an' all.

'Let's go!'

Fergus looked back and saw those startled, anguished eyes. The panic in them reminded him of something . . . some memory of bleak nights which he had found hard to endure. He had often woken up in that sort of panic when he was smaller, after his mum died, struggling to breathe, feeling that every choking breath was going to be his last and the darkness around him was endlessly smothering.

'Undo her nose . . . Go on Nobs . . . '

'Get out you pisser . . . '

And they were gone out the back door but Fergus had time to sneak back and rip the brown stuff from her nose – Jeez, it must have been agony, brought half her moustache away as well – before he leapt the fence at the end of the garden and joined them.

And now he is desperate to shout a warning but the trio come nearer, walking through the shades of grass until he can see their silly faces and if he doesn't take cover they will spot him as well.

The woman is wearing stiletto heels, the man has a patterned golfing sweater and a carrot-coloured beard. The boy must be twelve or thirteen, dressed in blue jeans and a caringly washed and ironed white T-shirt. Just an ordinary, boring, stupid bloody family, dreary and proper, looking for somewhere private to piss.

He can see them laughing together, the cretins.

If only he'd set off ten minutes earlier.

Now it's too sodding late.

Fergus feels his heart tremble. He dare not take hold of the ban-dog's collar.

He has tried that before, and backed off pretty damn quick.

And then the ban-dog senses them.

Every muscle in its body is taut. Its gaze is hostile. Its ferocity ripples like a sheen across its back.

This is the ban-dog's patch and these people are intruders.

Fergus feels himself being hurried forward, rushed along towards some destination already determined and beyond his control, and his body is weak with anticipation.

As the family breaks in through the feeble saplings at the edge of the wood they split up, each searching for their own private space. Believing themselves to be quite alone they call to each other and it's like a song between them, replacing all the missing birds.

Fergus and the ban-dog watch silently as the woman comes nearer, looking round before hitching her skirts and bending to squat. They hear the piss as it bubbles onto the sunless grass, and then she calls, 'Christ, that's better,' and from a distance, they hear the man laugh.

Perhaps the ban-dog will follow Fergus's lead and keep quite quiet and still.

But then the creature beside him utters the most uncanny, unbelievably horrifying sound, wilder and more savage than anything Fergus has ever heard.

Fergus breaks out of his place in the undergrowth and shouts, 'No!' as loud as his lungs will let him, and the ban-dog either mistakes the command or ignores it as the woman looks up with her skirts round her waist and is faced with a horror which renders her helpless to move or speak.

She would have fled if she could.

Fergus, so aware, even sees how she closes her eyes briefly, before widening them again, big and staring, full of sickly terror. She knows exactly what's going to happen.

'No!' screams Fergus again, but the dog is beyond hearing.

It rushes at her in a vicious turmoil, brawling, raging, spinning her onto her back under the boiling mass of its rage and weight. With shattering force it goes straight for annihilation, tearing into her throat and face with its gleaming fangs, ripping the flesh from her windpipe until blood spurts from the gaping rents, the brutal wounds. She flails on the earth beneath it as her limbs are pulled and her joints torn from their sockets, kicking her legs, thrashing with her hands in a welter of pain and desperation.

But against the primal ruthlessness there is no defence.

A soft moan comes from her. But her face is gone. No more than a grotesque broth of splintered bone.

The springy masses of hideous lacerations bump about like pieces of rubber as the dog continues to gnaw and tear at its weakening victim, now dragging at her opened stomach, now piercing the skin between her widespread legs, fastening its teeth, turning the soft and dark triangle into a jagged crimson slick. Blood pours from the welter of wounds. Reduced to nothing but meat and yet the woman is still alive, her torn hand with its tensioned fingers jerks skywards every so often, not warding it off any more but as if to embrace her murderer.

Fergus can scarcely breathe now as, in the next instant, the creature tosses his victim into the air as if she has no weight at all and in the dog's eyes shines a kind of perfect triumph, as again and again it throws up the broken pieces of gore which tumble and dance horribly to a music made out of limitless sound.

Soaked in sweat, Fergus is overcome by terror and loathing and he wipes a hand over his face with helpless desperation. He hears a high, fanatical laugh and looks around only to discover that it is his own. His head feels detached from his body and is whirling in the air somewhere above him.

'Anita? Anita? What's going on?' The man's voice rings in and out of the stunted trees.

'Anita?'

Hasn't he heard? Doesn't he know? Doesn't he sense that his wife is no longer one of the living, but the dead?

'I thought I saw this strange guy calling something . . . have you . . . ANITA!'

'MUM!' shouts the boy in the cared-about T-shirt, like that

fiendish brat who sits on the loo in the Andrex ad. 'MUM!' as he thrashes through the undergrowth.

KEEP AWAY!

The awful knowledge enters Fergus's mind and takes time to find the saner regions and settle – there might be three killings done here today.

He gives a shivering, involuntary spasm.

Like a zombie, like a man of wood, he turns on his heel and moves swiftly away.

Sentenced to hell.

Fergus leans back to feel the warmth on his skin and the breeze on his cheek but he cannot get rid of the stench of blood which fills his nostrils.

It feels like eternity before he reaches the edge of the wood, at the opposite end to Fingles Ponds.

He hears shouts from behind him, but Fergus does not pause, or turn round, he is programmed to walk on.

He does not bother to check any more for he knows that, in time, the dog will find him and follow.

28

It is late afternoon and here they are, messing about in the foyer of the Holiday Inn, drinking cocktails.

Can this be real?

Can dreams really come true?

'Quite an occasion for you, young lady! I'm sorry, what did Michael say your name was?'

'Yeah! I'm really excited. And it's Kirsty.'

'Aha!'

Is this honestly happening to her – Kirsty Maggs of 16 Montpellier Court, dragged into those leggings with a sleeveless top so short that every crease and wrinkle in her body from waist to ankle is emphasised in lurid pink, attracting the most defended eye? And there's Mum looking happier than she has ever looked in her life, almost as if she has never gone desperately to the kitchen tap with a glass and a handful of Ativan.

And it's all happening so fast. Kirsty finds the pace quite shocking. Back in that other world of hers it would have taken a year to prepare for a venture as enormous as this – and it has been exhausting – but now, with the racing over, here they are mingling with the crews of the big racing yachts, with Michael's parents, and Mark's, and Jamie's and Charlie's, chatting away as if this is just another ordinary occasion.

The kiddies are out in the hotel garden, being minded by the hotel nanny!

Kirsty's face is as pink as her leggings. With one hand she

sips a mixture of strawberries and champagne, while resting a rollie between the fingers of the other. It is all quite intoxicating, she is already tottering, and she wishes she had not worn her highest heels.

They sprang Sheralee out of the hozzie at lunchtime, no problem, just as Michael said it would be. And there she sits looking frail on the luxurious sofa beside the grandfather clock, chatting away to the rear-admiral with the handlebar eyebrows, staggeringly commanding in his braid, as if she is used to hob-nobbing with the great and mighty.

Here comes Michael's imperious father. He looks like a tsar. 'And you two are sisters, Michael tells me.'

'Yeah. And that's our Mum over there.'

'Have you met Michael's mother? Darling! I say darling, come and see who Michael is taking with him.' The snob. He looks genteelly horrified.

'Oh my dear, do have one of these,' offers Michael's mother, kindly, noting the mean little cigarette.

'Don't mind if I do, ta,' Kirsty giggles fatly.

They have put the flat keys in an envelope and posted them back to the council.

And the most incredible thing of all is that in a minute they will say goodbye to everyone and be off!

Naturally poor Sheralee was shocked when the party arrived at the hospital, and even more taken aback when Kirsty explained the plan.

She opened her eyes in alarm. 'How can I possibly?'

'You're up and about now, aren't you, having baths on your own, going to the toilet, what's the difference?'

Sheralee lounged on her hospital chair with her hospital nightgown shamelessly gaping at the front. She feels safe in here. Safe and pampered. If she was given the choice she would never leave. You could see that her breasts are double the size they used to be. Typical. Now that she doesn't care. 'On a bus?

What sort of bus? You're out of your mind, Kirsty. Just because you're besotted again . . . '

'I thought I was frigid.'

'Okay, so he turns you on, but that doesn't mean you can pull up your roots and chase off after him on some madcap scheme. You're not just a piece of flesh! Think about the kids! And then there's poor me and Jason.'

'Sheralee!' Kirsty was furious. 'What d'you think's going to benefit the kids more – a stagnant few years in Montpellier Court, running along the landings, playing down on that piece of grass trying to leap the dog turds? Or a time they'll never forget, I don't care how little they are . . . savouring the flavour of hot markets, those big fat yaks with snow in their beards, inscrutable eyes staring from foreign faces, and the way the sun sets over mountains; imagine, Sher, they'll probably even learn to swim! And then there's the company. You should see Jason with Jamie. You really won't believe it. He follows him around like a dog . . . '

Dulcie Maggs stood toothless beside her daughter's empty bed, gripping the brown rubber sheet with convulsive excitement. Disturbed by a fit of hysterical coughing, yet every now and then she nodded . . .

'Jesus, Kirsty,' cried Sheralee, shocked to the core, for such inspirational talk did not sound like her overweight, moaning, bronchial sister. She was speaking in many tongues, probably repeating that man word for word. 'What do we do for money?'

'Michael says we won't need much. He says that taking a few extra passengers won't be a problem and he's arranged with Mr Hardy-Brown for Jason's compensation claim to be put forward so we have something to fall back on when we get home. The bulk goes in petrol anyway and he says that smoking and having children is a way of abusing our bodies, it is not a sign of fertility, but sterility of the soul, and it's time we were shown some other way.'

'Bleeding heck. And what about you, Mum?' Surely somebody can see Sheralee's point of view, and Dulcie is hardly the type of person to be influenced by alternative jargon. 'You've only been out of the country once and that was to Benidorm. You're afraid to come out of your flat! You hate being around people!'

'I did, Sheralee, yes, you're quite right and I admit it. But since your accident nothing's been the same . . . Michael says our poverty has led us to our despair, don't you see, I would never have needed my Ativan unless I'd had so much struggle and stress.'

'I just don't believe this. You're both bloody barmy. And anyway, they won't let me out of here!' stated Sheralee flatly. Relieved.

'They can't stop you. Michael says you can get up and walk out of here any time you like, and our attitudes have been deliberately programmed to give us these feelings of natural inferiority. All buses and shopping bags. The more they do to you the more you let them!'

'Michael hasn't met the nurses.'

But Kirsty sensed her sister succumbing. She hurtled on. 'Michael and the rest of them are waiting outside prepared to do battle on your behalf. Look, Sheralee, look! Look out of the window and you can see the bus! Don't you see, we're being rescued, Sher. The prince has come . . . and he's offering more than we ever dreamed of.'

Kirsty's exultation shone like a beacon from her puce, illuminated face. Her eyes blazed. Sheralee had to tread carefully. 'Why d'you think Michael is doing all this for you, Kirsty?'

'You're saying that I'm a fat, ignorant cow and that he's a fraud?'

'No . . .'

'Yes, Sher, that's what you're saying, and don't you think I didn't think that first of all? Oh yes, of course I did. I've been led to believe that I'm bloody well worthless all my life, just as you have. Just as Mum has. I thought he was having a laugh with his mates . . . easy come easy go, let's have a few pokes at this little tart before we move on to something more interesting. But I just didn't care, you see. I didn't give a toss about what Michael might be doing, and I still don't. I only knew that he made me happy and I wanted to be happy and comforted and feel pretty for one last time . . . ' And Kirsty stopped with tears in her eyes, embarrassed and strained by trying to express what she could only feel.

'And what now? What d'you think now?'

'Okay, this might be a kind of crusade and Michael admits that he is a great crusader. But I think that Michael really, truly does care about me. He says he does, and he doesn't lie over things like that. Michael is brave, and free and generous . . . '

After a while, watching her sister's discomfort and the spreading blots of black make-up, Sheralee said, 'But it's scary, Kirsty.'

'Not half as scary as it would be if we turned this opportunity down. Don't you see, if we did that, they would have bloody well won. This way – we can dance on the sand!'

Sheralee managed a weak laugh. 'We can jump over those bloody great geysers!'

'We can lean out when we drive through Paris, feeling the wind in our hair, like in the song.'

'We can swim with the dolphins. We won't have to go round Safeways on Friday and see if they've got any out of date sausages.'

Sheralee sat forward with her hands gripping the arms of the chair. She breathed in heavily as she made the decision. 'Hand me my clothes.'

Then she pressed the emergency bell and confronted the impatient, 'Now then Sheralee, dear, what can we do for you?'

It was all so exciting!

The kiddies fell all over their mother when Sheralee came home. Jamie took them off to play while the three women tried to decide what to take. Dulcie had fetched the few things she wanted on her way over to the hospital before lunch.

The woman opposite, the neighbour with the phone, Mrs Crosby, opened her door and flicked her sharply interested eyes.

'You're back then. I was beginning to wonder. And what with all the business of feeding the cats . . . '

'I'm only visiting to collect my things. I am going away, Mrs Crosby, and I might not be back for quite some time.'

'Oh, it's a fortnight is it? And where, might I ask?' asked Mrs Crosby jealously.

'Round the world and back again,' sang Dulcie.

'Huh! You! You can't even answer your own front door!'

'That's the joy of it,' said Dulcie, 'I won't even have a door. I'm going by bus.'

'You want hospital treatment, dear, that's what you want.'

'And wouldn't you like that, Mrs Crosby, wouldn't that give you a sense of snooty superiority? Somebody else going batty first. But I suppose you're right. I am being carted off, in a way.' And Dulcie laughed and said no more.

Her cats were the main problem; she shed a few tears over the cats which had kept her company for so long. But the sensible matron who runs the old folk's home along the road where Dulcie sometimes does some cleaning happily agreed to take them. They will not go out any more. They will be indoor cats, fussed and cared for, sleeping under blankets of hand-knitted squares. Having their waste shovelled away, sharing the fate of most of the residents.

There wasn't much at Montpellier Court when you considered that five people lived in these two flats.

'Why don't we just empty the drawers and shove everything in black bags?'

'Good idea.'

None of the spare bits and pieces were worth keeping and the kitchen-ware, beds, tables and chairs were provided by the council anyway. There was nothing at Montpellier Court to which they felt an emotional attachment.

'Where are the babies going to sleep?'

'In those pull-down bunks on the top deck. They've got sides. They can't fall out of those. And they'll probably sleep better than normal because of the constant rocking motion.'

'I don't understand,' asked Sheralee, curious, 'why we have to go so quickly? Why couldn't they have waited for a week, say, and then we could have organised everything so much more easily?'

'They want to be off before their appointment at the cop shop. They don't want to get involved in statements, now that it's not necessary any more. Once they're asked for their statements he's had it.'

'What about us then?'

'I refuse to aid and abet the prosecution of poor Mrs Oliphant. I refuse to wait around to testify against her. That poor woman has enough on her plate at the moment and I'll say no more. And, as Michael says, if you're going to go, sod it, you might as well go.'

'Kirsty, you don't think he's going to marry you, do you?' Sheralee had never seen her sister so much in love, and she'd seen her bleeding too many times already.

For a split second Kirsty's softness hardened into sadness. But then she said, 'Getting married is far too unfashionable these days, Sher.' And then, 'Don't you think he looks just like an Indian?'

Sheralee laughed. 'And you're his squaw.'

'No,' said Kirsty quickly, 'that's the whole point. For once in my life I don't think I am.'

With a rustle of expensive fabric and a rich perfuming of the atmosphere as if a rose bed is on the move, the friends and family of Michael, Mark, Charlie and Jamie move forward as one to wave their precious offspring off on their big adventure.

The fluorescent bus is brought to the front of the Holiday Inn, attracting quite a crowd.

'Oh jolly good! What marvellous fun,' says one. 'Oh to be young again, Sebastian.'

'Well, I'm not young, and I'm going,' says Dulcie Maggs, feeling slighted, climbing aboard with her knitting bag and all dolled up in her best. She is wearing the navy blue beret with the tiger's eye hatpin, the one she picked up in the sale from Dorothy Modes. She thinks it gives her rather a touch of *savoir faire*.

Her bunk, upstairs, is the only one which has been curtained off. At her own request.

'Jolly good sport, that's what I say, frightfully eccentric,' says the man in the striped Bermuda shorts, regarding the lined and bent old body with a fair degree of surprise. It looks as if Michael is taking his char along with him. His char, two scrubbers and their offspring. How marvellously bizarre.

Nobody seems much bothered by the fact that they might not see their sons again for two or possibly three years.

But then we must remember that they are used to waving goodbyes without shedding tears because, from the tender age of seven, all these boys have been waved off three times a year with their trunks from various London platforms. Whereas one has to ask what deadening influence has been caused by Dulcie's tearful farewells – when Kirsty and Sheralee set off for that school trip to Yorkshire, for example.

A few years roughing it – securely funded through Cooks – will finish these sons of England off and drain this rebellious streak from their systems. When they return they will be ready to settle and follow their fathers' successful footsteps.

All the windows are opened wide and Charlie has decked the

vehicle with some of the yacht club bunting, creating a carnival spirit.

The babies, Billy and Kelly, are strapped securely into makeshift safety seats right at the back of the bus, waving colourful little windmills. The whole area has been cordoned off, a thick mat of foam under the blankets makes a soft and spacious play-area. Their toys are dotted about on the floor where they have already been thrown.

The hotel nanny, a sweet and natural girl from the country, is cleaning them up, freshening their faces before the off.

Jason won't get on until Jamie does. He lags behind, waiting while Jamie the Communist bids a formal goodbye to his financier father and *Vogue* magazine mother. With his missing leg (the appalling result of a skiing accident when he was three) let alone his outlandish values, Jamie has always been a bit of a disappointment to the couple. They have high hopes of this trip. At the moment it looks as though the boy will end up as a nursery nurse by vocation, but at least, presumably, he has ceased his worrying correspondence with Yasser Arafat.

'What is Michael up to, d'you suppose darling, with all these unlikely people?'

'Just a phase, darling, got to be gone through.'

'I suppose so, darling, but really . . . ' And Michael's mother, saddened by her cynicism, considers it rather cruel that Michael should demonstrate his political correctness by using these rather pathetic people – hasn't he learnt yet and when will the boy grow up, whatever he does he will never budge his father. Her son is so transparent. Even when he was small he used exactly the same strategy, bringing home not only the most unsuitable children for tea, but their whole families as well.

The rear-admiral salutes his pacifist son, well aware that this will annoy him. 'Now then Michael . . . '

'Father?'

'I needn't tell you . . .'

'I know more about Aids than you do Father, and I am fifty times as unlikely to get it.'

'I say.' The rear-admiral clears his throat and his eyebrows float to his hairline. He thrusts a crumpled fifty-pound note into Michael's workmanlike hands. 'And no more tattooes for Charlie, old man, you know how they horrify his mother. Maybe we'll fly out . . .'

'No father, please don't.' And Michael remembers a host of embarrassing sports days.

'Time to go!'

> 'On the shore stood Hiawatha,
> Turned and waved his hand at parting;
> On the clear and luminous water
> Launched his birch canoe for sailing
> From the pebbles of the margin
> Shoved it forth into the water;
> Whispered to it, "Westward! westward!"
> And with speed it darted forward.'

The bus jumps as Charlie cranks the gears.

There's a surge forward. 'Hip-hip-hoorah!'

'Byeee . . .'

'Bye darlings . . .'

'Bye everyone . . .'

'Take care!'

Oh what bliss.

Who says there is no such thing as true love? Kirsty Maggs is not that daft. If he honestly wants to faze his father Michael must make an honest woman of her, and take her kids as his own.

He will, in time. She knows very well that he will.

Just as soon as she possibly can, Kirsty is going to seek out some suitable clothes that make her look like Minnehaha.

So that they can step together – through the portals of the sunset.

29

Something dastardly – sailing away to another broken heart?

No, not for Kirsty. Not this time.

As the pink fluorescent bus makes for the coast with all its excited passengers singing and clapping and cheering inside it, reminding Dulcie of the war, Fergus Johnson, with his hunted eyes fixed directly ahead, senses the ban-dog prowling along behind him.

He does not need to look around to know that its jaws will be slicked with gore, its teeth shredded in it. He does not need to acknowledge the dog, or encourage it, he knows that by instinct it will follow. He blunders on through the undergrowth.

How the lethal creature crossed the road and travelled far enough along the verge to reach the disused railway track without being noticed does not matter now. Nothing much matters any more. The thing is here, and that is enough.

No-one can stop them now, but none the less, Fergus's ears are tuned to the faintest sound of a siren.

So overgrown, this must be one of the most secluded tracks leading between town and village in the countryside. A desolate, wasted place, it is obvious that not a soul had been along it today, and Fergus's old fag ends and lager cans still lie where he has thrown them. Lightfooted in his Reeboks, disreputable after his nights sleeping rough, unwashed and with his bristled chin, Fergus carries his leather jacket hooked on his shoulder with one finger. A mile further on and sheep nibble the grass as the pathway dissolves into a field, but Fergus knows the ban-dog will not be interested in worrying sheep.

He pauses to open the gate for the ban-dog, as an old-fashioned gentleman might pause politely for a lady, and the ban-dog, black and menacing, passes through and furtively slinks along the pathway round the tall wheat field.

It seems to know which way it is going.

Something dastardly – the innocent Oliphant sniffs his freedom.

Since his hearing this afternoon, when bail was denied him, Zak Oliphant has been waiting to be taken to the remand block at Exeter jail. Zak does not pace the floor, he has done all the pacing he is going to do and his corns are giving him hell. He has voluntarily removed his shoes.

But Zak is not alone in his miserable confinement. Cyril his hapless solicitor is sharing his lonely cell down underneath the police station, and sharing a host of promising looking news, too. For Zak Oliphant all is certainly not lost, in fact it begins to look as if he is going to come out of this smelling of roses.

'If you'd only calm down, Zak. These constant streams of abuse are not doing your cause any good. Now listen . . . For one thing it looks as if those students made up the squatter story, God knows for what reasons, that does not concern us now. Your wife has finally admitted that she was responsible for the hit-and-run accident outside the hospital last Tuesday, and that it was she who, foolishly, as she now agrees, passed that package of money to the woman's family.'

Zak looks grey and haggard this afternoon. 'That bastard Hardy-Brown probably bribed those students . . . '

'Zak! Will you please listen! It doesn't matter why they did it, but they misled Hardy-Brown and it was on the strength of that, and the Maggses' money, that he went ahead and published his editorial. The police have been through old

Hump Bass's disreputable patch and found nothing out of order. Just the four alsatians, well trained dogs apparently, and not particularly savage in the eyes of the experts. They ought to have been chained up during the daytime of course, but any one of them would quite happily pounce on a hand which happened to be mistakenly thrust through that fence, that is quite reasonable. Those dogs are not pets. They were probably only playing.'

'So really, the only pissing reason I'm in here is because of that damn fool Hump.'

'Yes. And now we've got Henry Lightfoot acting on our behalf, Hump's story will be believed when he takes his stand in the witness box, whatever he looks or sounds like. Once we've established that these other allegations against you are false, it will become quite clear that Hardy-Brown jumped to the wrong conclusions and caused all this trouble with nothing sound to base it on.'

'But what about that three hundred pounds in Hump's pocket?'

'That's quite likely to be the man's savings, just as he has been insisting from the beginning.'

'So they're reconsidering my bail application?'

'Yes Zak. They have to. Under the circumstances.'

'But my own bloody wife . . . ' Zak drops his head in his hands. They are almost too small to take the weight of it.

'I think Kimberley, bless her heart, considers you to be too strong to be damaged!'

'Huh. She always was a stupid bitch.' But Zak, in his crumpled, sweaty suit, does not look displeased with Cyril's explanation. He and Kimberley understand one another quite well.

'If you say so. I have also been led to believe that Hardy-Brown was rather over-optimistic with his expectations of a rush of complaints from your disgruntled old employees, let alone the ones still working at Fingles Ponds. They simply have not materialised. It takes a certain strength to stand up and be counted, even with the backing of a good man like Hardy-Brown . . . '

'Hang on, Cyril!' roars Zak impatiently. 'Hang on! What's this good man shit all about? The fart has made an absolute ass of himself.'

'Okay, Zak, okay, now calm down. What I'm saying is that all we have left, what it boils down to, is the crime you are supposed to have paid Hump to commit – pissing through the good editor's letterbox. Hardly the kind of vicious offence of which you were originally being accused.'

Zak smacks his exultant fist on his knee. 'It's looking good, isn't it, Cyril?'

'Yes indeed, it is looking surprisingly hopeful all of a sudden,' says Cyril, mournful at the best of times, but attempting a pasty smile, pushing back the lifeless hair of an ancient man. 'And you will certainly be out of here by tea time. But what does worry me, Zak, is who *did* carry out that original attack on the Hardy-Browns? If it wasn't you bribing those women to keep quiet, stealing guns and paying hooligans, then who is out there?'

'Quite frankly, Cyril, I couldn't give a damn.'

'No, but I think the police ought to be rather more worried than they appear to be. If there's some lunatic still wandering about . . . '

'Serves the bugger right,' scoffs Zak Oliphant, sitting back under his barred window and flamboyantly lighting a Havana cigar. 'As far as I'm concerned. I have always despised that ridiculous man.'

They are in the garden, Jemima and Hannah and Felix. They are lying on the rug together under the chestnut tree. It is a pretty picture and would make a good advertisement, Government funded probably, for British womanhood as it ought to be, or the old Milk Marketing Board. The two children are naked and Jemima might as well be for the good that tiny bikini does in covering her delectable body. With the best of nature shooting up greenly all around them, the scene could come straight from a *Country Life* calendar.

The good in us faces the bad in us over a dry stone wall.

'Hello, Fergus. I wondered when you would come.'

The echoes of that time three years ago . . .

'Hello, Fergus, I wondered when you would come.'

'How did you know?'

'I heard an item on the radio, they gave the descriptions of three . . . '

Fergus, still flailing to catch his breath, sobbed. 'I had to see you. There's been some trouble. There's two dead over in Thornton Avenue.'

'Did you say dead?' She shook her head bewildered. 'They didn't say dead . . . '

Jemima stepped back and Fergus followed her into the flat. 'Dead?' she repeated, paling, staring at him in absolute horror. 'Dead?'

'Yep,' Fergus leaned against the draining board of her model kitchen, panting, trembling beside the Kenwood Chef. His hair was plastered flat by the rain and his head ached from running. His body shivered and his jeans, wet from knee to ankle, stuck to his legs. There were splashes of blood on his jeans. 'Duncan got the man on the head with a golf club, the woman must've died soon after we left, she wasn't breathing properly when we went.'

'I am going to call the police.'

'No, Jemima, don't do that . . . '

'Fergus, I have to. Don't be ridiculous . . . '

'But you needn't mention me. I wouldn't have done it. Give me a chance to get away. I thought we could talk . . . '

'Talk?' she almost screamed, her hands to her head. '*But you did do it, Fergus*. Just by being there you did it.'

'Jemima! Wait! Listen!'

She turned and stared at him coldly. 'There is nothing you could possibly say that I would want to hear. Now, I will give you five minutes, Fergus, five minutes and no more. And after five minutes have gone by I am going to pick up this phone.'

His misery was complete. He felt an intolerable sick despair, both for what had happened at Thornton Avenue and at the flat a moment ago. The one sustaining hope he had had was that Jemima would take him in, help him to face the police, support him as she used to. The gate whined as he and the wind opened it together. The flood waters in the gutter ran along at his side as if they were keeping pace with him to see what was going to happen. The rain beat and stung his cheeks as if to say, 'You fool!' Dead leaves flew ahead of him, like ghostly, skeletal premonitions of doom.

They said he had ransacked her flat. They said he had gone wild and made that mess, even attacking Jemima herself, and he'd gone and left her bloodied and bruised all over. He looked at the photographs in genuine amazement. Her injuries looked worse than they were, they said, luckily for him. They said he tried to stop her from phoning and that's why he beat her up.

'Tell them!' screamed Fergus. 'Why are you lying? Don't let this happen to me!'

But she looked at him with disdain and contempt in her flashing green eyes, then the lids came down over knowledge she no longer wanted to see.

They said that he did it.

SHE said that he did it.

She told the police that Fergus killed the man at Thornton Avenue and that he was the one who strapped up the woman's mouth. She told them that Fergus confessed before he beat her up. If that asthmatic woman hadn't lived they would never have known the truth and they would have done Fergus for the murder instead of Nobby and Duncan.

Why did she do that?

Why did she hate him?

When did she start to hate him and why had she never said?

He was gone into some blinding desolation where nobody could reach him.

She told the curious police that Fergus told her those lies for attention, as usual.

She sent him the Reeboks in Durham, and the baseball cap, and packets of fags. The way she wrote, the way she behaved, no-one would think there was anything wrong. He smoked the fags but he put the clothes carefully aside, and kept them new until three years later when, good behaviour or not, he knew he would be released.

Three years of hell.

'Write to me, Fergus,' she wrote. 'Tell me how you are getting on.' When he did not reply to her letter she wrote again saying how relieved she was that, at last, Fergus was less dependent upon her, coping on his own as she had always wanted, and that she now felt free to move on.

'But come and see me whenever you feel like it, Fergus. Always remember that I am not just your social worker, but your friend.'

He kept her letters, too, every single one. The first one, nearly four years old, said she was getting married.

If Gerry ever found out. If Gerry ever discovered what she had done . . .

'I've been waiting for you, Fergus. I knew it was you.'

The beautiful softness of her voice stabs him deep in his heart.

'Why didn't you tell the police? Get me picked up before?'

'Oh yes, there was a moment when I thought I couldn't face it. I was all for taking the children and running away. Gerry was so certain it was Zak, but I knew . . . ' Jemima laughs wildly, 'and in the end it was Gerry who persuaded me to stay, isn't that funny? You had to come here, Fergus, didn't you? I don't know why you cleared off the first time. I was back soon after you left, you could have waited. I supposed you still take four sugars in your coffee? If the police had picked you up it would only have delayed this meeting for a few more years.'

He stares at her shyly, struggling. 'You look just the same. You haven't changed. You don't look any older.'

She answers, 'You do. You look quite a bit older. Filled out. Stronger.'

'Mummy, who's that?'

'Just an old friend of Mummy's, Hannah. Someone I haven't seen for a very long time. Now go back and play with Felix before I put him down for his rest.'

She knows he will not hurt her. He never could. Fergus was always putty in her hands.

'Hannah and Felix,' says Fergus, running his finger along the edge of his knife and trying to smile, to be cool. 'Nice names. Your sort of names.'

'Nice children, Fergus,' she answers witheringly, 'nice, well-mannered, gentle, sweet children.'

'Not tarred, not damaged . . . ' he chokes.

Jemima shakes her pretty head and the sun catches the highlights. 'No, nothing like that. Not here. Not in this place. We are protected from all that here.'

'Until I come along.'

'Ah yes, but I knew you would, you see. I knew you would come, but only when I was alone, and that's why I persuaded Gerry to replace his gun after you took the Purdy away, after you tried to frighten my children. You're not contaminating us, Fergus, you're not going to taint us, not again, not this time. Not in this pretty garden of mine.' And on her face is all the repellence and horror and fear that she has always felt.

He cries out, in a last burst of desperation. 'But I'm not an illness.'

She speaks for so many people. 'Oh yes you are. And once people like you get into the system you corrupt it, your evil seeps like a gas of degeneracy, your depravity oozes throughout humanity leaving a tell-tale smell behind it. If you were a disease you would have been eliminated long ago to save the species from terrible mutation. I had hoped they would lock you away for years behind high walls . . . '

'And that's why you lied.'

'I lied for your sake. Everything I ever did was for your sake. Dirt, you had to be removed from the streets if society was ever . . . Damnit, Fergus, don't you understand – I just wanted to be *RID OF YOU*!'

'Shit!' Now he can only croak and dribble. 'But I was a child . . . '

She rounds on him with the gun in her hands, '*No, you were never a child!* I was a child. I know about children. I know about childhood. You were dark, Fergus, and impenetrable, from some other place, you were never a child like me.'

But he sounds like a very small child. 'Margery Block didn't think that.'

'Margery Block was always a fool. People like Margery Block do more harm than anyone else. They act unwittingly as couriers for evil . . . '

He knows now. His despair is total. There can be no greater pain than this and he whispers, 'Why did you pretend to care?'

Jemima tosses her head and laughs lightly. 'Everyone has to make a pretence at caring, Fergus, surely you know that. But I care about myself, my friends and my family. And that's where it stops. And that's where fools like you, who honestly believe it's any different, go blundering on expecting others to look after you.' She challenges him with a sharp question. 'When have you ever cared, when did you ever give a damn for anyone other than yourself? You're worse than the most hypocritical of us. At least we try. We read the *Guardian* and *New Society* and give money to good causes, and campaign and fight and march. You don't do a bloody thing, you don't even bother to pretend! And now,' she says pleasantly, 'you come here armed with your puny little knife, thinking you're going to "cut us" – that's one of your more unpleasant little expressions, isn't it Fergus . . . ? I'm surprised you didn't bring the gun.'

The ban-dog raises its head above the wall. A moment of still horror and the smell . . .

Jemima falters, and makes a rush towards the children before she remembers she has something more powerful, and grips the gun tight in her hands.

'Mummy . . . '

Jemima hisses between her teeth. 'Don't move, Hannah, please, do exactly what Mummy says, and stay just where you are.'

'Why would I bother with a gun? Your gun won't stop this, Jemima. Nothing will stop it once it goes. Even I can't stop it. It's like my obsession, it can't even stop itself.' His voice breaks down. 'I love you. I love you. I love you.'

Her face is drawn with terror. Her voice is reduced to a harsh snarl. 'Love,' she sneers. 'You deliberately brought that evil thing here . . . you came with a devil beside you.'

Fergus, shaking with shock, feels his breath coming faster now. 'All I want is your love . . . all I've ever wanted is to please you.'

She laughs, and there is madness in her eyes right there beside the fear. 'Oh yes, people like you don't change . . . you're still in love with me and unable to hurt me, as the bad has always envied the good and gone round whining because their circumstances – childhood, bad luck, stupidity, all those pathetic excuses – prevented them from being like us. Your cry for sympathy disgusts me. But it's not circumstances, Fergus, you were born evil and I never cared about you . . . not more than I can care about the spider lurking under my freezer. I can pity it. But it still repels me . . . Call that damn dog off or I'll shoot.'

But the ban-dog, tense and unsettled, senses blood. It has fed once today and its appetite has been sharpened. As Fergus steadily climbs the wall, the animal leaps it in one bound like a horse taking an easy jump, and is sniffing in the garden, baring its teeth, attracted by the woman with the smell of fear coming off her. It takes a pace forward and utters a low and terrible sound . . .

'Call it off, Fergus . . . '

'I warn you, Fergus, call it off . . . '

Fergus's eyes shift from Jemima to the crouching dog. He watches how the blood-stained spittle drools from its ferocious jaws. Its odour rises like hot waves of hatred. From here it almost seems to be bigger than Jemima herself, a menacing shadow in all the soft green beauty of the garden. He understands how it feels. It wants to crush and grind, it wants to humiliate and break.

Dogboy, oh yes. He and the dog have come together and are one single mind. One purpose.

He loves her. He would call it off if he could.

Jemima already has the gun braced firm against her shoulder.

As the ban-dog springs towards her the echoes of the shot ring out like bells over meadows and hills, over nests in thatched roofs, over villages and streams and the sounds of radios in summer gardens, and ice clunking in glass jugs, and church spires and ancient yews, the smell of rubber paddling pools, and china teacups and pretty little country sign-posts that used to mark the gallows cross.

The second shot cracks out in shrieking defence of everything good and safe and respectable and happy and warm and not ever frightened or lonely.

30

To either side of the sun the hills turn purple. The fiery rim changes the Channel water to silver as it sinks beneath the horizon, and somewhere on the sea a couple of Indian lovers hold hands as they voyage into the evening vapours.

'Is there a representative of the RSPCA at the scene?' trills a frantic woman on the telephone to the local radio station which is broadcasting the drama minute by minute as it unfolds. 'I would not like to think that animal is without representation.'

'I am an animal behaviourist myself,' states a softly spoken man. 'And I have been calling the police and telling them repeatedly that if they would only deliver the dog to me, I would be able to alter its nature completely. They cut me off. Too busy to speak. It would be a crime if such a magnificent beast were to be destroyed purely because it has been mishandled and misunderstood.'

'They've got to catch it first,' says the DJ jollily, 'and don't forget this is already a crime. This dog has already killed one woman, and made an attempt to kill another. Surely you realise that animals like this have to be dealt with pretty severely.'

'It should never have been allowed into this country in the first place,' bridles a Mrs Pringle of Saltash. 'There are laws against this sort of thing, and I would like to know what the police and the customs have been doing all this time. Don't we pay them enough?'

'Well, we are still taking your phone calls, but for the moment nothing about the situation in the sleepy village of Middlehempston has changed. The man and the dog are somewhere in the infants' school building which is now surrounded by police, and I have been told that marksmen have been issued with weapons as an emergency measure. Let's hope they don't have to use them. Needless to say, members of the general public have been ordered to keep away and any immediate neighbours have been evacuated and taken to the village hall.'

In the street stands Mrs Haddock, cleaner to the Hardy-Browns and respected local gossip. There are exciting drips of blood on the road, marking the passage of the wounded ban-dog as it limped its way, with Fergus beside it, looking for a likely refuge after the shots, and the sirens that followed.

Several horrified motorists had sighted the ban-dog after it left the wood, searching for Fergus, and when the body of the woman was discovered – not so much a body but a tangle of guts and gizzards, a pathologist's nightmare – the chase hotted up considerably.

From where the little bunch stand they can just about see the flat roof of the new school extension, paid for by the PTA. Unfortunately there is a cordon further down the road so they can't get any nearer without looking like nosy parkers. 'That poor woman,' Mrs Haddock tells a group of casually gathered villagers. 'You realise that poor Mrs Hardy-Brown has been threatened by this man twice before?'

'No!'

'Oh yes, I had to help Mr Hardy-Brown clear up the mess after the first time.' She lowers her chins so they tremble while her eyes roll to the skies. 'I've never seen the likes of it before. You'd think some maniac had broken loose and run riot over all those lovely things of theirs. Lovely that cottage was, really beautiful, like a magazine picture. Nothing but an animal. I can't tell you what else he did, and Mr Hardy-Brown had to tackle all that as well . . . burnt that lovely bedspread on a bonfire in the garden, but it was all over the walls, the floors, the pictures . . . and oh, dear, the smell!'

They all turn and watch as another police van arrives, and the uniformed occupants jump out bearing riot shields and helmets, in military style. Nothing so exciting has ever reached Middlehempston before.

'They should be put down.'

'Of course they should.'

'Dogboy, they say. You remember that one? In all the papers.'

'Someone's responsible for letting him out! These judges need a good kick up the arse. What are they thinking of, letting them work at gone seventy while the rest of us have to pack up at sixty-five?'

'Perhaps if we moved a bit further down we could ask them what's happening. I mean, we need to know. We might be in danger, if those buggers manage to break out!'

Something dastardly –

Police surround The Old Schoolhouse, stark amongst the honeysuckle.

They are sending a doctor along in a minute to treat the occupants for shock. Hannah is making a daisy chain in the garden, watched over by Clara the elderly neighbour.

'I will never, ever, forgive myself!'

'Oh Gerry, don't feel like that. Don't even talk like that!'

Gerry strides round the living room, hair madly awry, stooped and desperate like a composing poet. His sandals slap against his heels. 'By my own crass stupidity I put the lives of my wife and my children at risk. What the hell sort of man am I? So blinded by my own convictions.'

'It was just very lucky that you bought the gun and that it was in a place where I could easily . . . '

287

'I wouldn't have bought the gun if you hadn't persuaded me. Oh, when I think. Thank God, thank God you did! And thank God you managed to load it, and work it!'

'A childhood trick that hasn't been forgotten. We used to follow the guns every Boxing Day, and I often loaded for Daddy. The lucky part of it was that I heard a scrambling noise behind the wall and I had the foresight to go and fetch it.'

Gerry smacks his intelligent forehead. 'Damn it, Jem, I was so bloody convinced that Zak Oliphant . . . ' He shakes his head wearily. 'And now it looks as if the case against him was nothing but a build-up of coincidences and misunderstandings.' He stops, and looks up from his pacings. On his face is a tortured frown. 'They've freed him, you know. They let him go this afternoon. He's only one case to answer, and they reckon he'll get off that.'

Jemima circles her distraught husband in her tanned, gentle arms. She squeezes him tightly. It is easy to get your arms round Gerry for he is a careful eater, and mostly vegetarian. 'Let it go, Gerry. You tried your best, and no-one can do more than that. If you hadn't been such a strong, dedicated person, I might not have had the willpower to deal with Fergus as I did. You pass your wonderful strength on to me, and your goodness to everyone who meets you . . . '

She makes him sound like Mother Teresa.

'I'm going to have to let the whole thing drop. We didn't even have the time to examine the books . . . Everything the police took has been returned, and they've even been forced to apologise . . . Imagine, Jemima.' And Gerry buries his suffering face in his wife's perfumed neck. 'He has triumphed again! Evil has won the day.'

Jemima stands back and grasps his arms. She stares directly into his eyes. Thank God he will never see evil, will never know that the evil in this is all down to her. She destroyed Fergus's life as surely as if she murdered him. She did it when he was eight years old and cannot endure the guilt any longer.

'Oh no, Gerry. You musn't think like that. Fergus Johnson is ten times more of a monster than Zak Oliphant, who is nothing more than a greedy, insensitive fool. You don't know Fergus like I do . . . '

'You never spoke about him, Jemima. You never told me . . . '

'No, I did not. Because I knew I had failed him. Because everything I tried to do for that boy was thrown back in my face. And then he attacked me on the night of the murder. Oh Gerry, it was all so awful, and I don't want that darkness to come near my life ever again. I tried to pretend it hadn't really happened, I suppose. I tried to forget it.'

'And yet he carried round this evil obsession. For three years he must have planned to come here when they released him. And you never suspected!'

'I loved that boy,' she lies, so easily. 'People like Fergus turn love into something rotten and violent and vengeful. He is bad, Gerry. Bad in the sort of way that you'll never know. And all we've got to hope for now is that they lock him away for the rest of his life, which is what they ought to have done in the first place.'

But how she wishes she had managed to kill him and exorcise the devil inside her.

Zak Oliphant watches the television news with half an eye while he attempts to cut into the piece of steak which Kimberley has prepared and cooked to celebrate his release.

There is a bottle of sweet red wine on the table between them. Red wine with red meat, although this particular meat is black.

'Oh Zak,' she says, for the umpteenth time, 'how can you ever, ever forgive me? I never imagined it would go as far as it did. When I think what could have happened to you. Oh, I was so frightened.'

'Well, now perhaps they'll all lay off me and let me get on

with my life,' says Zak, chewing the meat until it turns into a piece of softened leather in his mouth. He picks his teeth with his fingernail.

'We can all go back to normal,' trills Kimberley, 'and pretend this never happened.' She will never drink and drive again. All she is being accused of is failing to report an accident.

'Oh no, oh no, Kimberley, it certainly won't be like that. There are several people who have worked together to further my destruction, not least that Jesus freak Hardy-Brown. And I, quite rightly, expect some measure of compensation from the local community, and the authorities, for the damage to my reputation, not so much in the way of financial reward, not this time, but as Cyril pointed out to me, after I have made my next contribution to party funds before the next election, I should stand a good chance of being put forward . . .'

All Kimberley's bangles jangle. She throws down her gold knife and fork. She almost looks thirty again. 'Oh Zak!' She presses her hands hard against her fluttering chest. 'You don't mean . . . you're not suggesting . . .'

'A trip up to London, perhaps, my dear,' he beams, a shred of meat dangling between his two front teeth. 'Around about this time next year, a touch on the shoulder . . .'

'I do not believe you!'

He tackles a frozen sprout with his fork but fails to pierce it. 'Aha. We shall see. The possibility has already been suggested to me by several various eminent groups of people, and these little mistakes on the part of Hardy-Brown and his chums brings the likelihood closer than ever. Derek Hooper has been reinstated. No-one dare say a word against me. One more hefty donation and we should be home and dry.'

'I'd be a lady!'

'Yes, my dear, you certainly would.'

'Lady Kimberley Oliphant! Everyone would want to know me.'

'That's the way the cookie crumbles.'

'The Albany Country Club would probably invite me to join.'

'I'm sure their invitation would arrive by first class post.'

And she probably won't even bother to speak to those uppity neighbours, no matter how often they come calling.

'Oh, Zak, Zak, it's so good to have you home and I do so love you!'

Something dastardly –

The pussy willows on the nature table have turned dark and dry, all the life sucked out of them. Soon the children will bring copper-brown leaves, chestnuts and fire cones, reds and russets and yellows, and time will move on once more and then it will be holly and tinsel and fairy lights, and mistletoe cut from the local orchards.

As they sing round their little crib, the most helpful child in the class will place the baby Jesus. In a couple of years' time, perhaps, that special child will be Hannah.

The ban-dog's breathing is heavy but it fights to keep upright, fights to ignore the pain in its chest – it knows that it will go in the end, it understands about pain because pain has never been a stranger.

Fergus is slumped on the floor in the corner beside the nature table. You would think, to look at him, that he is the one who has been wounded. With his knife he prepares to cut another J in his arm.

He knows no other response to make.

Many strange thoughts struggle for birth, but they will not live, some dull knowledge inside him is denying them life. He wonders if he could staunch the bleeding in the ban-dog's wounds, but then he dismisses that idea. No point. After what it's done today they will not let it live, and why should Fergus care anyway.

This black bastard means little to him.

They are out there now, waiting for him. Every now and then they call to him through a loudspeaker and he's seen this sort of thing before, on telly. They use specially trained psychologists, apparently, particularly for prisoners holding hostages. Pity he hasn't got a hostage.

She must have told them his name.

'Fergus, you must come out of there. Our main priority is to deal with the dangerous dog you have with you. We believe it to be badly wounded, and its behaviour is likely to be extremely unstable right now. It's a danger to you, Fergus, let alone the local community. If you can hear me, Fergus, please open the window so we can talk.'

Like hell I will. Huh. They don't know much about the ban-dog if they think it is any more dangerous wounded than healthy.

Three years ago he would have opened the window. He would have told them to go and fetch Jemima. He would have said that she was the only one he was willing to speak to. And she would have cajoled him and humoured him until he gave himself up.

But today Jemima has tried to kill him.

Even to whisper her name is to take a sip of poisoned pain.

The ban-dog turns to face Fergus as it hears a noise outside the door. Somebody knows which classroom they are in . . . they've probably known from the start. Why do they take so long . . . why are they so slow to act? Fergus has been waiting here for over two hours now. Shaking in every limb, Fergus finishes chiselling the J in his arm, glad of the pain and the temporary relief it gives him.

'Fergus,' comes the hollow-sounding voice again. 'Will you please come out of the nursery classroom and close the door behind you. We need to deal with the dog. Please understand that it is imperative that we deal with the dog. We are not interested in you at the moment and any help you give us today will count in your favour . . .'

From his place on the floor Fergus shakes an angry fist, 'FUCK YOU!'

They are going to shoot it. Expecting him to stand to one side, they are going to burst through that door in a minute and shoot it. Although they are dressed in bite-proof clothing, their arms protected with thick padding, although there's no way it can really hurt them, they are going to kill it.

In front of Fergus the ban-dog staggers and a sob like a child's storms up in the boy then sinks again, and perishes. There is a blue film, like defeat, forming over the dog's pained eyes. Jeez, don't let it give up. After all that fight, don't let it give up now. It tries to focus on Fergus, turns dizzily towards him, and, with laboured breathing, it teeters nearer.

It seems impossible that it can walk. It must be going through agony.

Bright red blood courses from the gaping wound.

They are going to open that door in a minute. They are going to take aim, and fire. Fergus has only to get out of the way . . .

The ban-dog slumps, by accident or on purpose – it was ever a wily bastard – and ends up with all its dead weight propped against Fergus's knees.

If Fergus drops his knees then the dog will fall onto the nursery floor and all the fighting will be over.

So Fergus braces his legs to take the enormous weight, almost limp against him.

'Don't let them see you down, shithead,' Fergus whispers huskily.

With great caution, slowly, careful not to startle it, Fergus places his hand firmly on the soft black head so it may feel the comfort of a friend.

There is one gentle moment. A dog who has never been stroked licks the tears of a boy who has never cried.

The only way to freedom. To know it is a relief. It is time for them both to go and Fergus braces his shoulders. He laughs. 'Two dogs. Two shitheads. I'll hold you tight as I can. Hang on.'

Just one second later it's over.

They have God on their side. When they kick in the door there is no sign of Fergus. Just the dog, lolling, looming, leering helplessly. When they shout, aim and fire, releasing a wild cacophony of sound, the ferocious bullets pass through the dog and smack straight into Fergus's chest.

His love was flawed, but constant. At last Fergus was able to give her something that she wanted.

On the hills and meadows around Middlehempston the dusk falls, throwing its shadows into the silence. The note of a nightjar tears the stillness. Another dusk, the light goes out, and one more sun gone forever. There is bound to be a public outcry when the press find out about the ban-dog's miserable life. And I think that Kimberley Oliphant will probably hurry out first thing in the morning to order personalised Christmas cards – just in case.

also available from
THE ORION PUBLISHING GROUP
————————

The Normal Man £5.99
SUSIE BOYT
1 85799 421 3

Mothers and Other Lovers
£5.99
JOANNA BRISCOE
1 85799 248 2

Judicial Whispers £5.99
CARO FRASER
1 85799 377 2

The Pupil £5.99
CARO FRASER
1 85799 063 3

The Trustees £5.99
CARO FRASER
1 85799 059 5

The Good Doctor £6.99
CAROLA GROOM
1 85799 409 4

Stealing Beauty £4.99
SHIRLEY LOWE
0 75280 687 4

While the Music Lasts £5.99
ALICE MCVEIGH
1 85799 342 X

House of Splendid Isolation
£5.99
EDNA O'BRIEN
1 85799 209 1

Astonishing the Gods £5.99
BEN OKRI
1 85799 374 8

A Suitable Boy £9.99
VIKRAM SETH
1 85799 088 9

The New Rector £5.99
REBECCA SHAW
1 85799 731 X

Talk of the Village £9.99
REBECCA SHAW
1 85799 732 8

The Beautiful Mrs Seidenman
£5.99
ANDRZEJ SZCZYPIORSKI
1 85799 499 X

The Crow Biddy £5.99
GILLIAN WHITE
1 85799 204 0

Grandfather's Footsteps
£5.99
GILLIAN WHITE
1 85799 337 3

Mothertime £5.99
GILLIAN WHITE
1 85799 208 3

Nasty Habits £5.99
GILLIAN WHITE
1 85799 338 1

The Plague Stone £5.99
GILLIAN WHITE
1 85799 419 1

Rich Deceiver £5.99
GILLIAN WHITE
1 85799 256 3

All Orion/Phoenix titles are available at your local bookshop or from the following address:

Littlehampton Book Services
Cash Sales Department L
14 Eldon Way, Lineside Industrial Estate
Littlehampton
West Sussex BN17 7HE
telephone 01903 721596, *facsimile* 01903 730914

Payment can either be made by credit card (Visa and Mastercard accepted) or by sending a cheque or postal order made payable to *Littlehampton Book Services*.
DO NOT SEND CASH OR CURRENCY.

Please add the following to cover postage and packing

UK and BFPO:
£1.50 for the first book, and 50P for each additional book to a maximum of £3.50

Overseas and Eire:
£2.50 for the first book plus £1.00 for the second book and 50p for each additional book ordered

----

BLOCK CAPITALS PLEASE

name of cardholder ....   *delivery address*
                      ....   *(if different from cardholder)*
address of cardholder ....
....
....
....
     postcode ....   *postcode* ....

☐ I enclose my remittance for £...........................

☐ please debit my Mastercard/Visa (delete as appropriate)

card number [ ][ ][ ][ ][ ][ ][ ][ ][ ][ ][ ][ ][ ][ ][ ][ ]

expiry date [ ][ ][ ][ ]

signature ....

prices and availability are subject to change without notice